A COMMISSION ON MURDER

AN EASTERN SHORE MYSTERY

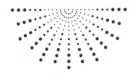

CHERIL THOMAS

Tred
Avon
Press

LIES, MORE LIES, AND
A LITTLE BIT OF TRUTH

A COMMISSION ON MURDER

One waterfront property for auction and three buyers — then someone narrows the odds.

Until the morning Garrett Bishop is murdered, Grace Reagan only has to worry about the house she can't sell and a business sliding into bankruptcy. She has four months left on her agreement to manage Cyrus Mosley's law firm, a plan that sounded easy enough in September when the weather was warm and she was optimistic. But Grace barely has time to regret the decision she's made before the man who can guarantee her success is killed.

Was the flamboyant, loud-mouthed Bishop shot by a hunter with bad aim — or by one of the many people who want him gone from Kingston County and don't care how he leaves? Grace knows that in some parts of the Eastern Shore strangers are guilty until proven otherwise. A near stranger herself, she must prove not one, but two of her clients are innocent of murder.

Welcome to Mallard Bay, Maryland, the little village where everyone has an opinion, but the truth is in short supply.

ALSO BY CHERIL THOMAS

Squatter's Rights

A Commission on Murder

Bad Intent

For Ronald Hohman Thomas
and his sweet girl,
Gracie Mae

"For he has been reported killed more than a score of times, yet his bloody corpse became reanimated through some witchery peculiar to himself."

Obituary of William 'Wild Bill' Hickok
  St. Louis Post-Dispatch
  15 August 1876

PROLOGUE

Friday Morning
November 10

The rifle was heavy.

Slippery, wet leaves and tree roots made slow going and weak sunshine did nothing to dispel the cold. It was a perfect day for correcting mistakes, clearing accounts. A perfect day for hunting. Too bad the hunter hadn't planned better, but some things couldn't be helped. When life hands you the perfect opportunity, you take your shot. So to speak.

Overhead, south bound Canadian geese called to each other in a crashing chorus, but the hunter wasn't tempted. Five minutes later, the desired target came into view, still far away but well within range.

Turn around. Let me see your face.

So. Not the perfect opportunity, after all. The bastard wouldn't turn around.

The hunter took the shot anyway.

Perfect.

CHAPTER ONE

"He can't be dead," Grace Reagan said.

"Looks dead to me." The police officer standing beside her sounded pleased. Corporal Aidan Banks hated being bored and a murder guaranteed excitement. Much better than writing parking tickets and wrangling drunk tourists.

"Maybe I didn't do CPR long enough. I should try again."

"He's gone." Banks kept a wary eye on the tall woman who stood next to him, shivering in the brisk autumn breeze. He'd put his uniform jacket over her shoulders when he'd found her pumping the dead man's chest in a frenzy. "You did what you could," he added, but only because he didn't want her to freak out until someone who outranked him arrived to take over.

"He was fine when I talked to him a couple of hours ago," Grace insisted.

"Not fine now."

There was no denying it. The man lying on the scraggly grass behind a decrepit house in the middle of nowhere was dead.

"Look, Aidan, I know I need to stay here, but could you check his pockets? He should have a contract with him and I have to get it."

Banks didn't bother telling her 'no.'

She knew better, but she had to try. "Sorry. I know you can't. I'm just going in the house to wash my hands."

"No."

They heard sirens, still far off but getting closer.

"I've got blood everywhere. I'm a mess. Look at me!"

Ordinarily, Grace with her curly dark hair and wide blue eyes wasn't hard to look at, but today wasn't ordinary. Unable to produce a response that wouldn't cause trouble, Banks remained stoically silent. He'd sacrificed his almost new jacket to a blood-covered woman and that was as far as he'd go. Tact was beyond him.

"Fine," she said when he didn't answer her. "I'll wait in my car."

"Stay where you are, just like the Chief said. He'll be here soon with the State Police."

Grace gave up and tried not to fidget as she waited for Banks' boss to arrive and tell her what she already knew — her ticket out of Mallard Bay, Maryland was officially canceled. She wanted to feel horrified, or at the very least *bad* for the dead man, but Garrett Bishop had been difficult from the first moment she'd met him. In the last week he had more than lived up to his notorious reputation, and now he'd gone and gotten himself killed, probably without signing the bid he'd offered her. If only she could get her hands on the papers he'd taunted her with this morning, she'd know if she still had a deal.

She took a step back and then another. And then heard tires crunching over oyster shells as vehicles pulled into the driveway at the front of the property. Banks was right. She wasn't going anywhere.

FIRST, THE MARYLAND STATE POLICE, THEN THE CORONER AND finally the MSP crime scene technicians claimed command of the old Morgan farm.

One man stood apart from the swarm of activity, but he knew all too well what was taking place. Violent death had been a part of Lee

McNamara's working life since he'd first worn a uniform in the Maryland State Police thirty years ago. Now that he was the Chief of Police in the small waterfront village of Mallard Bay, the human carnage which came his way usually involved vehicles, the occasional domestic battle, and in increasing numbers, opioid overdoses. While he didn't share his corporal's thrill at having a shooting to perk up the workday, he was relieved the victim wasn't a loss to anyone local.

Garrett Bishop had been stirring up trouble since he arrived on the Eastern Shore and McNamara was happy to have him gone by whatever expedient means available, but he didn't like seeing Grace Reagan involved. He'd grown fond of her over the last year and as the first person to find the body, she was already being questioned by the MSP team which had followed him out to the secluded waterfront property. Grace wasn't helping herself by asking everyone if they were sure Bishop was really, truly, dead.

The question wasn't as inane as it sounded. Garrett Bishop was wealthy, eccentric and prone to headline grabbing stunts which gave him fleeting fame and boosted stock sales in his video game empire. He'd been lost in an avalanche, hijacked from his corporate plane and held hostage by mysterious kidnappers. After each death defying event, Bishop's publicity team would say he'd managed to survive by his own cunning and skill. News commentators and comedians ripped him up, but the public loved it. Even if the farmhouse was creepy enough to host a murder scene, dying in a remote area of Maryland was anti-climactic for the flamboyant Bishop.

The Morgan Creek area wasn't in Mallard Bay proper, and the only role McNamara would play in the investigation would be to support the MSP as they saw fit. His professional instincts shouted instructions but he stood still, hands clasped behind his back. He was behind the fluttering neon yellow tape that ringed the crime scene perimeter. Ten years ago, Captain McNamara of the Violent Crimes and Homicide Division of the Maryland State Police might have been under the tent, his back turned to the local cops who were on the outside looking in. Today, Chief McNamara of the Mallard Bay

Police Department stood watch, on duty but far from the action. His only assignment was to keep the growing crowd of onlookers away from the investigation. He knew his place. He and Aidan Banks were a two man department with limited resources.

The first civilians to arrive had caught the emergency calls on their home police scanners. Smartphones notified everyone else. In a rural area where neighbors helped neighbors and volunteer fire departments were the best line of defense, both old and new technology were necessary. But sometimes, it wasn't only the emergency workers and volunteers who showed up to an exciting call. The crowd was gathering within sight of the official activity. Garrett Bishop's death wasn't only shocking; the aftermath was noisy. Cries of 'Over here!' and 'Tell us something, Mac!' were starting to erupt and McNamara knew his corporal was having a hard time. Not that Banks ever made anything easy.

With a signal to the MSP's lead investigator, McNamara left to lend Banks a hand with the agitated group. Corporal Banks had little empathy and less patience for his fellow human beings. The expression on his face as he aimed a glare over his shoulder at McNamara made the Chief speed up. One homicide was enough for today.

The standard 'no comment, active investigation' speech did nothing to settle the crowd. Neither did the Chief's down-home, 'Come on, folks, you know I can't say anything, but I need your cooperation' plea. For once his sympathies lay with the hot headed Banks. Both were substantial men, McNamara just shy of six feet and barrel chested, Banks shorter, but gym fit. None of which had any effect on the people who were arguing with them. McNamara was known for his companionable nature, and most of the crowd had watched Banks grow up.

"This is private property." The change in McNamara's tone worked where politeness had failed. He pointed north, where the narrow country lane wound out of sight. "If you don't want to wait up there at the turnaround, then move off to the other side of the road and quit heckling Corporal Banks. We're doing our jobs here. When I know something, I'll tell you what I can."

The grumbling people moved back to a clearing opposite the driveway entrance. Only one person ignored him and continued to take photos with her cell phone. McNamara stepped up to her and leaned in, hoping the others assumed he wanted to talk to the lone dissenter.

"Avril, seriously, what are you going to do with a hundred shots of an ambulance?"

"You don't know what I've captured with this." The tiny, arthritic woman ignored McNamara and the nearly apoplectic Banks and started walking around them, the artificial *clickclickclick* of the phone's camera punctuating her steps.

"I know what I'm gonna capture, you old —" Banks stopped when he saw his chief's face.

McNamara said, "I need a favor."

"You'll get my photos when I've seen them and not before," Avril Oxley said, but she turned to face the officers and looked past them to the curious crowd. "Vultures! Nothing to do and no brains to do it with. Just glomming onto whatever shiny object comes their way."

Banks gave McNamara a questioning look, but the Chief shook his head. The mixed bird metaphor wasn't worth it. Avril wouldn't appreciate the comparison to her fellow crime scene bystanders and when she was angry, it was impossible to schmooze her.

McNamara said, "Not the photos, although I'll need them."

The old woman gave him her attention and as always, he thought what an uncomfortable thing it was to be the subject of that sharp, if ancient, brain. He said, "I need to learn everything I can about Garrett Bishop."

A quick intake of breath and bloom of color on her wrinkled cheeks were the only signs Avril gave of the impact of his words. She sounded casual as she said, "Oh, so it is him?"

"I didn't say that. And I expect you to keep my request to yourself."

She ignored the underlying insult and said, "They already know." Again her gaze moved to the crowd. "How do you think I found out?

Rory Bailey told the new clerk at Baldy's and she was running her mouth to everyone in the checkout line."

Bailey owned the neighboring land, a farm which ran north to the state highway a half mile away. He and others had been vocal about their dislike for Bishop. McNamara scanned the crowd for the farmer.

"I got shots of everyone, just in case, but the killer isn't over there," Avril said.

"And you know that how?" Banks asked.

"Oh, pay attention. They're just background noise. Little Nosy Parkers who show up at the scent of excitement. Not one of them lives nearby or is truly concerned about Bishop. You check out Rory and see what he says. That's what you want to do."

Rory Bailey. McNamara made a note of the name and earned a brief smile from Avril. He felt sorry for whoever had to investigate every bit of local gossip and run down every neighbor versus neighbor grudge. He was suddenly glad it wasn't going to be him.

CHAPTER TWO

U ntil Garrett Bishop's death, a business sliding into bankruptcy, feuding employees and an incontinent dog formed the boundaries of Grace Reagan's life. She may have stumbled into a murder, but she still had the other three issues to deal with.

When the State Police finally released her, she went to her office and walked into a new war between the secretaries. Friday afternoon or not, they still had work to do, and she would tell them so right after she answered the phone. She caught the call on the fifth ring and tried to sound professional.

"Kastner and Mosley, how may I help you?"

"I'm gonna kill Mom if you don't get over here!" Her cousin Niki was trying to yell and whisper at the same time and sounded demented.

Grace closed her eyes and allowed herself a blissful moment imagining a homicide at the other end of the phone. Niki's mother was not Grace's favorite person.

"I'm not kidding!" Niki's volume went up. "You put her up to this and now there's a free for all in my living room. Your precious bidders may kill her before I get a chance to."

It was too much. Grace wanted to scream, but she only said, "What wrong with the bidders? Have they heard about Bishop?"

"What about him? He's the only one who isn't here, thank God. The rest of them are in a fight, though, and Mom's in the middle of it."

Of all the adjustments Grace had made over the past year, being nice to Connie Delaney for Niki's sake was the one which grated the most. It wasn't hard to imagine that wherever Connie was, there'd be trouble.

But Niki wasn't finished. "Dad's in Atlantic City, so he's no help. Besides, you promised to take Leo, remember?"

"I will, it's just —"

"Too late is what it is. That dog's lucky to even be in the garage considering his toileting hygiene. Get. Over. Here."

"I've been a little busy with a possible murder," Grace said to the dial tone in her ear.

On her way out of the office, she took a second to appreciate a sudden silence in the mostly empty suite of rooms which had once been a healthy law firm and real estate office. Even if the two secretaries — the only remaining staff — had stopped arguing, Grace knew it didn't mean they were working. She should talk to them and tell them about Bishop. Tell them it was time to pull together while they all still had jobs. But the day's events had drained her, and she had to get to Niki's inn. Monday, for sure, she'd put her foot down and straighten everyone out.

Just as she reached the lobby, she heard the arguing start up again. She pushed the button for the elevator. When it arrived, she stepped in, then leaned out and called, "Have a good weekend!" before stabbing 'close' and 'down'. The god of old elevators smiled and she made her escape.

Running from one fight to another, Grace scolded herself, but she kept going. If she didn't pull off the auction of the Morgan farm, Kastner and Mosley might be out of business and she wouldn't have any staff problems at all.

"STILL THINK THIS WAS A GOOD IDEA?" NIKI ASKED.

Her cousin's pale face and hushed tone worried Grace more than the yammering voices coming from the other side of Niki's kitchen door. "I never thought this was a good idea," Grace hissed as she eased the swinging door open to better hear the argument she'd have to referee. "I told Connie to do all of the communication by email and phone."

"That worked out really well didn't it?" Niki said as she peeked around Grace for a better look into the hallway. "I turned away normal, *paying* guests to host this little disaster. It's Waterfowl Weekend! I could have rented these rooms ten times over. Do you know what this will do to the inn's bottom line?"

"Nik, it's worse than you know," Grace turned back and let the door swing shut. "If we don't have a firm offer on the Morgan farm by Monday morning, we'll lose the listing. The bank won't give us an extension."

This was the last foreclosure sale Tred Avon Bank and Trust would give to Kastner and Mosley. The law firm had occupied the top floor of the bank building for decades and handled the Tred Avon's legal work. Now the bank was being swallowed by a national chain, and like all change in a small town, the merger affected many other businesses. Grace knew she was lucky to have a shot at this sale. If she hadn't been a licensed broker as well as an attorney, the property would have gone to White Marsh Realty along with the rest of the bank's business.

She was down to the last few days on the contract with a lot of interest but no offers that met the bank's minimum. The auction was a tactic which had worked for some of her clients when she practiced in Washington. Only back then, none of her buyers had been shot on the properties she was trying to sell.

"I'm sorry," Niki's anger seemed to leave her. She looked as tired as Grace felt. "The auction was a great idea, I know. But it's gone wrong from the start. Maybe Waterfowl wasn't the best time to do it."

It was a perfect time and it may still work, Grace thought. She was accepting bids on the property up until Sunday, the day after tomorrow. The date was deliberately chosen to coincide with the Waterfowl Festival in Easton. All things Eastern Shore were show-cased during the area's largest event. Festival attendees bought paint-ings, sculptures and, often, real estate as they fell in love with the small towns and villages in their fall splendor.

It had been Connie's idea to jazz up the auction by offering the three most promising potential buyers an all expenses paid stay at the Victory Manor Inn for the festival weekend.

Two rooms away, voices raised in volume.

"You need to do something," Niki pleaded.

"You don't understand. Something's happened. Something bad." The sound of shattering glass cut Grace's explanation short and sent her running.

"See! There she is! She can explain everything!"

Three angry people turned to face Grace as she entered the living room. After diverting all the attention to her niece, Connie Delaney knelt out of the line of fire and used drink napkins to scoop up the remnants of a broken glass.

A tall man with a ramrod straight posture and an angry expres-sion let loose on his new target. "Madam, I do not conduct business in this manner. And I certainly do not frequent inexpensive accom-modations. I was told —"

"Hey!" Niki's outraged voice cut through his tirade.

Grace looked around the room. Niki and Tall Guy were in a glare-off. Across from them, a couple sat as far apart as they could from each other on an overstuffed Chesterfield sofa. Her aunt was making a production of the busy work of glass removal. Grace had no idea how to break the news that these remaining bidders now had much better odds of winning the auction. The notorious Garrett Bishop's interest in the property and the auction had surprised and confused everyone. Bishop could buy anything he wanted. His 'maybe I will, maybe I won't' behavior had kept gossip flowing and wreaked havoc with Grace's nerves. Now he was gone and if she didn't handle things right, the other bidders might be, too.

Connie came to stand with Grace, but they were far from a united front. Both were tall women, but Connie's nervousness made her seem smaller. "Tell them, dear," Connie said, poking Grace in the arm. "Everything's going to work out fine, right?"

There was nothing to do but get on with it.

"Good evening, everyone. I'm Grace Reagan, and I'm happy to finally meet all of you, Senator and Mrs. Carter, Mr. Norse," she nodded briefly at each of them. "I apologize for the circumstances. I never meant for anyone to misunderstand the intent of the weekend. As I said in my letter about the auction —"

"Oh, dear," Connie stammered. "There may have been a problem. Apparently, the letters didn't arrive."

"They went out last week," Grace said, even as she could see the truth in Connie's expression of panic.

"What letter is this?"

Grace turned to Anton Norse, who still stood by the fireplace as if posing for a *Country Life* cover. She thought she detected a German accent in his clipped speech.

"About the structure of the purchase offers. As you all know, this farm is a rare commodity. We didn't advertise widely, preferring to limit the offering to a select list of individuals we thought would be interested. You were invited here for the weekend to give you one last chance to inspect the property and to —"

"Try and top each other's offers." Norse clapped his hands and gave a mock bow. "But your plan is not working, Ms. Reagan. Garrett Bishop isn't here."

"Mr. Bishop is very much in the bidding," Connie said.

"Actually, there's been a development I need to tell you about," Grace started.

Norse cut her off. "No surprise to me at all. I'm sure Bishop has pulled out of the bidding. I may follow him."

"Well, I certainly am." Jason Carter stood and made an impatient motion toward his wife.

Sandra Carter made a face at him. "Oh, Jase, sit down. Or better still, since you're up, replace my drink. I barely got a sip before my little oopsie."

"Before you dropped it, you mean?" her husband said. The senator was a decade younger than his wife and would have been a handsome man if his face hadn't been scarlet and his eyes pinched with anger. "I think you've had enough to drink and we're leaving."

"I'm not going anywhere." Sandra straightened up from her slouch across the sofa arm and tucked a curtain of streaky ash brown hair behind her ear. It's Friday afternoon and I'm not going back across that dreadful bridge in bumper to bumper traffic. A gin and tonic, Jase. Snap, snap. We've got a weekend in a lovely B and B," here Niki got a wide smile, "and if Mr. Obnoxious over there gets his panties in a twist and leaves, so much the better for us."

They all looked to Norse, who laughed and said, "Touché, madam. May the best bidder win."

Connie handed Sandra a drink that might have passed near a tonic bottle, but then again, maybe not. Grace could smell the gin from five feet away.

"As I said, I need to give you some news." Grace hesitated. She should have told them right away, and now she didn't know where to start. Sandra Carter's attention was on her drink. The Senator was mad, and Anton Norse was scrolling through screens on his phone. She tried again. "There's been an accident —"

"Good God!" Norse boomed. Bishop is dead!"

CHAPTER THREE

Grace had promised herself she would never work another weekend. She looked around her office and toasted the silence with her half-empty water bottle. Another grandiose scheme down the drain. True, she wasn't working a seventy-hour week and this Saturday morning in the office was uncommon. Nothing like finding a dead man to mess up a weekend.

She winced at the memory. Flashbacks and anxiety had kept her awake most of the night. The morning hadn't been much better. She was killing time with paperwork before meeting with the Carters and Anton Norse. And she was hoping to hear from her boss, Cyrus Mosley. She hadn't been able to reach him last night, and he wasn't answering his phone this morning. She needed to tell him about Bishop before he heard about the shooting somewhere else. Bishop's death was turning her auction into a circus. It remained to be seen if the excitement would be good or bad for business. Even a murder wouldn't stop a bank sale if she could manage to produce a viable offer.

She leaned back in the leather swivel chair she'd taken from Mosley's office and propped her sneaker-clad feet up on the corner of her desk. Lately, she'd been trying calming techniques to ward off panic attacks. The rapid thumping of her heart and jangled nerves were disconcerting but hadn't yet driven her to a doctor — just online to self-diagnose. One article purporting to cure any illness with positive thinking reminded her of a sampler that had hung in the kitchen of her childhood home. *Count Your Blessings, Not Your Problems.* The advice was trite but didn't require a prescription and turned out to be surprisingly soothing. However, once she started counting, she had to keep going until she had a satisfying list. She wasn't overly superstitious, but she figured failing at blessing counting could lead to bad luck and she had enough of that.

Blessings. She had a dog. Part of a dog. She was fostering a mostly non-house trained Chihuahua and Jack Russell Terrier mix for a local animal rescue group. Leo needed to be socialized, trained and generally calmed down to have a better chance at finding a forever home. Given his tendency to howl and have diarrhea whenever he was left alone, Grace figured she and Niki equaled 'forever' for Leo. He split his time between them and any friends they could persuade to help out. For his part, Leo took it all in stride, bestowing love and dog poop on everyone equally. Grace put him on her blessing list because he erased any stirring of her biological clock.

Almost no Saturday work and Leo. Two blessings. What else? She hadn't worn serious heels in nearly a year. She rotated first one foot, then the other, making air circles and smiling. Her feet hadn't hurt in months. The last new clothes she'd bought had been jeans from Target, but she could count them as a blessing for her bank account.

Even a few weeks ago, she would have capped the blessings list with 'No David.' She was no longer the work wife and not-so-secret lover of the senior partner in her former law firm. The newness of freedom had worn off and the loneliness which replaced it was taking some getting used to. She pushed David's image away and concentrated. Blessing counting was a tad stressful today.

Daily treachery was less overt. Could that be a real blessing? She decided it was. She didn't have to worry about up and coming associates looking to push her off the corporate ladder or partners who dumped their hopeless cases on mid-level attorneys. 'No bullies' made the list, and she decided to expand its power. She found a pad of sticky notes and wrote *Staff Meeting!* She underlined 'meeting', ripped the bright yellow square from the pad and slapped it on the top of her monitor frame. First thing Monday morning, she'd sit the staff down and set them straight. Filled with inspiration, she grabbed a legal pad and begin to list all the things she wanted to change in the office operations.

Grace had never supervised anyone before taking over the management at Kastner and Mosley. She'd taken human resources seminars but hadn't learned anything useful, such as how to handle coworkers who hated each other. She looked at the yellow notepad and felt her resolve slip.

She was trying to run a venerable law firm without any of its historical underpinnings. The letterhead said there were two partners and Grace F. Reagan, Esquire practicing under the Kastner and Mosley, LLC banner. The half page ads in the Chamber of Commerce annual yearbook suggested a bustling operation with professionals who could answer any question, handle any problem. Grace knew a more accurate representation of the current firm would be a middle-school locker room and girls yelling, 'You goin' *down.'*

The name partners, Paul Kastner and Cyrus Mosley, were theoretically still practicing, but a young wife with a yen to see Europe had made off with Kastner and a stroke had taken Mosley out of action. All of which left Grace as the only working attorney. For the time being. She checked the date on her phone. She had four months and three days left on the contract she'd signed with Mosley. Four more months in which she would try to force life into the dying firm and keep the few clients they had left happy while Mosley recovered. As if this wasn't challenging enough, she also had to move the firm out of the offices it had occupied for half a century and into a smaller building ten miles away in Mallard Bay. Most days she tried not to think about that Herculean chore.

A sharp 'ding!' from the direction of the lobby broke Grace out of her reverie. Finding Lee McNamara at the reception desk was a relief until she realized he probably had a good reason for showing up instead of calling. Mallard Bay's Chief of Police was well out of his jurisdiction.

He said, "Sorry to barge in on your weekend at the office, I should have called."

"You're always welcome," she said and meant it. The Chief had been one of the first people she'd met when she came to the Eastern Shore, and he'd become a good friend. "What's happened?" she asked. "Have they found out who shot Garrett?"

"No, sorry, no news like that. I ran into Avril with Leo at the Farmers' Market. She said she was dog sitting while you worked today. I need to talk to you and thought we'd have more privacy here than at the station."

"And here I thought you were checking up on me," she teased. "Let's go to the break room and I'll make coffee."

But the Chief wasn't making a social call, and soon Grace had a whole new set of problems to worry about.

"HAVE THEY AT LEAST MADE ANY PROGRESS?" GRACE PRODUCED mugs of coffee and McNamara made himself comfortable in one of the armchairs that flanked her desk. She took the other chair and waited for him to get on with whatever he'd come to tell her. His usually calm demeanor was missing today, and she was surprised at how disconcerting it was to see him tense.

"The State Police held a news conference about an hour ago. Bishop was identified and his death officially declared suspicious. He was shot. They also confirmed Bishop was at the farm because he was buying it."

Grace groaned. "That's not what I said to them! Now the other bidders will think I made a deal behind their backs before the deadline." She took a breath and pushed that concern aside. Maybe the Carters and Norse would be too busy trying to one-up each other to get bogged down in news reports. "He called and told me he had an offer for me, one I'd be happy with, but he refused to come to the office. He said if I wanted it, I had to meet him at the property."

McNamara sat back and looked at her curiously. "He said it like that and you went?"

She saw how it must look to him. Bishop had been obnoxious, but he was also an attractive man, in a dark, brooding sort of way. He wasn't tall but had an athletic build and a booming voice that turned heads. The sort of man who always drew attention and worked hard to keep it. The thought that her interactions with him might look less than professional made her uneasy.

She said, "He liked using double entendres. He was juvenile in that way. I believed him when he said he had a contract, so I went." When McNamara didn't respond, she added, "Did they find any paperwork on the body or in his car? If Garrett really had a contract for me, it would be with his corporation. If he signed it, might still be valid."

McNamara shook his head. "I'm sorry. It was in his front pocket and was damaged. But in any case, it wasn't signed."

Grace didn't ask how the contract was damaged. The Chief was watching her and she felt a blush warm her face. A man was dead, and her first reaction was whether or not he'd solved her problems before he drew his last breath.

"I sound awful, I know," she said. The memory of Bishop's body, crumpled on the damp grass, was never far from her mind. Odd details kept popping out at her. This morning she'd remembered his neck had been cold when she'd touched him and she'd been grateful his eyes were closed. "There was a lot of blood." She wished she could make herself shut up. "Do you know, they put bags over my hands and they wouldn't let me wash. I was so filthy! The officers wore those suits, the HAZMAT type, but they wouldn't even let me wipe my hands."

"Grace," McNamara gently took her hands in his. "You were in shock. Probably still are. Do you have someone to talk to?"

She thought about his question. It should have an easy answer. His hands were warm and his touch felt good. "I'm okay," she said.

He let her go with a gentle pat. "A shock like this can fester and cause problems if you don't deal with it head-on."

Now she felt foolish as well as crass. Not trusting her voice, she only smiled and smoothed her hair back from her face, tucking a loose strand into the French braid that tamed her wiry curls.

McNamara continued as if nothing had happened. "I know you gave your statement to the detectives yesterday and I'm not on the front line of the investigation, but I'd like to hear your take. Tell me about the bidders."

She was grateful for the change in conversation. "State guys are letting you play?" She meant it as a joke, but he didn't smile.

"I'm helping where I can," he said. He had his notepad and pen out and was waiting.

She started with the dead man.

CHAPTER FOUR

"Of course, you know Garrett Bishop's background. He was most likely to win the bidding because, as he repeatedly told me, he had the most money. He even had an architect drawing up plans for a compound of homes he would build after he subdivided the property. He was the first person to respond to our advertising mailing. He tried to cut the firm out of the sale by offering the bank a quick cash deal. If they hadn't already made the agreement with us, he might have succeeded." Grace felt better as she talked, gathering her thoughts and emotions and putting them to good use.

"Jason and Sandra Carter are from Virginia," she continued. "He's a state Senator, an insurance broker by trade, and she's an artist. Sandra was a sorority sister of Connie's back in the day and that's how they wound up with her as a real estate agent. You know Connie got her license, right? Cyrus insisted we help her out, even though I'm closing down the real estate division of the firm. None of which is pertinent, I guess." She stopped and watched as McNamara wrote.

After a moment, he said, "I did know, yes, but thanks for the background. Are the Senator and his wife in the same financial circles as Bishop?"

"I doubt it. According to Connie, Mrs. Carter has family money and likes to toss it around. The Carters also want to subdivide the property, but they plan to sell off the extra lots and renovate the original house as a vacation home." She paused to let McNamara catch up, but he stopped writing almost immediately.

"Anton Norse appeared out of nowhere about a week ago," she continued. "I don't know much about him. He's an agent for an anonymous buyer."

"Is that unusual?" McNamara asked.

"Not at all," Grace said, and then because she knew what he was referring to, she added, "There are all kinds of reasons a person would want to conceal their identity when purchasing a property." She'd used such a ploy to buy her mother's childhood home.

The Chief smiled. He knew her story better than anyone. "Why would someone send an agent like Anton Norse to buy the Morgan homestead?"

"I made some calls. Norse owns a company which specializes in finding and buying rare or unlisted properties. He promises a secure transaction and anonymity, or anything else. For a price, a buyer can get almost anything they want."

"Anything meaning?"

"I'm talking about real estate, Mac. If Norse is brokering anything else, I haven't heard it. But I have heard rumors he can make competing buyers happy with alternative deals, or ruin them if they refuse his best offer to go away quietly."

McNamara's naturally straight posture stretched out another inch. "Ruin?"

"Rumors."

"Of?"

"Bidders getting cold feet and pulling out suddenly. Banks removing financing from previously solid accounts. Rumors. But he isn't a welcome sight in a bidding war. Frankly, I had no idea what we were getting into."

"Pitting Bishop against Norse, you mean?"

"Inadvertently, but yes." The pit of anxiety opened again. This was why she felt worse with the official statement that Bishop's death was suspicious. What if her grand plan, her auction, had been the motive for a murder? "Connie decided Bishop or Norse might back out if they knew there were others invited to bid, so she told Marjorie not to send out the letters I wrote to them explaining the process." The memory of Connie's meddling brought a fresh burst of anger, but Grace concentrated on McNamara.

"Why would they back out?" he asked. "Don't people usually come to an auction expecting to bid against others?"

"Bishop and Norse didn't know it *was* an auction, or that the Carters were in the mix. Each believed they were in the cat-bird seat and only had to make an offer acceptable to the bank. Connie was afraid of upsetting them and thought an all expenses paid weekend during the Waterfowl Festival would keep everyone happy. She made the arrangements and only told me after they'd all accepted the invitation. She also didn't tell me she'd intercepted my letters from the secretary."

McNamara wrote many more squiggles on his pad than were needed to record her answer. She waited until he'd finished before saying, "What's going on? Don't tell me you think Norse got so worked up over the weekend auction arrangements that he shot Bishop so his client could have the property? These people fight with money, not guns."

The Chief shrugged. "Who knows? Maybe. That's not the avenue the state investigators are favoring, though." He smiled at her. "I think Norse will be free to bid if he's still interested after what happened to Bishop."

Grace looked at her watch. She was more nervous than ever now and wanted to get over to the Victory Manor Inn and see if Norse and the Carters were there.

"One more thing," McNamara said as she made leaving noises. "Help me understand what the big deal is about the Morgan Farm. I mean, I get the deep water and access to the Wye River, but the house is falling down. Doesn't look like a spot rich people would fight to own."

"Really? You want to talk real estate strategy?"

"I want to understand why there would be competition for the purchase."

"Oh. This farm is unusual because it can be subdivided into four waterfront building lots in an area where all the properties - even the farms - are already built out. The subdivision rights are grandfathered. Without them, there would only be one structure allowed, the existing house."

McNamara thought a moment and then said, "Sounds lucrative. So why didn't the former owners do that instead of letting it go to foreclosure?"

"A bad investment plan is what I heard. They only got as far as naming the project 'Morgan's Hope' and having plans drawn up. Apparently, they spread themselves too thin and just let it go."

"Nothing, in particular, stopped them from carving up the lots and selling them off?"

"You mean opposition of some kind? Not that I heard. But it wouldn't have been welcomed by the community. That area's very secluded and four more homes on what's now open land would be unpopular."

"So I've heard."

"Rory Bailey? Is that who you're talking about? You think a disgruntled neighbor might have caused the former owners to give up the property instead of fighting to develop it? Oh, wait! You've talked to Avril, right?"

McNamara laughed and closed his notebook. "As a matter of fact, I need your help with her and one other thing."

"What?" She was up and pulling on her coat.

"You may hear from someone in Bishop's circle regarding the sale. If you do, I want to know as soon as possible. Call me immediately if you see this man."

McNamara handed her a passport-style photograph of a fortyish man with an unremarkable face and short light brown hair. She could have seen him yesterday on the street or never laid eyes on him before.

McNamara said, "This is Quentin Bishop, Garrett Bishop's son. We haven't been able to locate him as yet. Father and son didn't get along."

"He's a suspect?" Grace looked at the photo more closely.

"Everyone's a suspect right now, but they have an interesting past. From what I've heard, their roles are somewhat reversed. Garrett Bishop is a daredevil who's even been declared dead a couple of times when he's gone missing. He's always beaten the odds until now."

"And Junior?"

"We don't know much about their recent relationship. Bishop the Younger was arrested a couple of years ago for attempted murder. Probably would have gone to trial if Bishop Senior had cooperated."

"He tried to kill his father?"

"That's what the files say. I'm tracking down a buddy in New York who worked the case. And please keep this to yourself, counselor."

Grace said she understood. If he was giving her the information, there was a good reason.

McNamara rose and stretched. "It's been a long morning and the afternoon isn't looking any better." He swallowed the last of his coffee and added, "If Quentin Bishop contacts you, don't meet with him, just call the MSP or me immediately. I want to know if you hear anything."

She frowned. "You really think he's dangerous?"

"Somebody shot Garrett Bishop and left him to die. You were alone with Bishop for a good stretch before Aidan answered your 911 call. If the shooting wasn't an accident, the killer could have seen you. I'm going to think every suspect is dangerous until we catch whoever did it."

"I don't like the sound of that." She hesitated, then asked, "Will you let me know the developments?"

McNamara smiled. "I always tell you what I can."

"Which means 'no.'"

"It means I'll tell you what I can. But you can help me with something else. Some*one* else."

"If Connie's causing problems, I have no control over her."

"No one does, but I meant Avril. She's taken an interest in Bishop's death and seems intent on stirring up trouble where I don't think any exists."

"And you expect me to do what? Control Avril? Because I've been so successful in the past?"

"She listens to you," McNamara said. "Let her vent, be her friend. What you'd do anyway, but keep an eye on her. She didn't look good when I saw her. She was too agitated, even for Avril."

"Sure. Why not? I've got Cyrus under one wing, may as well balance him out with Avril under the other."

"That's the spirit," McNamara said as he walked out to the lobby. "Maybe Delaney House could become the Old Curmudgeon's Home. You wouldn't have to sell it; it'd be a moneymaker."

"Oh, good idea. There are certainly enough old cranks around to fill it. I'll look in on Avril, but I have to run over to Niki's first and check on Norse and the Carters."

The elevator closed behind McNamara as Grace dug her phone out of her pocket. She'd turned it off when he arrived, and now it displayed calls and texts from Connie. Grace grabbed her purse, locked the office and ran down the stairs. She didn't waste time on the elevator or calling Connie, but drove straight to the inn and what she hoped were still viable buyers. She only had one more day to pull off the sale.

CHAPTER FIVE

J ason and Sandra Carter withdrew from the bidding, but a call from Anton Norse shut down Connie's histrionics and turned lunch into a cocktail hour at the Victory Manor Inn. The Carters had hung in long enough to make Norse take them seriously. A short phone call and back and forth emails resulted in a no-contingency contract and a six-figure deposit to Kastner and Mosley's real estate account. When all was done, Connie had sold the Morgan farm for two hundred thousand over the bank's minimum price.

Grace left mother and daughter with champagne and went home. She wanted to be alone to absorb the news. The firm would survive under her watch - at least for a little while longer. She had to find her boss and fill him in, and then she needed quiet. The day had been an overload for an introvert like her.

Mosley continued to be elusive. On the drive home, she left messages on his cell and home phones, the final one telling him he could call her if he wanted to know what was going on, she was through chasing him. "Invalid, indeed!" she said. "Whatever you're doing, stop it and call me. In the meantime, I'll handle things as I see fit."

That should do it, she decided. Mosley couldn't stand to be out of the loop on anything.

THE RESOUNDING SILENCE OF DELANEY HOUSE GREETED HER, AS IT always did, like a tangible thing. A heavy blanket of quiet, holding time in place. Years of memories, Delaney voices and footsteps vibrated gently in the absence of contemporary sound.

Most of the first and second floor rooms were sparsely furnished or empty. The twenty-four-room historical landmark had been on the market for six months, but the sheer size and the price were proving attractive only to curiosity seekers. After the local real estate agents, history buffs and most of the county's residents had traipsed through, there had been no offers, only a chorus of shocked reactions to the price. There was also a collective opinion that Grace would never get her investment out of the white elephant.

She refused to consider that they might be right. She'd loved the house from the moment she first saw it, although, at the time, it had been hard to distinguish the thrill of owning a masterpiece from total panic. A year ago, Delaney House had been a rotting shell of a mansion with a grave in the backyard. Not an inch of the historic property had escaped abuse and neglect over the past half-century. What Grace's estranged family had failed to ruin, law enforcement destroyed in investigating a murder.

Even now, the house and grounds were recovering under Grace's care. Once the major restoration had been completed, the never-ending list of small tasks and daily maintenance began. Fortunately, the contractor who completed the renovation project loved Delaney House almost as much as Grace did. A regular contingent of workers from Pannel Construction kept up the grounds and worked on Grace's latest projects.

There were times when she thought living in the enormous house might be causing her to develop agoraphobia. The empty rooms sometimes made her uneasy and drove her to the security of her third-floor apartment. The downstairs rooms and the large entry hall, with its cantilevered staircase and domed ceiling thirty feet overhead, were designed for a big family.

Four original rooms at the rear of the house had grown from a modest eighteenth-century village home to a twenty-first-century landmark. Sometimes, when Grace walked through the empty rooms accompanied only by the sound of her own footsteps, she felt slightly off balance, as if she was moving too close to the edge of a precipice. No matter how much she gave Delaney House, it always wanted more. Wanted what she couldn't provide. In a way she understood, but couldn't describe, Grace knew the house needed more people. Lovers, children, a family. She wasn't enough.

As she did each time she entered the house alone, she called out, "I'm home!" and heard the words echo. The first time she'd done it, she'd felt like she was declaring victory over the obstacles which had plagued the renovation. This pleased her so much she kept doing it. Every time she returned, she called fair warning to anyone within earshot - fair warning to the house - that the owner had arrived. She was always brave when she came through the front door. The house's beauty, uncovered and restored by her determination, greeted her, offering a daily reward for her hard work.

Grace walked through the house, admiring it - and reassuring herself she and Delaney House were alone - before ending her tour in her apartment. Located in the former nursery suite and perched at the top of the house, the apartment was her haven. But only after she'd double checked the locks and security systems on the lower floors could she relax in her cozy home.

The apartment's rooms were smaller than those below and were filled with a mixture of her prized primitive antiques and cheerful chintz fabrics. Niki said Grace's taste was Little House on the Prairie meets 1990s Laura Ashley. Grace ignored her cousin's sarcasm and thanked her for the compliment.

Shoes off and hair freed from the braid which had given her a headache, she was reviewing the contents of her mostly empty refrigerator when the front doorbell sounded. A check of the security camera icon on her phone showed a gray helmet of hair.

"Hang on," she called into the intercom as she jammed her feet back into her sneakers.

Ten minutes later, dinner was warming in the oven of the big downstairs kitchen. Avril's arrival had ended Grace's plan for a quiet, restorative evening, but Avril had brought homemade cheddar cheese ziti and a bag of salad. Dinner was solved. Avril had also brought Leo. She was the dog-sitter of last resort, but Grace had been desperate that morning. Leo didn't do well alone, the Victory Manor Inn was out, and the little dog had proven to be angst-ridden when taken to the office. He loved Avril, and he was one of the few beings she even tried to tolerate. Judging from the scowl on her face when Grace answered the door, Avril's tolerance was exhausted for the time being.

"If you and Niki took any effort with this dog, he wouldn't be a pain in the ass," the old woman said by way of a greeting. "It's your turn," she added, in case Grace missed the point when Leo tried to prove he could climb her leg to reach her arms.

Her relationship with Avril still surprised Grace when she thought about it. Her life had changed dramatically, taking her from the tenth floor of the Casper Building in Washington, DC, where she had maintained a healthy law practice and an unhealthy lifestyle, to the Eastern Shore, where she'd heard life was slow and sweet. So far she'd seen no evidence those rumors were correct, but she was willing to be proven wrong just any time now. Avril had been one of the first people she'd met in Mallard Bay. Despite Grace's many attempts to dislodge her, Avril had stayed stuck to Grace's side and showed no sign of moving on to a more agreeable companion. In fact, she seemed to draw energy from tormenting Grace, who so far hadn't been able to outmaneuver her octogenarian sidekick.

"I told you I'm taking him to obedience classes," Grace said. "Did you read the training instructions I gave you? You need to work with him, too."

Avril snorted, then said, "And I told you, I don't need training. I know what to do with a dog." She sat in the paddle arm rocker near the kitchen fireplace and continued to catalog Leo's issues and Grace's shortcomings while Grace readied dinner. For his part, Leo settled into Avril's lap, content to be stroked while being discussed and diagnosed. Periodically, he appeared to wink at Grace as if to say *Aren't I clever?* The wink was usually followed by a burp, and the whole act was probably gas, but it made Grace smile.

"Tell me why you were out at the Morgan farm yesterday," Grace said, in an attempt to change the subject away from canine digestive issues while they ate. "Mac told me you were there."

"I had information I thought he needed. You know, about Rory Bailey. I tried to tell you last week, didn't I? Rory's been all over town saying he won't let anyone subdivide the property. It used to be in his family, you know. The Baileys owned the entire neck of land until the 1980s."

Grace frowned. She did remember now that Avril was reminding her. She should have told Mac this morning, even if the idea of Bailey killing a potential buyer was preposterous.

Happy to have Grace's attention, Avril pushed on. "I went right out to the Morgan place as soon as I learned what happened. I wanted to cover things for you in case you weren't there. And when you were, well, I couldn't leave. The State Police were all over you. I thought you might be arrested and would need help."

"Me!" Grace pulled the ziti out of the microwave and carried it to the pine farm table which claimed the wall along the servant's staircase to the upper floor. "Avril, you were playing sleuth, admit it."

Leo was unceremoniously dumped as Avril stood up from the rocker. Fortunately, she was so short, it wasn't much of a fall and Leo landed as if the whole thing was his idea. "Well, you found Bishop, didn't you? Who else are they going to look at?"

"A lot of people." Too late, Grace realized she was being played. Avril would grill her until she had what she wanted.

"What does our Chief of Police have to say?"

"He's worried about you. Wanted me to make sure you're not overdoing things and are taking care of yourself."

"Oh, really? *That's* what he said when you met this morning?"

Grace dished out the food and shook her head. "Is there anything you don't know?"

"I don't know who shot Garrett Bishop, but I'm going to find out."

"Why Avril?" Grace sat down and suddenly felt the weight of the past two days settle across her shoulders. "Why can't you leave it to the police and —" she stopped, at a loss for words that wouldn't hurt her friend.

"Prop myself up in an easy chair and stay out of trouble so people won't worry about me?" Avril pushed the salad and ziti away and grabbed the package of Double Stuf Oreos she'd brought. "Look, Mom, dessert for dinner!" She put an entire cookie into her small mouth and looked like a boa constrictor as her jaws adjusted to the mouthful.

"I only meant I'm tired, and I can't get enthused about a murder investigation tonight. I found Garrett's body, Avril, and it was awful."

Avril kept chewing and dropped a ziti to the ever-hopeful dog at her feet. When she finally spoke, she said, "Tell me all about it."

CHAPTER SIX

M cNamara had been right. Avril was planning to move in on the police investigation, and nothing Grace said seemed to make any difference.

She tried for a calm tone as she poured fresh tea into Avril's cup. "The odds are someone connected to Garrett Bishop killed him. The police will be looking into a lot of angles." Grace was careful not to imply she knew more than Avril did. No sense giving her more motivation to snoop.

"But I'm the best person to figure out what Rory knows. I can look into a few others who had issues with Bishop, too. I can find out who hated him the most."

Grace's attempt to be the voice of reason faltered in the face of Avril's excitement. "Bishop wasn't here long enough for anyone local to hate him." She wasn't sure this was true, but it sounded good, so she kept on the same vein of logic. "And, you're talking about Rory Bailey, who just didn't want to see changes near his farm."

"Have you ever seen Rory mad? He was nearly arrested at a Town Council meeting once, for yelling about some proposed zoning change and threatening to sue everyone in sight."

"That sounds like you." Grace put another spoonful of ziti on her plate and dug in. The gooey cheddar and Brie cheeses chased away the calorie guilt of her second helping. "Besides, I didn't think Bishop's plan was developed enough to stir up this kind of reaction from Rory or anyone else. He talked a lot and did have an architect, but it was all in the 'what if' stage."

"You need to chase that pasta with some sugar," Avril pushed the Oreo bag toward her. "Your brain's clogged. Bailey's not only against Bishop's proposal to put three houses on a historically single family property, he doesn't want strangers wandering over onto his land and he knows that will happen if the Morgan farm goes residential."

"And you know this, how?"

"Rory's a distant relative. We spend time together, now and then. I'm sure I told you he worked with me against the grave hunters when they went after our family."

Grace began to see a glimmer of sense in Avril's words. A local genealogical club had a splinter wing of avid cemetery enthusiasts. They called themselves grave hunters and often ran into opposition from property owners who objected to having strangers combing over their family plots. Avril had been at war with the group for years.

"You don't understand the situation," Avril said. "Rory's even more private than I am. He's not letting anyone near his people."

Grace was not going to provoke an unwinnable argument by pointing out that all of Rory's 'people' were dead. Instead, she said, "Well, there's nothing we can do about it tonight, and I have a mystery right here you can help me with."

Avril sighed and rolled her eyes. "Well, I've explained what you need to do with this dog, so let me see. What else? I know: Why won't anyone buy this house? Because it's overpriced. Why isn't anyone looking at the house anymore? Because you're letting that idiot Connie show it. Why are these issues still issues? Because you don't really want to sell the house. Why? Because you love it. There. All your mysteries are solved."

They'd had the conversation a few times before.

"This is a new mystery." Grace rose and waved at Avril to join her. "Bring your tea, I've got something to show you."

"You've finally bought furniture?" Avril called after her as Grace led the way down the wide hallway which ran the length of the house.

Delaney House was shaped like a backward capital L. Walking from the kitchen down the spine of the L took them through three centuries of architectural styles. Grace never walked through the house without a sense of pride and gratitude. Pride at her restoration of a masterpiece, gratitude that her family hadn't managed to completely destroy it before she got there.

"Do you have to walk so fast?" Avril snapped as she entered the front parlor a half minute after Grace. The crumbs on her chin said she hadn't spent the whole time stumping down the long hall. Leo brought up the rear, hoovering up stray cookie bits.

Grace asked, "Do you remember the painting that used to hang over this fireplace?"

"Since I'm the one who told you about it, I'm guessing you know the answer. What about it?"

"I'm still looking for it."

"Good grief, girl. Why? If you're selling the place, you surely don't mean to include your grandmother's portrait with the house." She narrowed her eyes when Grace didn't answer. "And if you aren't selling, why would you display something she hated so much? She thought it was pretentious and not particularly flattering."

"Look at the wall over the mantle."

With a hiss of exasperation, Avril clasped her hands behind her back and studied the cream plaster wall. "I think it needs another coat of paint. Is the discoloration what you mean?"

"Yes."

"So, paint it."

"It's been painted. Four coats over fresh plaster." The front parlor had been damaged when a leak in the bathroom above it had caused the floor to collapse. The first time Grace had seen the room, it looked like a demolition site. "Every time, the shadow over the fireplace returns after the paint dries. Benny's guys are baffled."

Benny Pannel was more than baffled; he'd run out of suggestions. One of the older painters told Grace she just needed to get a large painting to cover the discoloration. His words had reminded Grace of her grandmother, Emma, and the portrait.

"Then buy a painting the same size," Avril said. "Don't torture your poor dead grandmother by dragging that monstrosity back into the house."

"You said it was elegant!"

"I know what I said!" After a moment, she added, "Emma felt it was a symbol of your grandfather's greed. I've always thought it was a harbinger of the misery that was coming to them. Why would you want it here?"

Grace didn't have an answer. Not one she wanted to share with Avril, at any rate. Her grandmother and uncle had sold off most of the family's valuables before Grace even knew her relatives existed. What they hadn't sold had disappeared before Grace bought the house. Little remained of her grandmother's estate by the time it was divided between Grace and her uncle, Stark Delaney.

Grace wanted to know what had once filled the rooms of her house. She was sure Stark and his son Winston were behind the missing heirlooms, but she hadn't found a way to prove it - yet. She'd never been successful in getting answers from Connie about her husband and son, and Grace didn't have the heart to question Niki about her family. Niki rarely talked at length about her father or her brother, and when she did, tears were usually involved.

"Or paint the room a darker color," Avril was saying. "Or better still, get a real contractor in here to assess the situation. There's probably some old wallpaper those Pannels didn't know needed to be treated to keep the dyes and paste from bleeding through."

It was getting late. Grace still had to walk Avril and, hopefully, Leo home and then clean the kitchen, removing any trace of their dinner on the off-chance Connie was on a winning streak and got a showing for the house. It would be after ten before she could think about bed. For a woman whose former life had rarely seen her in bed before one, a late night in her new circumstances usually meant insomnia. Which she would probably have, anyway. She wasn't up to the usual argument with Avril over Grace's support and employment of Pannel Contractors, a business which had cut its teeth on the restoration of Delaney House.

Avril wasn't going to let her get away with avoiding conversation. "What? You think the shadow is some ghostly manifestation of Emma's displeasure?" Avril looked around, as if assessing the possibility her long-dead friend might be within earshot. "All she ever wanted was the Delaneys to be rid of this place and here you are defying her. But let me tell you, she wouldn't be mad; she'd be proud of you."

Grace's tired brain perked up at the surprising idea. "Really? Why?"

"You're just like her in many ways."

"Oh, Stark says that, too. It isn't a compliment coming from him."

"It is coming from me." Avril put her fists on her hips and fixed Grace with a glare. "I knew Emma, the *real* Emma, as well as anyone. We were friends before she, well, you know."

"Before she went crazy," Grace finished for her. "You can say it."

"And you know she had her reasons," Avril shot back.

"Help me here," Grace said. "What is it we're fighting about?"

In an uncharacteristically tender move, Avril moved to Grace's side and reached up to pat her cheek and tuck an errant curl behind her ear. "Nothing. Only your cranky old friend wishing she had half of your energy and good health. There's so much I want to do and it makes me irritable when I see young people squandering their resources on the past. It's gone, Grace. They're all gone, now. Let the furniture go, let the portrait go. Let Cyrus and me go, too, if you need to. Try again with the handsome lawyer you left in Washington, but whatever you do, stop dithering, girl. Life's too short."

Later that night, as sleep did its usual disappearing act, Grace couldn't get Avril's grand speech out of her mind. She didn't feel like she was wasting time. She was helping Cyrus keep his firm afloat. It wasn't unreasonable to want to find antiques which had been in her mother's family and which should still be in Delaney House. A year and a half ago, her whole life had changed. It made sense to take her time in deciding her future plans. Avril's suggestion that she go back to David was ridiculous. It had taken her years to get out of her relationship with the controlling, insensitive jerk.

She had four good arguments, but she didn't believe any of them.

She *was* dithering.

And she'd let Avril distract her before she could find out how her meddling friend planned to help the Chief of Police solve the mystery of Garret Bishop's death.

CHAPTER SEVEN

"Sit down. Take a load off." McNamara tapped the chair next to his desk with the toe of his black oxford and sent the rickety wheels flying.

Aidan Banks caught the chair, wheeled it around and settled himself off to the side of the desk, dropping his head in his hands as soon as his rear hit the seat. "I hate this damned job," he moaned.

"Rough morning?" The chair routine and Banks' complaining were their usual greeting unless they had an audience. McNamara resumed his endless task of initialing the previous day's reports and waited for the complaint du jour. When Banks didn't respond, the Chief glanced at the corporal who, in rubbing his head, was massaging his curly hair into a blond fuzzball. Between reports, McNamara retrieved a bottle of Ibuprofen from a drawer and set it down on the corner of the desk.

"You, uh, might be getting a complaint," Banks finally said.

"A complaint about you?" McNamara's pen continued to scribble his initials and pages continued to turn, but the month-end statistics passed unnoticed under his gaze.

"This woman, I am sure she's blowing hot air. Nothing will come of it, but she pissed me off."

"How old?" McNamara asked.

"What difference does that make?"

"Your problems with women are in two categories, hormone-driven and everything else. I'm just trying to determine which avenue we're traveling today."

Red splotches blossomed on Banks' neck and spread upward. "She's old, uh, older. At least fifty and probably more, okay? And I was doing my job. She's been in town about twenty minutes and was trying to tell me it wasn't legal that Dodson Avenue is one way."

"Which way was she headed?"

Banks rubbed his head harder. When the Chief made bad jokes, it was hard to swallow the comeback. "The wrong one. She tore up the ticket and drove off."

"And you did, what?"

"Regulations say —"

"What did you do?"

McNamara wasn't writing anymore. Banks had his full attention.

"Look, Chief, we can't let some out-of-towner get away with breaking the law. Before you know it, we'll have a reputation for being easy on crime and then—"

"You went after her, didn't you?" McNamara said in a toneless voice. This would not end well. He thought, not for the first time, Banks could go far if he could only harness his ever-ready anger and direct it toward positive action. As it was, McNamara doubted he would see another promotion, and there were days when continued employment at any rank seemed unlikely. Aidan Banks had a temper which touched and poisoned every part of his life. And yet McNamara not only made allowances, he also coached, mentored, and tried to teach the younger man. Most days, he thought he was wasting his time.

"When did this happen?' McNamara finally said.

"Recently." Banks saw his boss' jaw clench and quickly added, "an hour ago."

"You're currently assigned to the Bishop investigation. As am I. Since we are the only two wearing badges around here, this means we are officially shorthanded. You could have turned this woman around and given her the warning without all the drama. We don't have time for drama, am I clear? I need you focused."

"Yes, sir. There's one more thing, though. The woman was Sandra Carter."

There was only one reason Banks would have kept the wrong-way driver's identity out of the initial account of his morning. Something worse was coming. McNamara studied Banks' red face and wild hair and made a guess. "You chased her."

"Yes, sir."

"You caught her?"

"Yes, sir. Well, technically, she stopped when she got to Niki's inn, *and* she got out of the car. You know protocol says when a perp gets out of the car—"

"You pulled your gun, didn't you?"

"I was only—"

"Answer me. You stopped a person of interest in a suspicious death investigation, someone whose cooperation we *need,* a Senator's wife, no less. You yelled at her, too. Am I right?"

Banks nodded, no steam left in him.

"She told you where to go, drove off, and you chased her through town. Lights and sirens?"

Another nod.

"And when she finally stopped and got out of her car *at the inn where she was staying,*" McNamara paused and took a breath. "You pulled a gun on her. Do I have the general idea?"

"Yes, but —"

"Unless the 'but' means she didn't call her lawyer, I don't want to hear it." An awful thought occurred to him. "She isn't out there in the cell, is she?"

"Of course not!" McNamara's expression warned him to drop the indignant protest. Banks slid a business card across the desk. "Mrs. Carter carries her attorney's cards like she needs them on a regular basis. And Chief, I ran both the Carters' background. The senator has a concealed carry permit."

"The senator, but not his wife?"

"Yeah. Odd, right?"

"No. Ever watch the news, Aidan? Politicians get shot while playing baseball, for God's sake. And the fact Carter has a carry permit has no bearing whatsoever on you acting like a fool with his wife."

Banks started to protest but knew he was out of tricks.

McNamara stood, stepped around Banks and crossed the small office, an exercise requiring only five steps. Opening his door, he said, "You made this mess and you're going to fix it. Come with me."

———

"ONE MORE TIME," MCNAMARA SAID AS THEY WALKED ACROSS THE lawn of the Victory Manor Inn. "You never mentioned Bishop, the investigation, or anything other than Sandra Carter's driving?"

"No, sir. I was pretty mad. Actually, the connection didn't hit me until I was, uh, in pursuit."

"Pursuit at high speed, through the business district and a school zone, in direct violation of protocol. And all for a traffic violation," McNamara reminded him, lest Banks think they were on even ground.

It was Sunday, so no school, but Banks knew better than to point it out. He'd done what he'd done, and he was getting tired of apologizing for it.

As they reached the front porch of the inn, McNamara said, "She never said anything about needing her attorney for representation?"

"Representation? No. She said she was calling him to crucify me for harassment."

"Well, okay, then." McNamara rang the doorbell. "If you say anything other than 'hello' or 'I apologize,' you're fired. Understand?"

A man to follow the rules when left with no other options, Banks gave a short salute and kept his mouth shut.

JASON CARTER OPENED THE FRONT DOOR OF THE INN AS IF HE OWNED it. A slender man, he nonetheless managed to fill the doorway with entitlement and righteous indignation.

McNamara smiled and extended his hand as he introduced himself.

"This the guy who threatened my wife with a gun?" Carter pointed to Banks, who clinched his fists but stayed silent.

Pulling his hand back, McNamara said, "An unfortunate incident. Corporal Banks is here to apologize to your wife, and I'm here to talk with you both about another matter if you have a moment." McNamara saw Niki appear behind Carter. He called good morning to her and got a wave before she turned and disappeared down the hall. To the Carters, he said, "I won't take much of your time. I'd like to get your take on Mr. Bishop's frame of mind before he left here last Friday."

The Senator hadn't taken his eyes off of Banks. "That ticket going away?"

"Already done," McNamara said.

Carter stepped back, allowing them entrance, but his scowl remained firm.

After what Banks intended to be a subtle once-over to determine that the senator wasn't armed, he turned his attention to slipping away from his boss and the Carters. His on-again, off-again romance with Niki Malvern was on at the moment, and he could use a sympathetic ear and other comforts. He was poised to disappear through the den and circle around to the kitchen, when Niki appeared with a tray laden with coffee and lemon scones and blocked his getaway.

As the food was being set out, McNamara turned to Banks. "Corporal, you have something to say to the Carters?"

Banks managed a strangled apology that sounded about as sincere as a used car sales pitch.

The Carters settled on the living room sofa, separated from police officers by a low coffee table and miles of attitude. Niki disappeared again, and Banks sat on the chair nearest the door. His only job now was to try to appear interested while the Chief did his thing. Banks knew from experience McNamara could sweet talk a lizard, but he thought the Carter woman could make him work for his money. Maybe this would be the day he would see the Chief stumble. With that possibility to look forward to, he took out his notebook and began to scribble.

The Carters helped themselves to the coffee and a scone each and ignored the officers. Sandra Carter had acknowledged Banks' apology with a queenly nod but didn't offer to call off the crucifying attorney. To complicate matters, a faint aroma of alcohol wafted from the couple. It might be coming from both of them, but McNamara's money was on the wife. She restlessly picked at a scarf around her neck. The colorful bird pattern against a yellow background looked like something an elderly woman would wear, but probably cost more than his car payment.

McNamara asked a few questions about the Carters' search for a vacation home in the area. Jason Carter seemed to relax a bit as his wife sniped about the scarce inventory of homes. "At least with the farm, we could renovate the house and have what we wanted. Subdividing and selling off the other lots could bring the net cost down into our range. We'd have a deep-water property at an inland price. Great views and practically no mortgage at all."

Sandra Carter managed her speech without slurring a word. McNamara gave her husband new consideration. Maybe it was the Senator who'd had alcohol with his breakfast. Not too surprising. They were on a vacation of sorts and had been through a rough couple of days. He nodded as if impressed with their plan. "I understand Anton Norse won the bidding?"

"Won! There was never a contest, don't you see?" Jason Carter leaned forward, his face earnest with what was obviously a passionate opinion. "Bishop could have bought us all if he'd had a mind to. We were here for his entertainment; I'm convinced of it. The 'winner,' as you put it, would have been whoever Bishop said the winner was. Norse strutted around like he would take the prize, but I don't see how."

"Then why were you here?" McNamara asked.

With a glance at his wife, Carter said, "Sandra wants a vacation home. I want a private place to hunt. We are genuinely in the market to buy, but Bishop and Norse would have to back out for us to win a property like this. So, to answer your question, sir, we came here to help Connie Delaney bilk a billionaire."

CHAPTER EIGHT

"Oh, don't be so dramatic, Jason! They aren't voters, so you don't have to exaggerate. Garrett Bishop has a lot of money, but it's millions, not billions." Sandra Carter put her nibbled scone back on the plate and said, "Chief McNamara, is it? My husband doesn't like to admit we don't have the kind of money to compete with Garrett and Anton Norse."

"You knew going in you would lose the bidding?" McNamara asked.

"Certainly," Sandra said. Her husband's face said this was news to him. A deep flush spread up his neck. "We've been looking for the right place over here for a long time, and Connie and I have been friends for years. Sorority sisters at Hudson back in the day. We've been through a lot of agents without any success, so I was thrilled when Connie got her license and could help us. When she asked if we'd come participate in the bidding, I said sure. Why not? A nice weekend and a chance - not a good one, but a chance - at a great deal."

"I thought we'd be dealing with an older attorney, that fellow, Kastner," Jason Carter said. "The firm's website says he's the broker. Then I get here and it's only Connie and some woman who claims she's an attorney. To make a bad situation worse, the other two bidders, forgive the bluntness, but it's true, they're strutting jerks. We were all stuck here in this small inn and it was really uncomfortable."

McNamara scribbled a bit more and then said, "If I could ask a few questions about Mr. Bishop? What was the first impression you had of him?"

The senator struck a contemplative pose as if preparing to deliver a stump speech. McNamara thought he'd practiced the move in a mirror.

"In my opinion," Carter said, "Bishop didn't know what the hell he was doing. You can't always tell a man's worth by his appearance, but Bishop looked more like a street artist - sorry, dear - than a successful entrepreneur."

Carter's apology to his artist wife sounded as if it was a frequent exchange. Apparently used to the disparagement of her fellow creatives, Sandra Carter ignored him. "He wore bad shoes," she said as if that settled the issue.

Her husband needed no encouragement to continue. "Garrett Bishop was all over the place. One minute saying he had to buy a boat and jet ski, the next out power walking - when was the last time you heard that phrase? And he talked non-stop about wanting to *consume* the area." Carter waved his long, slender hands in dismissal. "Said he'd done Nantucket and the Hamptons and anything further south was *bourgeoisie*."

McNamara thought Carter enjoyed using Bishop's pretentiousness to emphasize his own social standing. "I'm sure that statement would be a surprise to a lot of folks," he said.

"Jase is right. Bishop was awful. Such a fake," Sandra said. "He kept talking about tearing down the old house and building a compound on the Wye River side of the property. Said he would have a perpetual party - people could come and go as the mood struck them."

"Who was he going to invite?" Banks' voice caused both Carters to snap out of the conversation and glare at him. McNamara's look reminded him he would be fired as soon as they were alone. He made a show of concentrating on the notes he was supposed to be taking. So far he'd only jotted down every swear word he knew and 'blah, blah, blah.'

"I was told Bishop designed gaming software," McNamara said, refocusing on the Carters who reluctantly turned back to him, although their cooperative mood had vanished.

Sandra shrugged, which seemed to be her go-to pose. The scarf around her neck looked like crumpled tissue paper from her continuous pulling and twisting.

Her husband said, "So what?"

McNamara said, "Building a compound for a perpetual house party sounds at odds with what I've read about Mr. Bishop." When neither Carter responded, he added, "What I mean is, when he wasn't working, he was a daredevil prone to disappearing acts. I don't see him as a party kind of guy."

"I saw him as a fool," Jason said.

"A silly man without an ounce of originality," Sandra added.

Here the senator gave an unrefined snort. "Silly? Bishop didn't *need* to be original. He could have bought and sold us a dozen times over. He'd have outbid us for sure if he hadn't been killed by a stray bullet from a hunter's rifle."

"Is that what happened?" McNamara asked.

"Isn't it? I heard it on the news."

McNamara didn't respond. Jason Carter looked thoughtful, but his wife had gone pale.

Banks decided if he was already fired, he might as well say what he wanted. "Why did you stay for the bidding after you learned who you were up against and knew you couldn't possibly win?"

He got another round of glares, but Jason answered the question. "Because Anton Norse is also in the running. I thought the two money guys might get into a wrangle, get mad, and walk away. I wanted to be here to grab up the property in the unlikely event that happened."

Sandra quickly agreed. Her color was returning and she seemed anxious to explain. "I love coming to little Niki's place. Connie and I always shop and have fun, and this time I might wind up with the house of my dreams, so why not?"

Senator Carter made a sour face.

Banks made a note that Carter's wife embarrassed him with her *bourgeoisie* behavior. He made sure to use quotes around the big word. He also noted she'd left her husband out of her explanation.

"What was your opinion of Mr. Norse?" McNamara asked.

The senator's face closed up, smooth neutrality sliding into place. His wife just shook her head.

"Nothing?" McNamara asked. "You must have some impressions. Anything would be helpful."

"He's arrogant and hateful," Sandra said. "As soon as Connie told him what was going on, that we were all bidding, he got nasty. Really impossible to be around. We were so glad when he left."

"He's gone?"

"Not entirely. We wouldn't get that lucky." Sandra lowered her voice. "Poor, dear Connie was so embarrassed. Norse said he wouldn't stay here, at Niki's inn. He insisted on moving to the Inn at Perry Cabin over in St. Michaels."

"Is that where he is now?" McNamara asked. "In St. Michaels?"

"How would we know?" Her husband's hostile attitude was back. "We're still here. I wanted to go, as well."

"Why didn't you move to Perry Cabin?"

"Because this is a lovely place!" Sandra said, then added, "And as I said, Connie and I are long-time friends."

"That's right," her husband broke in. "Your good friend set us up as window dressing for the real buyers. She knew she was wasting our time."

"Stop it!" The hiss in his wife's tone drew the senator up short. "Connie is one of my oldest friends. We are in her daughter's house. Stop acting like an ass."

Banks found himself sitting up a little straighter, the mind-numbing boredom gone. Jason Carter *was* an ass. An ass with a short fuse who'd been embarrassed by Connie Delaney and Anton Norse. But it was the pretentious multi-millionaire Garrett Bishop who'd infuriated the Senator. Banks looked over to see if McNamara had made the same connection.

The Chief of Police was smiling. "You pulled out of the bidding, I understand," McNamara said.

"Certainly," Carter nodded.

"Oh, please," Sandra Carter said.

Banks reminded himself there were worse things than being single. Such as never having the last word, for instance.

But Sandra wasn't done. "My husband, the big hunter, decided the woodland acres were perfect for his needs. And I could have a waterfront house once we subdivided the farm. But Bishop getting shot brought up some unpleasant memories, didn't it, dear?"

The look Carter gave his wife got both police officers' attention, but it was quickly replaced by a wry smile. "Sandra doesn't think much of my shooting skills, gentlemen. There was an incident a few years ago —"

"An embarrassing incident," Sandra added.

"Yes, it was," her husband agreed. "You may have heard about it? I was hunting and hit the wrong target."

"You shot a cow, I believe," McNamara said.

"You did some research. Guess that's to be expected. I did, indeed, shoot a cow. Thank God it was the week after the election. The farmer wrote 'COW' on the sides of his animals in orange paint and let the press have a photo shoot. Not the same as Dick Cheney shooting his hunting partner, but bad enough."

Carter's self-deprecating tone lightened the mood until his wife cut through the chuckles saying, "Who wants to live so close to an active hunting area? Any fool could kill you while you're minding your own business. We might look for something a little less remote now. If we don't get the farm, that is."

"You told the MSP detectives you both were in the area when Bishop was shot," McNamara said.

"That's true," Jason said. "I wanted to walk through the woods. Get a feel for the land."

"And you, Mrs. Carter? Why were you there?"

"Jase promised me he wouldn't stay long, and then we could shop in St. Michaels and have lunch at the new restaurant on Talbot Street. I didn't want to walk around that smelly old house again, and thank goodness I didn't. Just thinking we were near the shooting has given me nightmares."

"Where were you exactly when Bishop was shot?" Banks asked.

The Carters glared at him, but Banks noticed the Chief was waiting for their answer. Maybe he wouldn't get fired today.

"I was in my husband's tank of a car reading a magazine," Sandra said. "He parked in some deserted pull-off area in the woods about, oh, a quarter mile from the farm. That tiresome woman with the state police kept at us until we'd pinned down all these details. Why don't you talk to her? I was waiting for Deadeye over there," she waved at her husband. "He can probably drag you through the woods and show you where he was when he heard the shot."

"I doubt I could find the exact spot," Jason said. "But I did hear the shot. I'd already started back to Sandy, and I speeded up when I realized I hadn't put my reflective vest on. I exited the woods over near Wales Point and walked on the roadside. Took longer, but safer than blundering around in the woods, right? A couple of trucks passed me, and the police found one of the drivers who backed me up, so I'm in the clear."

Sandra Carter stood and smoothed non-existent wrinkles from her skirt. "Yes, dear, we know. You may have shot a cow, but you didn't shoot the rich guy. Your re-election campaign is safe. Officers, I have plans for the afternoon. If you've finished?"

Banks didn't get to see Niki before he left, but then he didn't look for her either. After the Carters, he needed to be alone.

The ride back to the office was quiet. While Banks pondered the wisdom of commitment on any level, McNamara struggled with the uncomfortable knowledge he'd overstepped jurisdictional boundaries. Beyond trying to get his bone-headed deputy out of trouble, he'd had no reason to talk to the Carters. The Bishop shooting hadn't happened in Mallard Bay. The MSP had thoroughly covered the Carters' stories and were no doubt checking their alibis. They had thrown him a bone by asking him to interview Grace the day before, and while he liked to think his personal connection to her had helped produce some good background for the investigation, that was all it was. And he hadn't been asked to do anything more.

For the first time in years, McNamara regretted leaving the MSP. He was relegated to the sidelines - not in the game, but still itching to find the shooter who was too damn close to Mallard Bay to be ignored. He was a reasonable man, a rule follower. He didn't buck the system — he found a way to work within it. This was a State Police investigation. If he wasn't going to stay in his own lane, he would have to be careful.

CHAPTER NINE

T he shock of Bishop's violent death and the momentary spotlight on Mallard Bay threw everyone's life off-center. Departing Waterfowl Festival attendees were replaced by news vans and reporters. The country lane leading to the murder site became a mud pit clogged with traffic. By Tuesday, the media was mostly gone, but the tourist count was still up. Local business owners tried hard to maintain their 'we're all devastated by this shocking crime' demeanor while they rang up sales.

For the people at the center of the investigation, life changed in a different way. Being interviewed by the police was not as exciting as showing a cable news team the table where Garrett Bishop had sucked down his last round of Bloody Marys on the morning he was shot. Eventually, the hoopla died down. The Carters returned to Virginia, and Anton Norse departed for California. All three of them were at the end of a long leash held by the Maryland State Police.

The days after the shooting passed in a blur for Grace, thanks to the MSP, Cyrus, Avril, and Leo, all of whom demanded her time, information and attention. By Wednesday, she was more than ready for a diversion even if the only option was New Recipe Night with Niki.

Not content with being a good cook, Niki had aspirations of being a chef and was continuously trying out difficult recipes. Declaring herself to be a visual learner, she bypassed her bookcase full of cookbooks and used videos on YouTube for instructions. Having watched Niki in the throes of a video-led cooking session, Grace knew the real reason her hyperactive cousin liked the videos. A half-hour prep time could take all day as Niki took calls, texts and emails in between chopping, blending and baking. And then there was downtime with Candy Crush.

Grace took an antacid before she left the office.

Her contributions to the evenings were a bottle of wine and cleanup duty. And lying. Creative lying was her chief responsibility for New Recipe Night. At the onset of the dinners, Niki had been clear about the parameters.

"My parents will pick it all apart when I make this for them," she'd said. "I need encouragement and there'd better not be any silence coming from your end of the table, either, get it?"

Grace got it. Stark and Connie Delaney weren't acquainted with constructive criticism, but dished negativity with enthusiasm.

Following the instructions in a text she'd gotten from Niki, Grace took the flagstone walkway from the parking area in the inn's backyard around to the front of the house. Niki was waiting at the door.

"Welcome to the Victory Manor Inn, Ms. Reagan! I'm your host, Niki Delaney, please come in."

Grace remained on the front step. "What are you doing?"

"Giving you the full guest treatment. I'm stepping things up a bit. You're my guinea pig."

"Niki *Delaney*?" Grace said as she followed Niki inside.

"I'm trying that out, too." Niki's tone said the name change was still up in the air.

Grace handed over her wine for inspection and waited for more details. Pushing Niki rarely worked. Besides, she knew Connie wanted her daughter to take back her maiden name — not for familial reasons, but to capitalize on the family's recent notoriety.

She'd preached to Niki and Grace that they were letting a golden opportunity for publicity slip through their hands. Grace couldn't see the value in changing her own name nearly two decades into her legal career, but Niki was considering giving up her ex-husband's name.

As if reading Grace's mind, Niki said, "I know it doesn't make sense for you to change to Delaney, but it does for me. No one outside of Mallard Bay knows who Niki Malvern is. Delaney may be associated with a little bit of scandal right now, but at least people recognize the name."

A little bit of scandal? Grace wanted to laugh but settled for a smile as she gave Niki a hug. "If you want your birth name for whatever reason, you should have it. But remember, if you change your mind, you'll have to remarry Bob to get Malvern back."

This set off a round of *icks* and *yuks* from Niki and more teasing from Grace. The laughter carried them through Niki's presentation of artichoke dip and a vegetable tray of intricately carved radishes and carrots.

Grace held up a tiny radish basket and complimented Niki on the detail. "I hope this doesn't have anything to do with the Band-Aids on your thumbs."

"It took a while to get the hang of it."

Grace gently set the work of art back on the tray next to three other vegetable baskets and four carrot flowers. "Do we dip these into the artichoke stuff, or what?"

Niki frowned. "Do you have any idea how long it took me to make those? You don't eat them. They're for decoration."

"I thought that might be the decoration," Grace pointed to a glittery, green gift bag which sat on the counter. The handles were tied together with a gold ribbon.

"Nope, that's for after dinner."

Grace stomach rumbled as if on cue. "Is the artichoke whatever decorating something?"

Niki handed Grace a spoon and pointed to two small packets of saltine crackers on the kitchen table. "I thought I had some French bread to toast, but I must have used it all for the guests' breakfast yesterday. But you can have the crackers and I'll eat it with a spoon."

"Let's just have it with dinner. What is for dinner, by the way?" A delicious smell said something yeasty with tomatoes and garlic.

"Don't judge me," Niki said as she took a pizza box from the oven. "Like I said, the garnishes took a while and after the second accident," she held up her thumb, "I defrosted the spinach dip and ordered a pizza."

"Do the usual rules still apply?"

"Hell, yeah! I made this dip, ordered this pizza and sliced myself up giving you fine art to admire through dinner."

"In that case, Ms. Delaney, your presentation is flawless, your ingenuity remarkable, and your ability to make beauty in the face of mounting disaster is truly awe inspiring."

"Good work!" Niki grinned. "Now dig in, there's something I wanted to talk to you about."

"It's been a long day," Grace pulled out a chair and sat, even though she knew it would be smarter to plead exhaustion and leave. Niki's propositions usually involved work for other people.

"I know. Mom's kept me in the loop, it's all awful, but life doesn't stop. I mean, it did for Garrett Bishop. Oh, hell, I'm making a mess of this."

The pizza looked so good. Crisp crust and thin, curled pepperoni just the way Grace liked it. Niki preferred a thick crust and nothing but loads of cheese. Grace watched her cousin pick the pepperoni off her first slice and knew whatever was coming required a bribe.

Niki nibbled the crust and said, "You have a few months left on your agreement with Cyrus and then you'll need something to do, right?"

Grace took a big bite of pizza. She was going to need her strength.

"Anyway, you've got a lot going on now. I have a plan to help you get rid of your biggest problem and solve things for you in the long run."

"You're sending your mother away? Thank you!"

"Ha, ha. You're too funny. Actually, Mom came up with the idea, or the idea of the idea, if you know what I mean."

"No. But I rarely do, so go on."

"Come on, pay attention." Niki took a deep breath, set her slice of pizza down, and wiped grease off of a bandaged thumb. "The problem with my business plan is I've been thinking too small. I can cover my living expenses with the inn, but I work all day at it, and I don't have time to do anything else to bring in money. I really have tried everything I can think of and nothing is taking off like it needs to."

Grace relaxed and enjoyed a bite of pizza. So far, this was about Niki's work. And, so far, Grace could agree with everything her cousin had said. She took another bite. The crunch of the crust and the crispy pepperoni was delicious. The dip, not so much. She'd toss it in the trash the first chance she got.

Niki took the silence for agreement and hurried on. "But what if I concentrated on the parts of the business I do well and hire out the work I don't? What I mean is, I'm great at running a business. My accountant says I do everything the right way, and I do turn a profit, even a reasonable percentage. But with only four rooms to rent, there's a limit to what I can bring in. I added dinner as an option, but I'm not a chef, I'm just a good cook. When I make what I like, it's good. When I experiment, well, you know."

Grace did know. Niki's experiments were the only reason Grace took antacids.

"I've come to the conclusion the only way to make more money with the inn is to make it bigger."

Grace paused before helping herself to another slice. "Expand the building? Where?"

"No. Expand the operations. Add another inn to the business and run them together. I'd handle the business and as much of the daily chores as possible and hire a cleaning staff to do the housekeeping. If I could add five or six more rooms, it wouldn't just double my profit, it should triple it because I can sell to groups. That means I'd sell more room nights. You know, the rooms would be full more often than they are now. I studied marketing in college. I know how to package a product and advertise and everything. When it gets going, I'll hire a chef and add a meal package."

Grace pushed her plate away and poured another glass of wine. "Nik, look," she hesitated and then plunged in. "I want to be support-ive, but I don't see how buying a new inn is even possible for you, and you know my funds are tied up until I sell Delaney House."

Oh, crap! She realized what Niki wanted.

On cue with Grace's revelation, Niki said, "What if I could do it without buying a property?"

Grace drank her wine and let the silence between them grow.

"It makes perfect sense!" Niki said when Grace didn't answer. "Delaney House is huge and historic, and it's empty. All those rooms! We could be in operation and making money in a month."

"We?"

"You wouldn't have to do anything, I promise. I'd lease the house from you and you'd get fifty percent of the business."

"Nik, I'm selling it. It's on the market."

"Well, take it off the market for a while. Let me turn it into an inn, and then you can sell it as a profitable business for three times the price. I'd take my share of the profit and buy a new place for a new inn."

The idea had a certain appeal, but Grace wasn't going to say so. She was tired and the wine had gone down too fast. She knew if she so much as smiled, Niki would be ordering furniture and European duvets. "It's a lot. I'll think about it, but I'm not crazy about living in an inn."

"You'd be living in your apartment, same as now, only every creak in the house below you would be a paying guest and not some-thing you needed to worry about. But, hey, I'll drop the sell now. You said you'll think about it. And to help you decide, I've drafted a busi-ness plan and a financial projection."

The gift bag turned out to have a presentation folder with Niki's business proposal.

Later, as she got ready for bed, Grace realized she hadn't asked where Connie figured into the new inn scheme. Her aunt's ideas were always self-serving and never to Grace's benefit. That thought and the memory of Niki's hopeful smile kept her awake most of the night.

CHAPTER TEN

G race dropped Leo off with Niki on Thursday morning and arrived at the office determined to handle at least one problem on her own terms. Today was going to be a game changer for the staff. She needed to get the firm back on track.

The addition of ditzy, gossipy Connie to the two warring secretaries had been a disaster from the first day Mosley had insisted Grace give her aunt office space for her new real estate career.

"It's only for a few months," he'd said. "Connie has to work under a licensed broker, and you are the broker now that Paul's gone. No local agencies are hiring."

Grace told him no agencies were hiring *Connie* because she was a known airhead. But Mosley held firm and she gave in. Knowing Connie didn't like the arrangement, either, helped. It also helped that Connie had no intention of actually working and was rarely in the office. Still, even the little time she put in caused problems and added to the difficulty Grace was having in transitioning the firm from its two-partner operation to a sole proprietorship Mosley could run after she was gone. Once they moved to the smaller office in Mallard Bay, the tighter quarters would make Connie's presence unbearable.

Gone was the impressive, if somewhat outdated, firm Grace had encountered when she first came to the Eastern Shore. Kastner and Mosley had run separate practices under one firm. Each had their own clients and secretaries while they shared the support staff and common office areas. Lily Travers, who worked for Cyrus Mosley, was the polar opposite of Marjorie Battsley, who had tended to Paul Kastner's every need since he'd joined the firm forty years earlier. As the firm had downsized over the last few years, so had the staff. Only Lily and Marjorie - known to one and all as 'the Bat' or 'Old Bat' depending on the age of the person she was irritating - remained of what had been a staff of fifteen only two years before. Neither woman was picking up the slack with any enthusiasm.

Lily had greeted Grace upon her first visit to Mosley's office, but it wasn't until near the end of Grace's first stay on the Eastern Shore that she really got to know the young woman who was Cyrus Mosley's secretary, assistant and watchdog. While Lily helped Grace wrap up her first encounters with Mosley and the Delaney family, she'd undergone a transformation. Gone were the bar-hopping stiletto heels and short, tight dresses designed for another of the world's oldest professions. Somewhere along the way, Lily's game plan had changed. These days, she dressed more formally than Grace. Ironically, the sedate business suits and tailored blouses made her sleek waterfall of shoulder length black hair and large green eyes stand out in a way the party clothes never had. If she'd been ordered up from central casting, Lily Travers couldn't have been more different from the rest of the Mosley and Kastner staff, especially the office manager, Marjorie Battsley.

Marjorie, in her collection of 1970s-era Villager sweater sets and a single strand of pearls, was imperious and officious and all the more annoying because she was usually right about everything. While loathed by most who worked with her, Marjorie had an uncanny sense of timing and turned out impeccable work. Just as an attorney reached panic mode, Marjorie would appear with a brief, file, or deposition tape which had been hopelessly lost. Projects doomed to run over a deadline would be miraculously finished in the nick of time. Her appearance at the rear of a courtroom with a file in her hand was a spiritual event to a struggling litigator. After one of her magic tricks, the hateful nickname would be banished from the office lexicon within the saved attorney's hearing. Unfortunately, Marjorie couldn't contain her natural sarcasm, or the need to one-up everyone near her, and eventually the 'B' word would reappear.

Pretty, energetic, and intense Lily was the first staff member in twenty years to be hired by anyone other than Marjorie. The Bat ruled the staid world of Kastner and Mosley until Mosley hired Lily, and the battles began. As efficient as and possibly smarter than her nemesis, Lily lacked Marjorie's most useful asset. The Bat was ruthless, and Lily was young enough to be conquered.

Now, in the fading days of the once busy firm, Lily flashed like a neon warning sign to the suddenly untethered Marjorie. Once Kastner was gone, Marjorie had been left with all the abandoned chores of the former support staff. But the Bat was resourceful. She was related to half of the local population, including Mallard Bay's Chief of Police, as well as the sitting judges in three of the five midshore counties. Paul Kastner might be gone, but his few clients still demanded continuity and they wanted it from Marjorie.

At first, Grace shushed Lily's objections and listened to Marjorie's diffident suggestions on how to handle the Kastner clients. She also agreed to Marjorie's ideas for the office's operations, which naturally had to adjust with only one attorney at the helm of a two-person practice. Marjorie's suggestions made sense and seemed to work at the outset. They would still be working, Grace knew, if she and Lily would just lay down and let the Bat roll over them at every opportunity.

Lily moved into the role of Grace's gatekeeper and right-hand person. When Marjorie arranged things to 'best serve the clients', Grace realized too late that Lily had gotten the short end of assignments. Lily was the Executive Secretary to the managing attorney, but the Bat was still the Queen of Everything. Now, Grace would have to backtrack and set things right while maintaining what little progress the firm had managed to make.

She parked in Paul Kastner's space behind the Tred Avon Bank and Trust building in Easton. She'd been using it since her arrival, and it irritated her every morning that Cyrus refused to have his former partner's name removed from the concrete wall in front of her bumper. There wasn't a soul on the mid-shore who didn't know the great man had departed to a tropical tax shelter with a thirty-year-old blond, but parking space assignments were slow to evolve. Grace let the daily annoyance fuel her steps into the office. She'd called a staff meeting for nine o'clock and she was ready to make changes.

————

"WHAT DO YOU MEAN THEY WENT OUT TO BREAKFAST?" GRACE asked Lily as they stood in the otherwise empty conference room. "I called a staff meeting."

"They do that from time to time." Lily's expression said she was thrilled to tell someone who was as outraged as she was.

"Marjorie and Connie?" In the three months she'd been working for Mosley, Grace had tried to avoid the office gossip-fests. Now she realized it was often Connie and Marjorie laughing and Lily off to the side.

"Yeah," Lily's tone said *duh*. "I think it's when they plot."

"Plot what?"

"Do you have to ask?" Lily looked momentarily embarrassed at her lack of respect, but after a quick glance to judge Grace's reaction, she went on. "Connie doesn't spend much time here, you know, so the Bat keeps her up to date, only I'm sure her version of events is different than ours. They gossip, and Connie tells Marjorie what needs to be done with the few clients that Connie has. Haven't you wondered what the Bat does all day?"

"I assumed she was working for Paul's clients." It wasn't exactly true, but Grace wasn't ready to share with Lily that she'd been putting off tackling the mystery of what kept Marjorie busy when the phone lines were usually silent and the office was a tomb. Whenever

Grace tried to give Marjorie work to do, it went to the bottom of the Bat's never-shrinking pile of unnamed projects.

"Mr. Kastner's clients have mostly moved on," Lily said, as if Grace could forget. "For a while, Marjorie was busy copying files to forward to their new attorneys, and scanning and shredding our documents. She's very good at that. I think you should talk to Mr. Mosley. I'm not the best judge of anything else she may be working on."

"It's okay," Grace said, knowing it wasn't. She grabbed her tote bag and added, "When the Queen and Igor arrive, tell them to be in my office at two. If they can't make it on time, they can clean out their desks."

Lily looked like a kid who knows the promised pony won't really be there on her birthday, but she managed a wan smile. "It'll be two against one," she said.

"You can handle it," Grace called over her shoulder as she marched through the lobby on her way to find Cyrus Mosley.

CHAPTER ELEVEN

G race had been in a hotel room in Key West, bags packed and waiting for her car to be delivered when she'd gotten the call from Mosley. Instead of taking a puddle-jumper to the Caymans for the second stop on her long-awaited vacation, she'd driven straight back to Maryland and over the World's Scariest Bridge to the Eastern Shore. She'd known things weren't going well on the Mallard Bay home front with the Delaneys. Niki had sent daily texts with complaints and stories of family disasters, which only served to make Grace grateful for the relative peace of Key West. But when Mosley said he needed her, she'd headed north. It'd seemed the right thing to do, but she didn't examine the emotions behind her decision too closely.

How hard could it be, she thought when Mosley laid out his proposal. Manage the small staff and keep the firm running until he was able to work a full day again. But chasing down Cyrus Mosley had become a weekly, sometimes daily, chore. The more she needed him, the harder he was to find. Grace had stopped denying this suspicion and had given into the paranoia. Mosley had the ability to monopolize her life without leaving his rehab center of choice, the Mallard Bay Golf and Country Club. Driving a golf cart around the beautifully landscaped course was much more pleasant than working out in a medical facility, but she didn't see any physical therapy getting done. The fall weather had been mild so far, which meant lots of action on the golf course. And as long as the course was open, Mosley would be there in his winterized golf cart.

The Pro Shop was quiet. The early starters were already out, and Grace was able to sweet-talk the young attendant into letting her borrow a golf cart for an hour. She knew from experience that Mosley would be following the first round of players out to the furthermost reaches of the winding cart paths. She spotted the distinctive red and white striped awning of his custom cart through a copse of trees near the 8th hole.

She pulled her cart nose-to-nose with his in a small clearing over-looking a pond where three players watched the fourth try to save his ball at the edge of the water. As she expected, Mosley was talking on his cell phone. In a show of respect she didn't particularly feel at the moment, she waited until he finished the call before getting out of her cart and joining him.

"Bad business, this Bishop thing," Mosley said by way of a greeting.

A little of Grace's steam dissipated. The old Mosley would have been on his feet, inquiring after her health and thwarting any attempt she made to have a fruitful conversation until all of the protocols of politeness had been observed. But then, the old Mosley wouldn't be haunting a golf course he couldn't play. There were days when Grace doubted he'd ever had a stroke and a heart attack. And then there were times like this, when his short words, intense concentration and a pallor one shade warmer than death said he still hadn't recovered.

Sliding onto the seat beside him, she said, "Talking to your secret source?"

Mosley didn't answer, just tilted his bald head in acknowl-edgment.

One of the most disconcerting things about his recovery was his new baldness. Before the stroke, Mosley had sported the world's tallest comb-over. He'd cemented what was left of his hair into a bump, giving him a forehead which ran to the crown of his head. One trip to the barber had removed the hair vanity and, Grace thought, a lot of his personality. Now he was totally bald and had taken to polishing his liver-spotted scalp until it was shiny enough to signal search aircraft from a mile away. The sight of his suddenly small and vulnerable head still caught Grace unawares. Today, it caused a sudden moisture in her eyes.

She blinked, gave herself a mental shake, and got down to business. "Chief McNamara says Bishop may have been killed by his son. Apparently, they have a history of conflict. The backup theory is a hunter who probably doesn't even know he shot someone."

"That's what he told me, too."

She should have known Mosley would have called the Chief of Police. Or— "Mac called you, then?"

Another nod of the spotlight scalp.

Of course he did, she thought. "Well, we have the bank's property sold, anyway. I've checked Norse's financials and the deal is good. It's a no contingency contract."

"So you said."

She *had* told him all of this, and she'd thought he would be happier. Or at least more agreeable. "You should be dancing a jig instead of being so gloomy."

"I only shuffle these days," Mosley's smile took the self-pity out of the words. "I'm pleased. Connie did a great job. She says Norse wants more properties."

This was the first Grace had heard of further business from Norse. Or of Connie doing any work at all. She doubted any of it was true, and this was not the direction she wanted the conversation about her aunt to go.

"Did you remind her we're closing down the real estate business?"

"You're here for another four months. Let's see what she can do." His attention shifted to the golfers who were commiserating with the out of luck player.

"Actually, while we got the Morgan farm sold, the bidding

weekend was a disaster. Connie caused more problems than she usually does and nearly lost the two remaining bidders by counter-manding my instructions. I want to wrap up this association with her as soon as possible."

Mosley didn't acknowledge her beyond a brief nod.

She took it as a go-ahead. "And I'd like to talk to you about Marjorie, while we're on the subject of problems."

"Must we?"

His aristocratic tone erased her sympathy. "Not if you don't want to," she said sweetly. "I'll just handle everything myself. Tell me about those guys? Who's playing? Friends of yours?"

"Handle what?"

Another personality trait which had been lost to the stroke was Mosley's previous inability to have a straightforward conversation. The man she'd met on her first day on the Eastern Shore required a warm-up chat, many conversational digressions and a wrap-up lecture just to order lunch. Now he cut to the chase without preamble, sometimes leaving Grace scrambling to keep up. She was ready for him today, though.

"Connie and Marjorie. Don't give it a thought. I'll sort things out. Since I'm the only attorney practicing and Lily is the only employee who is actually working, we can cut —"

"No."

She waited, but nothing else followed Mosley's edict. She'd been expecting that, too. Mosley hoarded words now, at least when he talked with her. He didn't seem upset, just not inclined to say anything.

"Okay, we keep Connie," she finally said, as if he'd made the suggestion. She'd find another way to get rid of her aunt. "But the Bat goes. Lily's work is falling off because all the two of them do is argue. Now that she doesn't have anyone to supervise, Marjorie is insufferable. She ignores my decisions and obstructs Lily's work."

"Your decisions." It was a statement. And again, nothing followed.

"Yes, Cyrus. *My* decisions. I'm running the firm, remember? Such as it is, anyway. We do have some of the regulars left."

Thirty-two. They had thirty-two clients left in a firm which had once handled hundreds. Thirty-two apparently non-litigious, law-abiding, non-lawyer-needing clients. "The office is like a tomb," she said and immediately regretted her choice of words when Mosley's shoulders shifted up to his ears.

"We do have work," she hurried on. "But there isn't enough to keep both secretaries busy even part of the day. And I don't have time to drum up any business because all I do is settle their fights and try to ride herd on Connie." This was an exaggeration, but not by much. "Since we're closing the real estate division, I've found semi-nars for her to attend to build up her knowledge base and skills. She's also going to open houses to get her face out there. She was supposed to be holding open houses for me at the Morgan place, but she decided the house was icky and she doesn't do woods. The Bat had to do everything for her." Too late, she realized the trap she'd fallen into. Her own trap.

"Then Marjorie does work." Mosley said, never taking his eyes off the departing mulligan-taker and his team.

Grace hung onto her temper and tried again. "Connie is supposed to be job hunting and we just sold our last big listing. There isn't any work for Marjorie. Not *any* except answering the phone and making coffee. Look, we're paying two salaries—"

"I'm paying."

Grace sighed. "I can't turn a profit for you if you won't let me operate an efficient business model. *You're* paying my salary and I don't generate enough billable hours to cover it. *You're* paying Connie a salary and then full commission on top of it - who does that?"

"I do."

She barreled on as if she were speaking to a reasonable person. "Connie spends about two hours a week, two miserable hours, I might add, in the office and the rest of the time is doing God knows what. I have no idea what Marjorie is doing when she isn't tormenting Lily. Lily is now consumed with avoiding or thwarting Marjorie and I'm a damn babysitter."

"Things will pick up," Mosley ignored her arguments but finally gave her his attention. He shifted his newly thin body around on the cart seat to face her directly. "You're treading water for me. I appreciate it."

"I didn't take this job to tread water, Cyrus."

"Actually, my dear, you did." He took a deep breath before continuing. "I'll make it up to you. The work will pick up. Marjorie has a lot of contacts. We need her."

Grace considered each of his short declarations. Either he was being deliberately obtuse, or he was just humoring her. "No, we don't need Marjorie. Lily is the better secretary. Marjorie may have been once, but now, she's never on time and is constantly picking fights."

Mosley looked thoughtful for a moment. "She's bored," he said, turning to the course and a new foursome.

"Yes, she's bored! There's no work, Cyrus!"

"Find something for her to do. You're in charge."

"I need to be finding something for *me* to do to bring in money."

"Yes. That, too."

"*Fore!*" The call from the other side of a stand of trees was followed by cheers as a golf ball landed within a foot of the 8th hole.

"Did she get a new hair-do?" Mosley asked, still watching the golfers.

Grace looked at the back of his cue ball head and tried to decide if she'd heard him correctly. "She, who?"

"Marjorie. Her hair look different?"

This is it, Grace thought. Dementia. "Well, yes," she said but didn't elaborate. The Bat's usual stiff curtain of straight ash-brown hair had morphed overnight into a streaky blond beehive. If Mosley wanted details, he could get himself into the office.

But he didn't respond, so she added, "She's got some new clothes, too." The sweater sets had been jazzed up with a wide-shoul-

dered, 80s era navy blazer and a collection of above the knee poly-
ester skirts.

"Short skirts?"

"Yeah."

"Could be a problem." Apparently satisfied with the progress on
the green, Mosley turned to her. "With Marjorie, that's a tell. New
hair, new man."

"Man?" Grace had a hard time with 'Old Bat' and 'man' in the
same sentence, let alone in real life.

Mosley said, "New clothes, a serious new man. When they part
ways, she'll be cranky."

"You mean it gets worse?"

"Could. You should be prepared."

"No, I shouldn't!" Grace's last bit of patience evaporated. "This
is ridiculous! I'm not running an adult daycare! I don't have work for
Connie or the Bat and even if I did, I wouldn't want them doing it. I
can rebuild your practice and run a professional operation, or —" she
wanted to say, 'or you can find someone else to wipe noses and
supervise recess', but instead she just stopped talking. Mosley's
expression hadn't changed during her tirade. He seemed to be
looking just past her, or through her. Whatever, he wasn't listening.

"Look," she started again, only to be interrupted when his cell
rang.

"Read their employment contracts," Mosley said as he eyed the
screen, tilting it out of the sunshine for a better view. "Marjorie.
Connie, too." He answered the call, leaving Grace to gape at him as
he accepted a dinner invitation, promising to 'be there with bells on'.

Confronted with another bizarre image she didn't want, Grace
got out of the cart and checked her own phone, which had been
vibrating like mad for the last five minutes. Three missed calls and
five texts, all from Lily, ran down her home screen. In increasing
degrees of panic, they all amounted to the same message: *Please
call. Need you to call. Get to the office as soon as you can.*

Oh, she'd go back. She'd go back and find those contracts, find
the loophole that would void them and fire the two slackers. Mosley

might be senile, but she wasn't. When she drove around Mosley's cart, he smiled and waved as if sending a child off to school. She stomped on the accelerator only to be rewarded with a brief hiccup and an unsatisfying amount of speed.

Another text *ding* vibrated in her pocket, but she didn't look at the phone until she'd returned the cart with a generous tip to the attendant.

Police are here with a warrant. What do I do?

Grace punched at the office icon on the phone and ran.

CHAPTER TWELVE

"They say they're looking for evidence, but that's all they're telling me." Lily stood next to a state trooper, a mulish expression on her face. "I haven't taken my eyes off of them." She handed Grace a folded sheaf of papers.

They were in the hallway outside Connie's office. Inside, one woman was emptying a file cabinet while another was photographing the office. They turned to Grace when she started to enter the room.

"That's far enough," the trooper said. Both women held up badges.

"Ms. Reagan?" the taller of the women, a slender redhead, motioned to the warrant Grace held. "Everything is explained in there. If you have any questions, you can call this number." She handed Grace a business card.

"If I have any questions? Are you kidding me? You're going through confidential files in a law office! You can't do this." Her brain had been racing, trying to put the pieces together. She had several guesses as to what was happening, and she didn't like any of them.

"Your secretary said this office is the real estate arm of your firm?"

"Yes, but —"

"Then it's not a law office, is it? Please read the warrant, Ms. Reagan," the redhead's partner said. She gestured toward the file cabinet she was unloading. "We'll be taking these documents and Ms. Delaney's computer. Once we've examined the contents, whatever we don't need will be returned to you."

Grace tamped down her anger and thought fast. "I need time to look at the warrant."

"Take all the time you want," the redhead said.

"Please stop until I understand what you are looking for."

"I'm sorry -"

"Unless," Grace broke in, "this warrant says you're authorized to search privileged documents subject to attorney-client confidentiality."

The women exchanged looks.

"Ms. Reagan, I don't want to be rude," the redhead's expression said she was fine with rude, but she'd give civility a shot. "Let's start over. I'm Detective Marbury, this is Detective Simmons," she nodded toward her partner. "We have a warrant to search the real estate offices of this firm. We will be removing files and computers from this room and the two adjoining ones, neither of which have been identified as being a part of the law firm."

"What are you looking for?"

"Let's allow Detective Simmons get on with it. We can talk in your office."

"Or not." Grace unconsciously adopted the same stance Lily maintained from her post in the hallway. Arms crossed, stubborn glare. "If my office isn't listed in this warrant, you aren't going into it. You are, however, going to tell me what you're looking for and why."

Marbury didn't flinch. "We have reason to suspect Connie Delaney may be involved in a crime and we are looking for evidence."

"What kind of crime?"

"If there are any other areas of this building Ms. Delaney might have access to, you can save us time and yourself some inconvenience by telling us now."

"Connie Delaney is a newly licensed real estate agent who has worked for this firm for less than three months." Grace said, knowing she wasn't answering the question. "She hasn't had time to produce much in the way of files or paperwork, so what you're removing isn't covered. Connie just uses this office, and these files are coincidentally housed here."

"The warrant specifies 'materials in the vicinity' of Ms. Delaney's office." Marbury said. "You may want to read it."

Grace joined Lily and the silent trooper and scanned the warrant.

"Good thing Connie and the Bat don't do any work," Lily whispered.

"Where are they?" Grace asked, realizing for the first time that the relative silence in the office meant Connie and Marjorie weren't anywhere nearby.

"Never came in." Lily's eyes widened. "Do you think they've been arrested?"

Grace glanced at the trooper to see he was watching them. She checked the brass nameplate on his chest and said, "Trooper Dodd, I assume my associate and I are free to go elsewhere?"

"Please stay with Trooper Dodd," Marbury answered for the silent officer who looked like he would love to go elsewhere, too.

"We'll be over here." Grace pulled Lily into the lobby, out of earshot, but still within the officer's view. Turning away from him, she said, "Do you have any idea what this is about?"

"No. Except you had an odd voicemail on the main line this morning. I didn't check the calls until after you left, or I would have told you."

Grace could feel the trooper's eyes on her back. She motioned for Lily to lower her voice. "Who was it?"

"A man who said he was Mr. Bishop's accountant. He sounded mad and demanded Connie call him immediately. He said she had to return Mr. Bishop's deposit."

"He wants *Connie* to return a deposit? I talked to a lawyer from

Bishop Industries on Monday and refunded the bid deposit by wire transfer."

"Sorry," Lily said, whispering again. "I don't know anything more. Connie was really happy on Friday morning, but then she'd just been shopping and you know that puts her in a good mood. And the Bat always looks like she just stole my lunch, so it's hard to tell if they were up to anything more than usual."

"You mean like accepting money from Bishop?" Grace was stunned. "You can't mean it."

"No." Lily said, but she didn't sound convincing.

"Don't say that *anywhere* else." Grace ignored Lily's hurt look. She'd apologize later. "Have there been any other questions about Connie's honesty? I mean that you've heard."

"There are lots of rumors about her."

"Forget our family stuff. Are there any rumors that might relate to why the police are here?"

Lily shook her head.

"Have you ever seen her in those files in her office?"

Detective Marbury emerged from Connie's office with a box in her arms.

"Hold it," Grace whispered to Lily. "Don't say anything, understand?"

Lily nodded as Marbury joined them. "Detective Simmons is finishing up. She'll give you a list of everything we're taking. We'll need to interview both of you at the State Police Barracks. You can ride with me."

"You can talk to us here," Grace said, keeping her tone conversational. "We will cooperate with you fully, but you will not be removing us from this office unless you have cause to arrest us." She and Lily waited as Marbury appeared to assess her options.

"We can talk here," Marbury finally said.

It was a small victory, but it was something. Grace had practiced law for fourteen years without dealing with the police, but all of that changed when she came to the Eastern Shore. Most of the time, she was able to forget Mac and Aidan were law enforcement. She thought Marbury and Simmons probably wore their badges to bed.

Simmons led Lily into Connie's office and Grace got Marbury. Her questions were perfunctory and all of a theme: Who handled the money that came into the office? Who was the signatory on the firm's accounts? Was there a cash box? How many real estate clients had they dealt with in the past year? How many complaints?

After ten minutes, Grace broke in and asked, "Where are Connie Delaney and Marjorie Battsley?"

"No idea," the detective said. "Now, tell me about the petty cash?"

"Then I am most concerned," Grace said in an exaggerated tone. "You haven't asked to see them, all of your questions involve them and you don't know where they are? That tells me they could be in danger. Or, they're being questioned somewhere else."

"That doesn't concern you. Let's finish up here and you can get back to work." Marbury's expression didn't change, but there was a shift in her posture.

"We're done." Grace said. Then she strode across the lobby to the door of Connie's office, repeated herself to Detective Simmons.

"You're making a mistake," Simmons said.

"Possibly," Grace agreed. "We'll see. You've been given the access granted by the warrant. You are not questioning anyone else in this firm without an attorney present. I represent Ms. Delaney, Ms. Battsley and Ms. Travers. If you have Ms. Battsley and Ms. Delaney, tell me now."

Simmons smiled and Marbury shook her head.

"Big talk," Simmons said, "but, okay. We're done."

They left, but without telling Grace any more than she already knew. Which was nothing.

CHAPTER THIRTEEN

S he found Mosley, Connie and Marjorie huddled together in the parking lot of the State Police barracks. Mosley'd traded his golf cart in for his gold Lexus, which Grace hadn't known he'd been released to drive.

"Well, I'm glad I rushed over here to save you two," she said, thinking it was no wonder the detectives had laughed at her.

Far from being embarrassed, Connie and Marjorie seemed downright irritated.

Mosley said, "I was going to call as soon as I got things straightened out here."

Grace said, "Things are straight here? Good. Now maybe you can fix what happened at the office."

Mosley glanced around and waved her closer.

She gave them a brief rundown on the office search and the questioning she and Lily had endured. When she was finished, Connie looked alarmed but Marjorie never lost her defiant glare. Mosley studied a pothole in the pavement.

"Keeping in mind I will hear everything sooner or later, someone needs to tell me what's happening."

Mosley said, "It's complicated," at the same time Connie said, "It's family business."

Turning to Marjorie, Grace said, "I can't help you if you don't tell me what's wrong."

For a second, there was a crack in Marjorie's composure. Then the Bat left without a word, stalking off to a black pickup that was idling nearby. The driver wasn't recognizable behind the tinted glass, but Grace felt two sets of eyes on her as the truck rolled away.

It was hard for Grace to believe Mac shared anything with Marjorie Battsley, let alone a family connection. But she knew Marjorie was his sister-in-law. "Did the Chief come down?" she asked Mosley.

"He called. It helped. I need to sit down. Can we do this tomorrow?"

Grace yanked the left rear door of the Lexus open and said, "Sit. Talk."

Mosley hitched up the waistband of his slacks and said, "Not a good time."

Connie saved them from the argument by wailing *'Take me home!'* and starting to cry. If she'd been a dainty crier, she might have gotten her way. Since she was an open-mouthed squealer, she was easy to push into the back seat of the Lexus with Mosley. Grace drove, which meant they went to the office for a showdown.

"I DIDN'T DO ANYTHING WRONG!" CONNIE SAID FOR THE TENTH TIME as she sipped the coffee Mosley had insisted Grace make.

"You took money from a bidder! Yes, you did something wrong!" Grace tried not to yell and failed. Connie's sniveling had worn out her last nerve, and Mosley's apathy about the situation was making her crazy.

"It was corrected as soon as it was brought to my attention," he said in a prim tone.

"And when did that happen?" Grace demanded.

"Yesterday. Bishop's firm had their money as of noon today. There is no crime."

"No crime? What the hell was he paying her for?"

"There was some confusion," Mosley said.

"Then Connie can explain it to me."

Through her still dribbling tears, Connie said, "Bishop told me he was going to need someone to shop for him. He wanted a boat and information about local contractors. And he said once the house was done, someone would have to decorate it. We agreed I could handle all of it for him, and he gave me the money against future services as his agent. I deposited it in my account because I was doing the work, not the firm. Now I have to give it back, but Stark thought it was a regular commission and paid bills with it."

"A regular commission? How could he think that? Until last Saturday, you'd never had a sale!" Grace recalled Lily saying Connie had gone shopping on Friday and felt her blood pressure rising to an unhealthy level. "Besides, why would Bishop pay you now?" she asked. "He couldn't be sure he would win the bidding."

"Oh, please!" Connie said. "He's Garrett Bishop. Of course he'd have won the bidding."

"And you don't think it looks bad that you took money from him right before the auction?"

"You're not my boss!"

Now, even Mosley looked at Connie in surprise.

"Really?" Grace said. "That's what you've got? I'm not the *boss* of you?" She turned to Mosley. "She's ridiculous, Cyrus, but she's not dumb. Something else is going on. We had two State Police detectives going through her office and they brought a trooper for additional enforcement. They took files and her computer and wanted to go through the rest of the office, but I wouldn't let them."

Mosley's wan parlor became almost translucent. A large blue vein on the top of his head throbbed.

Connie put her face in her hands and lowered her head to the table.

"What?" Grace demanded.

It was Mosley who answered her. "You're correct. The police think it's more than a deposit."

GRACE MADE HERSELF LISTEN TO MOSLEY WITHOUT INTERRUPTING him. In the start and stop of his new verbal shorthand, he explained what Connie had done. They talked over Connie's still-bowed head as if the weeping woman weren't there.

"The money was a gift," Mosley said and frowned at Connie. "She asked Bishop for a loan. He said she didn't have to repay it. He wrote her a check."

"He gave her twenty-five thousand dollars as a gift," Grace said and looked at her aunt with new interest. "A gift which was coincidentally the same amount as the bidder's deposit."

Connie's head came up and she mopped her face with a tissue. "This is all your fault, you know. If Stark had gotten his full inheritance, we wouldn't have any money problems. Now if I have to pay Cyrus back for covering me with Bishop's people, Niki will lose the inn."

Grace had been ready to argue about the inheritance nonsense, but she was stunned into silence at the news of Niki's inn.

"Oh, Connie," Mosley said. "What has Stark done?"

"You mean after spending all of our money on our drug-dealing son?" she snapped.

Grace sighed. Connie had a right to be angry about her husband enabling their son to the point of almost bankrupting the family. Grace saw the whole story even before Connie could get the words out. Stark Delaney was a bully whose addictions were all legal, but nonetheless devastating to his family. He'd passed the gene to their son, Winston.

"A few months ago, one of his plans to win big gambling in Atlantic City failed, like they all do, and Stark went into a bottle of Jack Daniels, like he always does. He isn't due for his annual trust fund payment until December 31 and we were behind on the house payments. He made Niki mortgage the inn and repay us for the money we gave her to remodel it. A temporary arrangement, of course."

Mosley was finally angry. "Her grandmother gave her that money," he said in a voice that warned Connie not to challenge the statement.

Never one to read emotional cues, Connie wailed, "It should have been ours! Emma even told Stark to tell Niki it came from us."

"Because she knew Niki wouldn't take money from her." Grace couldn't stand it any longer. The entitled behavior that was the Delaney family hallmark made her seethe. All of them except Niki would take whatever they wanted as their due.

Connie ignored her, directing her plea to Mosley. "Anyway, we were going to make the payments on the inn. And I'll be making good money soon. It won't cost Niki anything to return the money to us for a little while."

Once Mosley would have pounded the desk and called Connie out. It worried Grace when he just shook his head and closed his eyes. She said, "Let me understand this. You took Niki's money and paid your own mortgage, which was how far in arrears?"

"Four months."

"And Stark paid the mortgage on Niki's place with Bishop's money."

"Well, no. We had other bills that were older. He paid those. He'll pay Niki's new mortgage next week."

"Really? With what?" Grace asked. "How much of Bishop's twenty-five thousand is left?"

"I don't know," Connie's petulant whine was back.

Grace reached across the conference table to Connie's purse and sent it flying into her aunt's lap. "Call the bank. Get the current balance on every account you have. Order all but twenty dollars in each to be issued in a cashier's check made out to Cyrus."

"Oh, I couldn't. Stark —"

"Do it now," Grace said. "You're going to repay Cyrus for bailing you out with Bishop's firm. I'll make sure Niki doesn't lose the inn."

Connie looked first at Grace and then at Mosley's averted face. She dug out her cell and made the call.

CHAPTER FOURTEEN

T he temperature had dropped in the late afternoon, and McNamara was happy to have a good reason for a roaring fire in his den. He didn't like being wasteful, but he'd make an exception for wood fires even when they weren't needed for warmth. He just enjoyed them more when he could cut the thermostat back.

He sat in his favorite chair, a cracked leather, high-backed, winged monstrosity he'd rescued from the basement when his grandparents had owned his house. His feet were propped on a delicate needlepoint-covered stool which had spent the first years of its life on display in his late wife's sitting room. In his tenth year as a widower, McNamara had his house arranged just the way he liked it. Most of what he owned was not only useful, it was in use. The superfluous had been gifted away or worn out long ago.

McNamara organized his work in much the same way. Some of his best thinking was done here in his den, in this chair, staring into a fire and mentally peeling away the irrelevant from the questions he was trying to answer.

He'd spent an hour with Grace Reagan, discussing the investigation into Bishop's death and listening to her describe the 'gift'

Bishop had given Connie Delaney and the resulting search of the offices of Kastner and Mosley. He'd made a few calls after she left the office and now sat with his notes, trying to sort the truth out of the tangle of information he'd been given. A cut glass tumbler with an inch of single malt scotch kept him company. It didn't matter that the killing was another agency's investigation, McNamara couldn't let it go. Mallard Bay wouldn't let it go, either. Rumors were growing, not dying out. Everyone wanted the killer unmasked.

Avril Oxley had caught him at the station earlier in the day and wouldn't leave until he'd taken another look at her photographs. He'd maintained a polite interest as long as he could, then printed out a dozen photos that Avril thought were important. He promised to add them to the 'case file' and hoped she never found out he didn't have access or authority to do any such thing. Now, McNamara looked over them again without the distraction of Avril poking at his arm and explaining what he was looking at. He still didn't see anything useful.

A view of the back of the ambulance waiting for Bishop's body. The crowd at the foot of the driveway. The front porch of the old Morgan homestead. A slightly blurred, long distance view across a farm field of what Avril claimed was Rory Bailey's house.

"See?" Avril had exclaimed as she pointed at the spot. "Talk to Rory. He's the closest neighbor, and he's had a hard time with people crawling all over his property since the murder. He's mad about that, but he saw a lot of folks before the murder, too. He's bound to have seen something useful, but he won't talk to those State Police. They sent some woman over there to see him and you can imagine how Rory took to that."

McNamara could, indeed, and Desiree Marbury had confirmed that she'd gotten nowhere with Bailey. She'd jumped on McNamara's offer to interview the farmer, but he hadn't had much more luck. Bailey had talked his ear off, but with a litany of complaints about trespassers, developers and the world in general.

He'd gotten better results from his own corporal. It hadn't been hard to get Aidan Banks to talk about the loan his girlfriend had made to her parents. Banks readily confirmed Niki could default on her mortgage because her parents hadn't made the payments. Ordinarily loyal to a fault, Banks only needed the Chief's assurance that he was looking into Connie Delaney and the Bishop shooting. To Banks, Niki always came first, but punishing her troublesome parents and drug dealing brother ran a close second.

The most interesting revelation came from Grace. Cyrus Mosley had immediately repaid Bishop's business for the gift or bribe or whatever the twenty-five thousand turned out to be. The State Police had descended on his firm as soon as they could get a search warrant. It looked like Mosley, one of the area's most respected attorneys, had tried to cover up a crime, or at the least something unseemly, for an employee. Or Connie was playing both ends against the middle, wheedling money out of Bishop and then Mosley.

Connie Delaney belonged to a group of humans McNamara thought of as floaters. People who drifted in the river of life, grabbing what they could, even drowning others, to keep their own heads above water. Swimming didn't appeal to a floater if they could use someone else for ballast. Unfortunately, in marrying Stark Delaney, Connie had joined another a floater. They'd spawned one of their kind before Niki, a champion swimmer, had been given to them by some celestial being with an odd sense of humor.

It was no surprise at all that Mosley, a world-class swimmer and lifeguard (McNamara knew he needed to explore his excessive use of water analogies), would bail Connie out of trouble. Mosley had been rescuing one Delaney or another for more than sixty years. McNamara hoped the old lawyer really did have a bottomless bank account. He might need it to save Connie and her family this time.

He picked up the biography of Wild Bill Hickok and opened it to where he'd left off the night before. He'd first read the book years ago and it came to mind as he'd studied the background material he'd found on Garrett Bishop. It was a line from the legendary frontiersman's obituary that was stuck in McNamara's head. He flipped forward to the introduction and a quote from the August 15, 1876 edition of the *St. Louis Dispatch*. It wasn't the folk hero's life which mirrored Bishop's, it was his death, or to be precise, his near-deaths, plural.

He read aloud: *"For he has been reported killed more than a score of times, yet his bloody corpse became reanimated through some witchery peculiar to himself."*

Like Wild Bill, Garrett Bishop was known for a flashy lifestyle and many brushes with death. McNamara had found two reports of Bishop's exploits which had necessitated rescue missions. Once he'd been missing for a week after causing an avalanche in a restricted area. Another time he'd been the subject of a massive search after his plane, which he'd been flying without a license, crashed in Alaska. Also like the legend of Wild Bill, Bishop always became reanimated after his near disasters, but nothing could save either man from a bullet in the back. Hickok had been shot by a man he didn't know. But Bishop? The possibilities were limitless and the shooter could be anywhere by now.

The doorbell brought him out of his reverie and to his feet. A glance at the mantle clock told him he'd been woolgathering for nearly an hour and he wasn't sure if he'd accomplished anything, other than a better feel for the murdered man. The doorbell blasted again with two long rings. With a sigh, he gave up his quiet evening and opened the front door to a smiling face and the aroma of roasted garlic chicken.

"Give me a hand, Lee, this pan is heavy and the lemon pie is still in the car." Marjorie Battsley gave him a quick peck on the cheek as she swept past him into the house.

CHAPTER FIFTEEN

S tripping Stark's and Connie's accounts only returned a third of the twenty-five thousand Mosley had repaid to Garret Bishop's firm. Connie would have to work off the rest, a prospect that made Grace tempted to pay the debt for her. For the immediate future, Grace sent her unwanted employee to open houses and seminars and filled the rest of Connie's time with online sales courses, all of which could be viewed from her home computer.

The office move was set for Thanksgiving week in the hope of not disrupting what work the firm had left. This gave Grace little time to break down and pack up a business which had been in operation for a half century. For the first time in months, there was more than enough work for everyone.

Initially, things went smoothly. Mosley owned a pretty Victorian house on the harborfront in Mallard Bay. A commercial tenant used the first floor as an art gallery but was moving to a larger building in St. Michaels. Grace's contractor friend, Benny Pannel, was able to spare a carpenter and the painters needed to do a fast remodel of the new law office. The move was on, assuming Grace could keep the wagon train on course.

She found the contracts Cyrus had given Connie and Marjorie, as well as one he'd given Lily. He'd protected all three women with identical tightly worded clauses restricting termination of employment to 'for cause' only. Should the firm let them go for any other reason, substantial severance benefits would be triggered. Grace figured she had cause aplenty to fire Connie, but the Bat would make out very well. When she explained the situation to Lily, she was pleased to hear her secretary suggest a compromise.

"If you can get her to cooperate, I think the Bat would be an asset in the new operation," Lily said. "When she isn't arguing with every breath, she does super work."

"Cyrus says she has a new man."

Lily nodded. "The new hair, new clothes thing?"

"That's a real thing?"

"Yep. Marjorie's dating Rory Bailey, didn't you know that?"

"What? Bailey, the guy who owns the land next to the Morgan farm? That Bailey?"

"They hooked up after he was in here to talk to you about what might happen with the property when we sold it."

Grace winced, partly because of the sour memory of her meeting with the angry farmer, but mostly at Lily's reference to Marjorie 'hooking up'. She pushed that thought away and said, "Well, shouldn't she be in a good mood?"

"That's not how the Bat rolls. The longer she's with the guy the crankier she is. When she breaks up with him, then she gets all attentive to the job."

The resemblance to black widow spiders came to mind, but Grace stayed on topic. "Are you saying you're willing to keep trying with her?"

Lily hesitated, then said, "There have to be boundaries and she has to respect them. I don't answer to her, and she leaves my work alone. You know it will never happen, right?"

GRACE WAS STILL CONSIDERING STAFFING OPTIONS AS SHE LAY ON

the floor behind the reception counter on Friday morning. There was no other way to sort and disconnect the rat's nest of wires that tethered two ancient computers. She'd just decided to rip out the hard drives and leave the shells when the elevator dinged.

"Mr. Mosley, please." The words were clipped, the tone haughty. "This *is* his office?"

As she was unfolding herself to get up, Grace heard Lily say the office was relocating and Mr. Mosley wasn't in. Her offer of help was cut short.

"That's not acceptable. I have a meeting with Connie Delaney and Mr. Mosley."

If Sandra Carter was surprised to see an attorney pop up front behind the counter like a jack-in-the-box, the senator's wife hid it well. "Connie said you might be here, Ms. Reagan."

Grace bit back a dozen questions and led their unexpected visitor to the conference room. "I'm sure Mr. Mosley will be here any minute," she said as she cleared boxes from the table. She could hear Lily leaving a message on Cyrus' cell phone.

"And Connie?" Sandra asked.

Grace hesitated. "Connie isn't here. But I can help you with whatever you need."

Sandra made a show of looking at her watch. "We had dinner last night and she said she would meet me here at ten."

"Last night?" Grace asked, but before Sandra could respond, the answer walked in.

"Oh, good!" Connie gushed as she dropped her purse on a box by the door and moved in to air kiss Sandra's cheek. "Gracie has been keeping you company. Cyrus can't make it this morning, but we don't really need him. He got all the information he needed at dinner last night. I have the contract with me and we can get started." She opened her briefcase and paused. "Gracie dear, I have it from here. Ask Lily to bring in a coffee tray, will you?"

Contract?

Connie and Sandra were looking at her expectantly. Connie's eyes shone with satisfaction.

Grace smiled, rose obediently, and lied. "Happy to. But Cyrus called just before you got here. He asked me to go over the contract." She held out her hand.

"Oh, that's not necessary," Connie said. "It's already been signed," she paused for another 'gotcha' smile, then went on. "I only need Lily to notarize our signatures and make copies. *After* she's gotten the coffee. I really need it after the late evening we had." She and Sandra laughed.

"She's right," Sandra said, smiling. "Your aunt can drink anyone under the table. She could in college and she's still a champion today. I need coffee for my sympathy hangover."

Connie's delighted grin slipped. "Don't tell all my secrets, Sandy. Gracie will think I'm awful." To Grace she added, "Coffee, dear. Now please."

It was Grace's turn for a genuine smile. "I will, *Aunt* Connie. Coming up. But you know how Cyrus is, just an old a stickler for details. He said it wouldn't do to have an error that could void the contract. Especially worrisome with one executed under those conditions. It'll only take a minute and I'm happy to help."

In the file room, Grace read the contract, shaking her head in amazement. The firm would act as a buyer's agent for Sandra and Jason Carter in the location and purchase of a residential property. Sandra had agreed to a percentage fee twice the going rate and a non-refundable deposit.

Connie had brought in a paying client.

"NO! ABSOLUTELY NOT!"

Grace was hot, tired and dirty. She sat on the floor of the file storage room, surrounded by stacks of dusty manila folders and detritus from long ago legal battles. It was ten past three. Mosley had wandered in nearly five hours after Lily had left her message on his voice mail. In his new, abrupt way, he'd announced that Connie needed space in the new Mallard Bay office.

Lily materialized in the doorway, her eyes large with concern. Adding another body meant Lily would be sharing space with either Connie or Marjorie. Or both.

From her seat on the floor, Grace watched them and wished she had the energy to laugh. Mosley was wearing his 'I'm oblivious to any problems you may think you have' expression, and Lily looked like she'd seen the devil. Since Grace needed both of them, she took a swig from her water bottle, then a deep breath, and said, "I'm sorry, Cyrus. I shouldn't have yelled. We're exhausted and I'm a bit short-tempered."

This worked for Mosley, but Lily said, "I can't work like this anymore."

The little file room went from crowded to packed when Grace stood up. She was the tallest one by a head. "We need to talk, Cyrus," she said. And then, because Lily showed no signs of backing up, she added, "in your office, please."

But Lily didn't move.

"I will handle it," Grace drew out the words.

Lily crossed her arms.

"Wouldn't all three of us be more comfortable in the conference room?" Mosley asked, looking at Lily.

With a final pointed look at Grace, Lily turned and led the way down the hall.

In a whisper which could be heard in the next block, Mosley said, "What's wrong with Lily?"

CHAPTER SIXTEEN

A t first, nobody gave in. Then Mosley ended the argument by grabbing his chest and slumping down in his chair. The paramedics who arrived shortly thereafter didn't seem overly concerned but whisked him away to the relative safety of the emergency room.

When Grace found him on the golf course on Monday morning, drinking coffee and chatting away with a foursome waiting for the 10th tee, she wanted to hug him and slap him, in that order.

Mosley didn't even try to deny the fortuitous timing of his 'cardiac event'. "I've had some angina. Needed to get it checked. And we got Lily on board as a bonus."

"And you see nothing wrong with that?" Grace demanded. "I hope you have to pay double for the ambulance ride! And what's this *we*? *I'm* not on board. I don't even know what you want us to do."

Mosley's gaze drifted to the first of the foursome who was preparing to swing. "A clean start. Everything by the book. No shortcuts." He paused as the golfer took the swing and sliced it to the left. "Shame," he tsked.

Grace tried to find his logic without grilling him any more than she had to. Angina wasn't a heart attack, but he wasn't in any shape for a fight. She'd known Connie would be at the Morgan farm settlement with Norse's buyer, and she was resigned to 'mentoring' whatever that turned out to be, but Cyrus had to be made to realize he couldn't stuff three staffers who disliked each other into a small space and not see fireworks. She decided to try empathy. Nothing else had worked.

"Is it that you feel some responsibility to provide for Connie?" she asked.

Mosley's slight nod might have been a 'yes', or a palsied twitch.

"You don't owe her or Stark anything. She's dishonest, Cyrus. We can't have her working for us."

Legally, this wasn't true. The state police had returned Connie's files and computer. They would not be filing charges, for the time being, anyway. There was nothing in Connie's work that connected her or the firm to Bishop's death. Bishop's 'advance' to Connie looked crooked but for now was being put down to poor judgment.

"It isn't in the firm's best interest to cut her loose," Mosley said. The foursome had moved on and Mosley sat, hands on the golf cart's steering wheel as if undecided about starting it up.

"What?" She took a breath and tried again. "How can it be in our best interest to keep her? I'm trying to work out a solution for Marjorie, but Connie will cut our throats the first chance she gets."

"Keep your enemies close, m'dear," he gave her a rare, wide, denture-filled smile, then said, "Connie-" he took a moment. "Connie was a sweet child - you know?"

Please don't fade out on me, Cyrus. "I'm sure she was," Grace said, even though she couldn't imagine it. "But she isn't sweet now. She doesn't like either one of us and she's made it clear that if we let her, she'll take everything we have."

"You don't know the real girl."

"She is *not* a *girl*. I know the Connie who lives and breathes today," Grace'd had enough. "There may be sad reasons why Connie is the manipulative witch that she is, but understand this, Cyrus, *I don't care.* Period. I'm not working with her. I don't think I can make this any clearer."

"Okay." Mosley started the cart and looked at her expectantly. "I have a meeting at the clubhouse. Walker Berg needs a codicil for his will. He has a new wife."

Grace tried to decide if this last comment was code of some kind. "Are you saying no Connie?"

"You and Lily don't have to work with her."

"What? Are you setting her up somewhere else?" She'd meant it as a joke, but Mosley only smiled. And she didn't get another word out of him.

"I CAN'T BELIEVE HE FAKED IT!"

They were packing up the last of the books in the office library. Lily hefted a 1968 edition of *Black's Law Dictionary* as if she was contemplating throwing it.

"At least he had to go to the emergency room to get rid of us," Grace said. "And I'm pretty sure I won the argument this morning."

"Only pretty sure?"

Grace told her about Mosley's cryptic comment.

Lily gave her boss a pitying look for her unreasonable optimism. "He's up to something, I know it."

But nothing happened. Mosley didn't make changes and Connie stayed away. As soon as the Easton office was packed up, Grace gave Marjorie an unannounced two-week vacation. It was the only way she could think to get the Bat out of the way while Lily set up the new office. From the firm's anemic income, Grace managed a healthy bonus for Lily. Cyrus applauded her ingenuity, but Grace felt like a coward. She didn't have any other options but rewarding Marjorie's bad behavior didn't sit well.

The physical labor of packing for the move and the stress of juggling the personalities involved took its toll. When Avril announced on Wednesday that her oven had died after thirty years of heroic service, Grace declared it a sign Thanksgiving either had to be postponed or moved to a restaurant. There was no way she was letting Avril take over either kitchen at Delaney House. Avril's methods of cooking involved every item in the kitchen and many from other areas of the house. For once, Avril gave in without an argument.

Mosley pulled one of his magic tricks, securing a prime table at the country club and Grace was back home in time for a long nap. She couldn't remember when she'd enjoyed a holiday so much.

Buoyed by the pleasant day and a rare good night's sleep, she faced Friday morning, their last day in the Easton office, with enough energy to pull everything off and still have part of the weekend left to recover.

Her enthusiasm flagged in the funeral air of the old office. The walls seemed taller, the halls longer and the absence of work, of vitality, drained all the color from the formerly stylish rooms. Mosley was a no-show, which made things easier. Lily and Grace made jokes about their echoing voices, then played music and worked as fast as they could.

They skipped lunch, and were so determined to finish packing the files in the back storage room, they didn't hear the elevator's ding. When Grace rounded the corner from the real estate wing with fresh cups of coffee, she ran right into the arms of a stranger. She managed to stay upright but ended up wearing the coffee.

"Sorry! I did call out." The tall man backed up, hands in the air. "Let me help, are there towels?" He looked about at the empty reception area.

There were no towels and the tissues in her jeans pocket did little to mop up the spill. Grace was uncomfortably aware of her soaking wet shirt as she introduced herself.

Summoned by the unusual sound of voices, Lily saved the awkward scene by settling their visitor in the conference room while Grace got out of her wet shirt and put on the flannel hoodie jacket she'd worn into the office that morning.

As the last hours of Kastner and Mosley, LLC ticked away, she sat in a packed-up conference room wearing stained jeans, an old jacket and a wet bra and talked with Garrett Bishop's son.

CHAPTER SEVENTEEN

Criminal law wasn't Grace's specialty unless you counted developers and warring neighbors as criminals. And while her clients occasionally strayed from the bright line of the law, for the most part, she only helped them through benign, if sometimes uncomfortable, issues. Quentin Bishop wanted her to keep him out of jail.

"I'm afraid I have no contacts in the area and I've been told I need legal representation now?" he said.

Once she could concentrate on him instead of her wet clothes, Grace saw that the younger Bishop looked nothing like his father. A good six inches taller and at least fifty pounds heavier, Quentin had sun-streaked hair and light blue eyes. The photograph McNamara had shown her didn't do him justice. The differences between father and son weren't just physical. Unlike the bombastic Garrett, Quentin's voice and manner were soft and hesitant. His sentences were spoken as questions and he seemed to be looking for some kind of assurance from her before saying any more.

Grace waited and let the silence grow. She'd have known why the police wanted him even if McNamara hadn't told her. The authorities' desire to find and grill Garret Bishop's son had been discussed in a front page news article in the *Star Democrat*, not to mention all over Mallard Bay.

Finally, he said, "I know my rights, Ms. Reagan, but I'm a stranger in a strange land, if you will, and I need someone local to represent me."

Grace explained she wasn't a criminal attorney. "I am really very sorry for your loss, but we're in the middle of moving. The new office won't be operational until next week and even if it were, we practice family and real estate law. I'm not sure why you chose me, but I can recommend someone else." She thought she saw a flash of Garrett-like irritation cross Quentin's face, but it was gone before she was sure.

"My father dealt with you, right? I mean on a business level, right? Or maybe you were friends?"

"Friends?" Grace was taken aback. Quentin was leaning toward her now and seemed intent on getting an answer. "I knew your father, obviously. He was bidding on a farm my firm is selling. We were business acquaintances."

He studied her for a moment and then smiled as if he'd settled some issue in his mind. "I do need some legal advice. If I promise to be a low maintenance client, will you take me on?"

Grace thought the engaging look he was using probably worked with most women. He wasn't a handsome man but there was something very appealing about him. She wanted to think it was more than just the aura of his wealth, but she needed new clients. Wealthy new clients. But she hadn't forgotten Chief McNamara's warning; Quentin Bishop was a possible murder suspect.

She said, "Not to be indelicate, but with your family connections, I should think an attorney would be the least of your concerns."

"My father has attorneys. Present tense. They stay his, or his estate's, even in death. I need someone to represent my interests and they aren't necessarily the same as my father's. Other than for my foundation's work, I haven't needed an attorney in a long time, and you came highly recommended."

She tried not to take offense when even his compliment was spoken as a question. "Really?" she asked. "By whom?"

"My father, for one. According to his business manager, at least. And I checked with a college buddy who's from this area. He said you were in all the papers a while back - in a good way." He gave her the engaging smile again. "Plus, I looked you up. Impressive resume."

She did have an impressive resume, but she didn't believe for a minute that Garrett Bishop's business manager would recommend the firm Connie Delaney worked for. With the thought that the son might just be as manipulative as his father, she pulled back and waited to hear what he had to say.

"Look, let me try this again," he said. "All I need is for you to be with me if the police interview me. Listen to what they have to say and if you think I have anything to worry about, then decide if you can represent me further. If not, maybe you'll help me find someone else."

She noticed his voice was stronger and the questioning speech pattern was gone. She asked if he'd heard from any law enforcement officials.

"A few. I decided to get into town before returning their calls."

Grace shook her head. "I'm sorry. I'd like to help you, but I can't. However, if you want a reference, I can make a call."

Before she could say more, they heard the elevator's ding echo through from the empty lobby and then Lily's overly loud greeting to McNamara. She managed to refer to him as 'Chief' twice in the same sentence.

Grace winced at the timing, then stood and said, "Mr. Bishop, for reasons I can't go into right now, it would be a conflict of interest for me to represent you in anything to do with your father's death. However, I am going to make an exception for the next few minutes only, understand?"

With a glance toward the conference room door, Bishop said, "Yes. Thank you."

"I can recommend an attorney who can help you, but in the

meantime, you need to understand your rights, so listen carefully. The police have arrived and you shouldn't say a single word."

———

USUALLY, NOTHING GRACE DID SURPRISED MCNAMARA. THE WOMAN who'd appeared in Mallard Bay a year ago and turned the town upside down rarely did what he expected her to. But he'd been frank with her about Quentin Bishop. So much so, he'd later felt guilty for scaring her more than she already was. A meeting at the courthouse across the street gave him an excuse to pop in and check on her and what did he find? Bishop sitting in her office and Grace doing her lawyer thing as she introduced them. McNamara didn't like it at all.

"I'm sure you can understand, Chief," she was saying, "Mr. Bishop has just arrived in town and tells me he's here to cooperate with the investigation. He'll be available for questioning but he needs to talk to his counsel first."

"Ten minutes," McNamara said.

She raised an eyebrow but didn't answer.

He wasn't going to lie to her. "The State Police will be questioning him. Since I'm here, I could talk to him first, maybe clear everything up before the room gets too crowded."

"I appreciate the heads up, but I doubt they, or you, have a warrant."

McNamara hesitated. It was an odd scene. The conference room smelled like old books and lemon oil, comforting even in its disarray. In the same fashion, Grace was dressed for Saturday chores - dirty ones, but she still projected strength in her calm, unmoving demeanor. McNamara thought Bishop was lucky to have her for his attorney, even if she had been the one to find his father's body. He couldn't imagine how she planned to work around that detail. He said, "I'll need to know where he's staying."

"She looked at her watch. "It's getting late. Mr. Bishop will call you as soon as he checks in somewhere."

"I can't guarantee the MSP won't pick him up first," McNamara said.

"If the State Police had a warrant, you'd know it. They'll have no reason to get one when you tell them he's not going anywhere. They don't have any evidence against him."

"Is that so?" McNamara smiled, but he wasn't happy. Bishop's face had changed at Grace's words. It looked as if he was surprised to hear her confident statement.

SHE MAY HAVE TEMPORARILY TAKEN HIM ON AS A CLIENT, BUT GRACE wasn't comfortable enough with Quentin to suggest he stay at the Victory Manor Inn. Niki would be mad if she learned about the lost room rental, but Grace would sleep better knowing he wasn't under the same roof as her cousin.

The Inn at Perry Cabin was out since Anton Norse still held a room there and the Tidewater Inn was full. The Egret Inn in Mallard Bay was convenient and elegant, even though Grace was sure Bishop was used to livelier surroundings. She made the reservation for him under her own name and gave him directions.

She also made a call that secured an attorney for Bishop.

"Did you mean it?" he asked as they rode down in the creaky old elevator. "What you said about the police not having any evidence against me?"

Grace studied him, looking for some sign of artifice, but saw nothing other than a tired, nervous man who was back to talking in questions. "It was a guess. I have no way of knowing for sure, but if they had any evidence there'd be a warrant out for your arrest. And Chief McNamara would have never left me alone with you."

"Like that, is it?"

She had no idea what he meant, but she suddenly realized she also didn't know why McNamara had come to see her.

CHAPTER EIGHTEEN

Quentin Bishop's new attorney was with him when Grace arrived at the Egret Inn later that evening. She saw them before they saw her and was grateful for the few moments she had to gather her thoughts. The two men sat in a corner of the bistro, heads down, drinks half gone. David Farquar was talking, a concerned expression tightening his handsome features.

She'd done the right thing even if it felt wrong. David was a litigator and an excellent criminal defense attorney. Handing Bishop off to him solved her ethical conflict, but she regretted having to give up a potentially lucrative case. She regretted even more that her heart rate tripled at the sight of David.

They'd talked several times since she'd come back to Mallard Bay to run Mosley's firm. David had made the first overtures and Grace had told herself - was still telling herself - she responded because she needed to keep the professional connection. Eventually, she'd have to sign on with another firm or open her own. She couldn't burn all her bridges with Farquar, Mitchum and Stoltzfus. An attorney with no references wasn't marketable. Besides, it had been long enough. It had been months since they'd fought and longer still since he'd really upset her. She was an adult and she'd act like one.

She was glad she'd worn the pencil skirt and silk cowl-neck sweater from her Washington wardrobe. Her feet gave warning tingles from the Christian Louboutin heels but she was glad she'd worn them, too, as she crossed the room to meet her former lover and his new client.

David saw her first, his business poker face registering genuine pleasure, something which once would have made her smile for days. She gave him a real smile in return and chided herself for being happy that he'd dropped everything and come when she called. Both men stood. Quentin was tall, but David was taller. Grace enjoyed the old, and rare, feeling of being small and delicate as David pulled her in for a hug.

Bishop looked surprised but only said, "I'm sorry about this afternoon," as they all sat and David waved a waiter over for Grace's drink order. "Ordinarily, I wouldn't have just walked into your office, off the street like that, without an appointment. I plead jet lag and five messages from my assistant saying I needed to get legal representation as soon as possible. I told David you came highly recommended. I understand the situation you're in, and I'm very grateful to you for calling him."

Not a single question, Grace thought as the server brought her glass of merlot and fresh drinks for the men. "Then you've had time to talk?" she asked.

"Yes. After our phone conversation this afternoon, we thought it was best to meet face to face, and for David to be here for my meeting tomorrow with the police. I'm so pleased you could join us for a late dinner. It's the least I can do to thank you."

"No need to thank me," Grace said. "But I'm glad to talk with you again. I didn't get a chance earlier today to give you my condolences. I didn't spend much time with your father, but he was an interesting man."

It had taken her a long time to come up with those few words. Saying something nice about Garrett Bishop felt hypocritical and speaking the truth was unkind. The only thing she'd liked about the elder Bishop was his offer to buy the Morgan farm property.

"Yes?" Quentin seemed surprised. "Well, thank you for that. He *was* interesting, in the way of poisonous creatures and madmen."

The server's arrival with menus and a discussion of dinner orders saved Grace from making a response. When the men had settled on steaks and Grace on the grilled rockfish, David picked up the conversation and turned to business.

"I've explained to Quentin that you and I worked together for a long time, and I'm happy to represent him. But the problem is, I'm really backed up with other clients right now. I'm hoping we can answer the questions the police have and wrap everything up tomorrow."

Grace realized both men were waiting for her to confirm that this was possible. She felt a rush of irritation. This was one of David's ploys which had annoyed her to no end when they worked together. He'd make a positive, but absurd, statement and she would have no choice but to point out the unpleasant truth. He'd look like the savior when he came up with a solution to her negativity. Well, she *had* initiated the whole situation.

"It's possible," she said. "Quentin, you understand it's not a good idea for me to represent you because I'm a material witness in the investigation of your father's death?"

"A material witness?"

"Yes. A material witness is someone whose testimony might influence the outcome of a trial. Your father died at a farm my firm was selling and he was there to meet with me. I found the body. As far as I know, I don't have any information to help the police in their investigation, but I've spent hours with them and I've told them everything I know."

David was looking impatient, but Quentin seemed shocked. "You mean, you're a suspect, too?"

Grace shook her head. "No. I shouldn't be, anyway. Fortunately - for me, I mean - I was in a client conference all morning until I left the office to meet your father."

"You mean during the time he was murdered. Your alibi is definitely better than mine," Bishop said.

"Let's move off this topic," David said. "Grace is quite correct in explaining why she can't represent you. And since she isn't your attorney, we'll need to limit our conversation this evening. She's an officer of the court and will be a witness for the prosecution when someone is finally arrested. You don't want to say anything to her that you wouldn't mind having repeated from the witness stand."

"So you've said." Quentin Bishop gave Grace a rueful grin. "Even though he seems very pleased to see you, your friend here wasn't in favor of this dinner. I insisted you join us and I must apologize for making things awkward. If I can ask just a few questions about my father's death, I promise we can talk about anything you like while we eat."

Grace looked at David, who nodded but maintained his stern expression.

Quentin twirled the ice in his drink for a moment, and then said, "This is a blunt question since I can't lead up to it with an explanation of the relationship I had with my father, but here it is. When you were with him at the end, did he —"

"How did he die?" David broke in.

Although he frowned at the interruption, Quentin didn't object.

Grace understood David's concern and why he'd stopped his client from asking anything along the lines of did she think his father had suffered. It would be a natural question from a grieving relative, but a dangerous one from a suspect.

She was equally as careful with her answer. "I don't know any more than you will after you and David meet with the police tomorrow. I arrived at the property, saw your father's car, but couldn't find him. When I walked around to the back of the house, I saw him on the ground and ran to help him. I thought he'd tripped or something. I knelt beside him and tried to find a pulse, but he was gone. I called 911 and started CPR just in case. I'm sorry." It was more than she should have said, but nothing that wasn't on the record.

Quentin seemed taken aback by her brief description of his father's death. "But he was shot! Wasn't there blood?"

"Let's not—" David started.

"Too late." This time the client shut his attorney down. "I already asked and I want an answer."

Grace recognized the tone Garret Bishop used when he wanted something. She thought about those minutes on her knees in the grass beside the dead man and heard McNamara's voice. *Do you have someone to talk to, Grace?* She didn't look at David, but at Quentin as she said, "At first I didn't see any, or didn't notice."

Last night, she'd had the dream again, the one where she found Garrett Bishop and saw his lifeless hand laying in the grass. The cuff of his navy blue shirt was spotless where it met his wrist, but darkened to a damp black further up his arm. She remembered his hands were clean, but hers were stained with his blood.

"Grace?"

David's soft tone and worried look made her blush. "Sorry," she said and sipped her wine. "It's pretty fresh." She winced at her poor choice of words, but the men didn't seem to notice.

Quentin said, "I'm sorry for asking, but I have to know. It's hard to explain."

Grace didn't think he was sorry, only frustrated, but she continued. "After I started CPR, I saw the blood." Turning to David, she added, "Garrett's injuries were described in the news reports. Quentin can read all of this."

David nodded and his frown lines eased a bit.

Bishop drained the last of his drink, then said, "I heard the State Police think it could have been an accident. A hunter with bad aim."

"My guess is that's why there's no warrant for your arrest," Grace said.

David said, "Let's move on."

Grace agreed, but his client ignored him.

"He was a difficult man to be around," Bishop went on. "Always doing what you least expected and usually not in a good way. Such as flying here to dicker over a piece of property he didn't need. I can't imagine why he wanted it."

"Have you seen it?" Grace asked. "The house is derelict, but the site is beautiful. A one of a kind in that area."

"I'm sure it is, but unless some conflict was associated with it, the bidding wouldn't interest him. My father, not to boast but to give you context, has four homes. They're very different from each other. All they have in common is he had to fight to get them. Arguments with owners who didn't want to sell, anything smacking of a contest, my father would jump on."

"Then the bidding would have appealed to him, wouldn't it?" Grace could feel David watching her, but he didn't interrupt.

"Possibly, but unlikely at those prices. If Dad had wanted it for some reason, he'd have just bought it."

"Garrett said he *was* buying it. I went out to meet him because he said he had a contract for me that would top any other offer."

For the first time, Bishop appeared to be emotional. His eyes reddened and he cleared his throat. "Dad left me a message the week before he died. He said we were going to have a family Christmas here next year. I ignored it. The last family gathering we had was five years ago."

The arrival of their dinners broke the awkward silence that followed. When the servers left, David asked Grace about the Morgan farm and the other bidders. As she described the Carters and Anton Norse, she tried to realign her thoughts about how each of the buyers fit into the equation.

"Wait a minute," she said as a thought occurred to her. "Quentin, you said your father never went after anything unless it was a challenge."

"That's true," Quintin agreed and resumed pushing bits of steak around his plate.

"Anton Norse is an agent for a buyer from the west coast. I don't know who it is."

Quentin put his fork down and said, "You think that was the attraction for Dad? He wanted to best Norse or his client?"

Grace shrugged. "Maybe, who knows? Your father was staying at The Inn at Perry Cabin in St. Michaels. Then Anton moved there right after your father died." All of which sounded odd as she told it. Why hadn't she seen that before?

David frowned. "Do the police know?"

"Yes. Norse must have an alibi. He wasn't arrested."

"And now he has the winning bid," David said.

"Never heard of him," Quentin said without hesitation. "My father may have known him, though. He'd challenge anyone, and it would have amused him to see this Norse try to win the bidding."

David smiled for the first time since he'd hugged Grace. "Well, then," he said. "Our first question is, would losing bother Norse enough to commit murder?"

CHAPTER NINETEEN

"**Y**ou could have warned me about the redhead!"

It had been so long since David had raised his voice to her, Grace was momentarily stunned into silence. Then the old reflexes roared to life. "Good morning to you, too, sweetie. Yell at me again and you can talk to a dial tone."

That line had worked better when they were on landlines in DC and *had* dial tones, but it still did the trick. After a few more seconds, she got an exaggerated sigh and an insincere 'Sorry'.

Since it was all she would get, she moved on. "Did Detective Marbury give you a hard time?"

"She tried, but I controlled the situation."

This was David-speak for 'I pulled it out of the fire at the last minute, but a lesser attorney would have been lost.' Grace rolled her eyes and said, "I'm sure you did. What did she do that moved you to interrupt my morning to vent?"

"She's fixated on Quentin's relationship with his father. Do you know anything I don't?"

Grace was working from home in an attempt to wrap up a few billable hours for paying clients before meeting Lily at the new Mallard Bay office. It infuriated her that David would just stomp into her work time without even asking if she was free. If their roles had been reversed, she'd still be trying to get past his secretary *du jour*. It was an old argument not worth repeating.

"Many things, David. I know so much you don't, it would take hours just to list the subjects. But if you're asking if there's anything about Garret Bishop's death that your client may have failed to share with you, the answer is, I doubt it. Unless … do you know he threatened to kill his father a while back and was under suspicion of murder until Dear Daddy made a reappearance?"

"I knew that before I crossed the Bay Bridge."

"But you think he's keeping something from you?"

"Of course he is!" David was yelling again. "He's a client! Have you ever had one who told you everything? Now, I need you to brainstorm with me."

She laughed out loud and loved the feeling it gave her. "Sorry," she said. "I'm busy and you have minions. Put them to work."

"Then have dinner with me tonight," he said without missing a beat. "I'm staying over, so let me take you out. I'll give you all the DC office gossip you've missed, and you can tell me about working with Grandpa."

"Cyrus isn't that old," she said and laughed again. Cyrus *was* that old. "Pick me up at seven. I'll give you a tour of the house before we go."

She had missed him, a little anyway. The idea of showing off Delaney House excited her, but she knew it wasn't the reason for the butterflies in her stomach.

THE REST OF HER MORNING WAS PRODUCTIVE. WHEN SHE GOT TO THE new office, the movers had delivered the first load of the furniture and equipment and Cyrus had made a rare appearance. Grace found him stomping around, shouting orders at Lily, who was setting up her computer and ignoring him.

"Thank goodness you're here!" Lily said when she saw Grace.

"Do something with him, please. He needs to go to the golf course and torture someone else for a while."

Grace was surprised at the level of agitation from the usually unflappable Lily. Then Cyrus roared, "This is unacceptable!"

They found him in the next room holding an empty plant pot and kicking at clods of potting soil. A bedraggled fern lay a few feet away. "I can't find anything!"

"What are you looking for?" Grace asked. She didn't like the way he looked. His face and neck were a blotchy red and his hands shook.

"Everything." His voice dropped. "I'm looking for, for — everything."

A pot of tea, an hour of cajoling and teasing by Lily, and a light version of her morning's events from Grace turned the panicked old man back into Cyrus Mosley, Warrior at Law, but it wasn't a smooth transition. By the time Grace dropped him off at the Mallard Bay Golf Course, he looked better but his hands still shook. He'd refused to go to his doctor or his home. The golf course was the only place Grace thought might soothe him. She didn't want to think about what would happen when the course closed for the winter break.

"Give us two days," she said as she walked with him from the parking lot to the cart barn, "and you'll see a transformation. You'll be able to find everything."

"Everything?" It was the first word he'd said since they left the office.

"Johnnie Walker in the lower right-hand drawer with two glasses."

He grunted and said, "Blue label. I know how much is in the bottle."

Grace laughed and hugged him. "There'll be a new bottle, Cy. It's been a rough week."

She stopped to pick up strawberry muffins and the caramel

coffee that Lily liked. She would have to avoid such treats once the stress of the move was over, but right now her will was weak. The muffins were superb and the coffee was the best she'd had since leaving DC If she and Lily had to shore up their flagging spirits, at least they had help close at hand.

The muffins and coffee worked their magic and relative peace lasted for nearly two hours. Grace was at Cyrus' desk when she heard an unmistakable trill of laughter announce Connie's arrival. She made it out to Lily's office in time to hear Connie say, "Oh, it's alright, Lily dear. I don't expect to find my office ready, yet. You've got a long way to go before that, don't you?"

Grace swallowed the scathing remark that flew to her lips. Sandra Carter was with Connie and both women looked as if they were floating on the fumes of a long, alcoholic lunch.

"Gracie!" Connie squealed, "Look who's here! Sandra came down for the weekend! We've been shopping and to brunch at Morsels, and now we're off to see some listings, but I thought I'd show her around our new digs first." Connie stayed by Sandra's side, aligning herself with their client.

"I'm always amazed at the quality of merchandise in this little town," Sandra said. She loosened and then retied a bright yellow scarf around her neck. "I bought this last time we were here. Isn't the little bird pattern adorable? It's from that darling dress shop down on the harbor. Connie bought one just like it, but she's lost hers." Sandra shook a finger at her friend. "You're going to have to cut back on the bloodys at lunch if you keep losing things."

"Will you stop telling that story?" Connie said and immediately colored. "Sorry. It's just so frustrating. I didn't lose it, but I don't know what happened to it."

"Same difference, lovey."

"I'm sure it will turn up," Grace said, breaking the growing tenseness.

"Of course it will!' Connie said. "Now let's get our first new client out on a house hunt, shall we?"

"How disappointing. I thought I would be the first new

client?" Quentin Bishop stood in the doorway and took in the box-filled reception and the four women who'd turned to look at him.

Connie recovered first, gliding toward him with an outstretched hand. "Welcome to Kastner and Mosley! I'm Connie Delaney and I'd love to help you."

Quentin took her hand but looked around her to Grace, who ready to explode until she saw his comical expression.

"Cyrus Mosley and Associates," she said, correcting Connie. "Just like on the business card I gave you, Quentin. And this is Connie Delaney, a local real estate agent." Before Connie could protest, Grace went on to introduce Sandra and Lily.

Quentin said, "Ladies, a pleasure. Grace, if I could impose upon you for quick consultation?"

The large back office was the least crowded room and offered the best chance for a confidential conversation. Grace sat on the corner of a desk and waited while Quentin opened a slim briefcase and took out a file folder. Handing it to her he said, "These are affidavits from four impeccable sources that will testify I was in Sweden from the first of November until two days ago. I did not kill my father, Ms. Reagan."

Grace sat the papers aside. "I was clear with you yesterday. I'm not employed by David Farquar and I'm not your attorney."

"David's representing me with regard to my father's death. I'd like you to represent me in some unrelated matters. David has the originals of those affidavits, but I wanted you to have copies. I want you to have proof I'm not a killer. I want—"

Quentin had returned to the question-speak speech pattern and looked so embarrassed, Grace wanted to reassure him, but she kept quiet.

"It's important to me, personally, that you believe me," he finished.

Grace studied the man in front of her and tried to connect the dots of information she had. No pattern emerged. "You told me you live in San Francisco. You'll only be here while the investigation into your father's death is being completed. Why can't you use the attorneys you have back home?"

"You're here. I have to be here. I like you and want to work with you. It's as simple as that."

It wouldn't be simple at all, but she wasn't in a position to turn down work. She let the issue drop for the moment and turned her attention to the affidavits. The stationary told her what she needed to know. The American ambassador to Sweden was one of his three witnesses. At the time his father was killed, Quentin had been at a fundraising conference in Stockholm, negotiating a sponsorship with an international pharmaceutical company.

When she finished reading, Quentin said, "I had a fight with my father in New York two years ago during a difficult point in our relationship. I lost it. I said I'd kill him, and I did it in public. You know about that?"

Grace nodded. She could understand Garret Bishop infuriating someone to the point of making a threat. Quentin seemed well mannered, even diffident. He was handling his current circumstances, if not in stride, at least with apparent calm and common sense. Which only meant he could control himself when necessary.

She said, "I imagine that was bad for your business, whatever it is."

"I manage an educational foundation in California. My reputation is everything to me and I nearly wiped it out in one evening. Life and business went on afterward, but not without damage. Once Dad and I had a reputation for volatile behavior in public, it was as if Dad was determined to keep it up. He's been arrested several times since, all outlandish stunts. And every time he did pulled one, it made my job harder."

"And what do you do in managing your foundation?" Grace asked. As interesting as his story was, he hadn't gotten around to what he wanted from her. He was eating into her afternoon and she needed to sign him up as a client or move on to billable work.

"I convince wealthy people to give money to provide educational programs for underserved areas of the community."

"Underserved areas of San Francisco?"

"And other places."

She thought the man could not have been more vague if he'd refused to answer her. He had a curious expression on his face and seemed to be waiting for her next question. She said, "As long as it doesn't involve your father or his death, I'm happy to represent you where I can. Does that help?"

Quentin smiled and held out a hand. "Deal. I'll set up an appointment with your secretary. I need some documents notarized and I'm considering a funding request which is a little outside my comfort zone. I'd like your opinion of it."

Grace pushed away McNamara's warnings and the objections David was sure to raise and took Quentin's hand. She was still holding it when Lily knocked and opened the door.

CHAPTER TWENTY

They emerged from Grace's office to find Connie waiting for them. The atmosphere quickly deteriorated from professional to playground.

As soon as the front door closed behind Quentin, Connie turned on Lily. "Why don't you tell Grace what you said to me?"

Lily didn't back down. "I *said* there's no office for you, and you can't have mine."

"She is out of line, Grace. *And* she called me a vulgar name."

"I did not."

"You did, too. Whispering counts!"

"This is ridiculous. Connie, why are you doing this? It's embarrassing." The sympathy in Grace's voice silenced the argument. "The movers dropped your things off to you."

After a moment, Connie seemed to reload. "Marjorie and I don't need as much space as before. I told Lily we could share. This room is fine for both of us. Lily can take another office to herself."

Grace said, "When did you talk to Cyrus last?"

"He's been calling me, but I haven't had time to deal with him. Sandra insists on shopping when we're not looking at houses and I have to keep her happy. Someone has to work around here."

Grace looked at Lily, who shrugged and said, "If you're thinking what I think you're thinking, I'm out of here."

It was a powerful statement for the usually deferential Lily. They'd crossed a line in their relationship, Grace realized. She said, "Connie, let's go in my office."

"I think I'll call it a day," Lily said.

———

CONNIE DIDN'T TAKE THE NEWS WELL. "I HAVE THE REAL ESTATE division's only active client and you're firing me? I'm your aunt!"

Grace stared at Connie, finally saying, "Seriously? You want to play that card?"

"Cyrus hired me and you can't fire me."

This was, unfortunately, true.

"I'm not firing you. If Cyrus chooses to pay you to learn the real estate profession and show a few houses on behalf of the firm, that's his business. But I run this office and you don't work out of here. Period."

"Where do I work?"

Grace so badly wanted to give Rhett Butler's 'Frankly my dear' speech, but she said, "As I have explained before, you have a list of online courses to take to give you more skills. You can do them from home. You're licensed, so you can show property to Sandra. For the time being, your paycheck will continue to appear every Friday. But, and it's a big *but*, so pay attention, Connie - we are closing down the real estate end of the business. Except for Sandra's account, we have closed it. There will be no future work for you here, so make the most of Cyrus' generosity. Get some experience and maybe another sale under your belt before you have to job hunt. You need to get busy, understand?"

Connie stood and grabbed her purse. "Fine. I'll take my clients and go."

"No, you won't. Sandra and Jason Carter signed a contract with the firm, with Cyrus." She held a hand up at Connie's squeal of outrage. "Connie, do you understand how lucky you are? After what you did, asking Bishop for money—."

"I did *not*. He offered. I made a mistake. Why can't you give me the benefit of the doubt?"

Grace thought of Niki. And of Mosley. Of love and ties that bound her mother's family together in a way Grace would never understand. A way that didn't include her. She said, "I don't want to hurt you. But as long as you work here, I'm the broker you're working under. If you make another *mistake*, it might be one which could cost me my license."

"You're exaggerating!" Connie sat back down. Her brown eyes were huge in her pale face. When the artifice was peeled away, she just looked scared. "What am I going to do?" she asked.

"There'll be the fee for the sale of the Morgan place. After we deduct the money you still owe Cyrus, it will still be a nice amount. And you'll get your fee for any sale you make to Sandra."

"That's big of you, but you still need an agent. People might still contact us — you — because the old firm did real estate."

Grace shook her head. "I have a license, remember? I'm licensed to sell real estate as well as to practice law in Maryland, Virginia and DC"

Connie's mouth was open, but for once, she appeared speechless.

Grace took advantage of the rare opportunity. "You need to get a job in a firm that can support you. You'll do well." She managed this last part with utter sincerity. Connie would do well because she'd take out her competition by any means necessary.

"Sandra won't work with you."

"If she won't, she won't. But what she *also* won't do is work with you - not for at least six months. Cyrus isn't totally soft where you're concerned. You also signed a contract with him, remember?" Grace found her briefcase where she'd dropped it behind a box of books and took an envelope out of the side pocket. "I thought I might need this. I made a copy for you."

"I know what it says." Connie took the envelope and put it in her purse. "Well," she took a deep breath. "Let's regroup. How do you want to handle this?"

"What?" Grace was prepared for histrionics, not rational conversation.

"We're still family, Grace. You know what Stark will do if I run home crying and say you threw me out. I don't want to deal with it. You and Niki are close and I don't want my girl upset again. I'm also pretty sure Cyrus isn't the one insisting I work from home and wrap things up with the firm. Am I right?"

"It doesn't change the outcome."

"I understand." Hands clasped behind her back, Connie began to pace around the cluttered room.

Grace remembered the first time Niki tried to explain her mother's personality. *She lies when she doesn't have to. It's all about appearances with her. She lies about little things.* Grace tried to decide how much of the Connie she was watching was just a show.

Sincere or not, Connie was caught up in her performance. "We can call it an amicable parting of the ways. I'll keep showing Sandra properties and earn my fee. I won't be in the office, but I'll sell her a house. She and Jason are desperate for a place and he gave her carte blanche. I haven't shown her anything under a million."

Grace had to work not to smile at her aunt. Connie was on the rebound and remaking the situation to work to her benefit. "Sounds good," she said.

"You're going to wish you'd worked with me, sweetie, because I always come out on top. Now watch your auntie and learn."

Connie's about-face reminded Grace she had never looked at Niki's business proposal for an inn at Delaney House. With Connie on the prowl for new ways to make money, avoiding Niki's pie in the sky dream was risky. If Connie and Niki were in agreement about the inn, it would be better to know what each of them was planning so she could be prepared. As soon as Connie was gone, she found the folder with the plan for Niki's bed and breakfast empire and began to read.

At first she was relieved. The plan sounded realistic and well researched. Grace saw Niki's solid ideas and business training were enhanced by her natural enthusiasm. If Grace had been a dispassionate outsider, she'd be considering the offer. As it was, she couldn't read a paragraph of the document without imagining the disasters that could result from putting Delaney House back in Delaney hands.

At least she could tell Niki she was thinking about her proposal. Maybe a buyer would turn up before Grace had to admit which way her thoughts were going.

CHAPTER TWENTY-ONE

M cNamara's day started early with a call out to a domestic violence complaint. Putting a local businessman in handcuffs in front of his neighbors guaranteed a lot of phone calls and paperwork. Not that it would have been a good day, anyway. The anniversary of Merri's death was always a challenge.

By noon, he needed a break. Leaving the office to Banks, he picked up a turkey sandwich at the Three Pigs deli and drove out to Morgan Creek. After bumping down the rutted lane, he pulled into the driveway of the farm where Garrett Bishop had died. This trip wasn't about the investigation, but he couldn't pass up an opportunity to take a quick look around.

He was struck anew by the incongruity of the deteriorating farmhouse and its stunning setting. The midday sun was merciless in showcasing every flaw in the long abandoned structure while sharpening the gray-blue tones of the water that flowed past it. Willow trees and a grand magnolia said someone had once cared enough to landscape the yard around the house. He tried to imagine four houses here, soldiers lined up, claiming nature for their own.

He was glad the laws had changed, limiting development near the water. Except for the years spent climbing the State Police command ladder on the western shore, he'd lived in the same house in Mallard Bay all of his life. He'd adjusted to seeing farms produce their final crops in subdivisions and shopping centers, and while he appreciated having the same shopping opportunities as the rest of the developed world, it was enough already. How many grocery stores and WalMarts did they need?

He walked around the old, squat Victorian. Wide porches on three sides gave it a squarish look. It was a medium-sized house that looked bigger than it was. The gabled tin roof angled this way and that, rising to a peak over the attic, and falling in over the back porch. Gaps in the siding, broken windows and rotting steps were testimony to the years and lives it had seen. The house was crumbling and the process had been hurried along when the MSP investigators tore it apart. They'd been thorough but found no evidence inside the house that they could tie to either the victim or the shooter.

Just as when he'd studied Avril's photos, there was nothing of interest see, but McNamara stood where Bishop had died and turned slowly until he'd had a look in all directions. He spent a long moment scanning the woods, imagining the person who'd fired the killing shot. Had the killer's day been considered a success or a failure? Had a hunter gone home empty-handed and unaware of what had happened, or had a killer's mission been accomplished?

He turned around to look at the water, but the peacefulness of the view was gone and the crisp fall air couldn't account for the chill he felt. When the back of his neck began to tingle, he turned and walked to his truck. This wasn't what he'd come for.

A FEW HUNDRED YARDS PAST THE MORGAN FARM, THE NARROW country lane turned to gravel and widened into an area big enough for vehicles to pull off and park or turn around. This was Morning Rise Point, one of many access points to the thousands of miles of shoreline along the eastern side of the Chesapeake Bay. Morgan

Creek and a smaller, nameless branch of water curled off to the left, fading away into a marsh, which in turn became solid ground.

Ten years ago, he'd parked here, lifted a kayak out of his pickup and taken Merri's ashes out on the water until he reached the spot where he'd proposed to her. He'd left her there, not tossed into the morning breeze, but sprinkled over still water. She'd floated away, leaving him at last in a widening skim of pale ash, moving slowly, but going all the same.

He came every year on the anniversary of her death, not to mourn her, but to slip back to a time when he was one of two. Out on the water he talked to Merri in a way he couldn't on land. For a few hours, he was twenty-five again and his girl sat behind him in the kayak. He caught her up on recent events and told her how he saw the coming months unfolding. For her part, Merri was sympathetic and encouraging, if short on return conversation. He felt her presence as he once had when she anchored every hour of his life.

He talked to his wife at home, usually as he put in his miles on the treadmill. In the first year after her death, he kept the conversations internal. This was not only unsatisfying but caused him to focus inward, listening for her responses. At his core, he was a reasonable man who craved order in his life. Stumbling through the days and lying awake through the nights, always listening for Merri, caused a chaos he couldn't tolerate indefinitely.

It was Marjorie who broke his cycle of waiting and constant disappointment. On the first anniversary of Merri's death, Marjorie appeared at his front door with a picnic basket and an order. A year of self-centered grief had left him well-armed in denial tactics, but no protest he mounted could sway Merri's big sister. Marjorie, who couldn't have looked less like his slender, elegant wife if she'd tried, manhandled him out of his recliner and into his truck.

Leaning through the passenger-side window, she'd said, "Listen, Lee. This crap has got to stop and I mean now. Merri is miserable and yes, you jerk, you're not the only one who talks to her. She's mad and I'm mad and you can't tell me the State Police are gonna let you glide through another year looking like you're waiting for the

Apocalypse. The end has come and gone, big guy. You survived. Deal with it."

He hit the horn so hard, Marjorie jumped like she'd been shot. Then she came at him again, hitting the side of his truck with the flat of her hand. "No!" she screamed. "You take this damned truck and your damned kayak and the double-damned lunch I made for you and you get yourself down to Morning's Rise and out on the water. Merri's got a few things to say to you and you're gonna listen. You've had too many blessings in life, Lee McNamara, too many blessings! You think you're entitled to them, that's what's wrong with you. You had everything with Merri and now you're like the rest of us. Go dump your self-righteous misery in the water and get yourself back here. There's work to be done."

Shame did what sympathy couldn't manage.

The first anniversary of the worst day of his life was the last day he was Lee, husband of Merri, half of a whole. He returned from the water that evening, sunburned and exhausted and different. The second anniversary saw the new Chief of Police of Mallard Bay taking a weekday off to go kayaking in the morning and coaching a Little League game in the afternoon.

Merri McNamara took up residence in her husband's introspective hours but let the time between visits lengthen. She never missed their date on the water, though. And she could always be counted on to send advice when he needed it, even if sometimes her sister was the one who did the talking.

This day, when his mind was so occupied with the Bishop investigation and its various moving parts, he just let Merri's presence warm and soothe him. There were no revelations or inspirations, but he felt better as he dragged the kayak up on the riverbank and let it drain off on the grass at the water's edge.

He wasn't ready for work or people. He tossed the mostly uneaten sandwich out to a couple of ducks and decided to take a walk back to the Morgan farm. Something about the place bugged him.

MᴄNᴀᴍᴀʀᴀ ᴡᴀs ᴀʟᴍᴏsᴛ ᴛᴏ ᴛʜᴇ ᴅʀɪᴠᴇᴡᴀʏ ᴡʜᴇɴ ʜᴇ ʜᴇᴀʀᴅ ᴛʜᴇ distinctive sound of a rifle slide being racked. He jumped from the side of the road into the culvert, rolling to his knees and pulling his pistol from his shoulder holster as the nearby blast set off a barrage of squawking and flapping of wings. He yelled, not trusting the DayGlo orange vest he wore to set him apart from a ten-pound goose. An answering shout from the woods acknowledged him.

He was back on the road and brushing himself off when Anton Norse emerged from the tree line twenty feet away. The grin on the big German's face said he wasn't at all unhappy to have sent the Chief of Police into a ditch dive.

"This is legal hunting, yes?" Norse asked. "Trying out my new land."

"The property you are buying is over there. These woods are posted." McNamara didn't know what made him angrier, Norse's smugness or his own heavy breathing. It'd been a while since he'd used his basic training moves.

"I bought rights here, too." Norse used his shotgun to indicate the woods behind him.

McNamara studied him a moment before re-holstering his gun. You're too close to the house. Lots of people in or near these woods. You need to study up on local regulations for discharging a firearm. Natural Resources Police enforce the laws around here."

"Yes, yes. Your, what do you call them? Your Fish Police. You have many police."

It didn't seem to be the time to point out there wasn't nearly enough law enforcement for the thousands of acres the DNR had to patrol. McNamara kept his tone mild as he said, "People are killed every year by careless hunters."

"Oh, yes. You refer to Mr. Bishop. Perhaps he did not jump as fast as you?"

McNamara reassessed the situation. Norse had been watching

him when he fired the gun. "Perhaps we should go to the police station to discuss that very possibility."

"When you have grounds for an arrest, sir," Norse said. He smiled, gave McNamara a nod and turned back to the woods.

The Chief let him go, waiting until he disappeared from sight before following him.

Norse crashed through the undergrowth, crunching leaves and snapping off twigs. McNamara had no trouble following him straight through the narrow neck of woods to a small parking area near Baker's Landing where Norse climbed into a large pickup with a camouflage paint job. He took his time securing the shotgun and settling himself. When he finally started the engine, Norse lowered the driver's side window, looked directly into the woods and gave a smart salute.

Pushing Norse's arrogance out of his mind, McNamara turned around. He had another hour and a half of daylight and he made the most of the time, studying his surroundings as he slowly made his way toward the Morgan farm. Twenty minutes later, he stood next to an old, scarred pine.

When he'd photographed the tree and the area around it, he closed the camera function of the phone and sent a text to Banks. Cell service this far out was spotty. The text went through and was almost immediately acknowledged, but his follow up call failed. His work radio was in his car, but he wasn't going anywhere until the MSP crime scene techs arrived. For another hour he kept watch over a shotgun shell and a yellow scarf as the sun moved west and shadows darkened the woods. It gave him plenty of time to think.

CHAPTER TWENTY-TWO

G race was exhausted but she couldn't come up with an
excuse to get out of the dinner with David.

She didn't want to rekindle their romantic relation-
ship. Most of the time she was sure about that, except at three in the
morning and odd times during the day when her guard was down.
He'd let her love for him wither until it was well past dead. Surely a
small cupful of nourishment couldn't bring it back.

Calling David for Quentin had only been an act of professional
kindness for a stranger, nothing more. Now she wanted David to
disappear and leave her heart in one piece and her ego satisfied.
Since he was still in town, she put on a dress he liked, pinned her
hair up and dabbed on the perfume he'd given her on their last
Christmas together. If she was going, she was going flat out.

He arrived with Champagne and a hug and a smile so sweet, she
was worried until he said, "The student surpasses the master. Well
done, Grasshopper."

Relief flooded through her. He was talking about Quentin
Bishop. "I was astounded when he showed up at the office," she said.
"I don't think he'll be giving me much work."

"He mentioned it to me," David said. "He said he likes to have a lawyer with local connections."

She heard a note of condescension in his words, but ignored it. "Do you want the tour or the wine first?"

They took the tour. David said all the right things, but Grace could feel his impatience. It wasn't until they were on the third-floor landing and he looked over the curved mahogany railing to the first floor below that he seemed genuinely engaged.

"Whoa. Cool," he said. "It'd be a tumble from here, huh?"

Grace was grateful for the crass comment; she'd been feeling a little mushy.

"You can try it later if you like," she said. "But right now, let's finish the tour and go eat, I'm hungry."

"How come you don't live in the main part of the house?" he asked as he followed her onto the third floor and into her sitting room. "I mean, this is great and all, but compared to downstairs, well." He took in the cozy sitting room with its kitchen alcove before continuing on to the threshold of her bedroom. "I see you hung onto the sleigh bed."

Grace stayed in the short hallway between the rooms. Bedrooms and David used to equal only one thing. The sleigh bed had been a bone of contention because David was too tall to fit in it and had to sleep sideways.

"I brought all my favorite pieces and sold the rest," she said. "I don't need twenty-four rooms and I don't want to furnish them, either. I'll sell when I find the right buyer."

"And leave Mallard Bay?"

"I don't know. I like this area, and it's close enough to DC so I can get in when I want." She immediately wanted to kick herself. Why had she said that? She hadn't once wanted to go back over the bridge since she'd arrived. She'd gone when she had to, but she hadn't liked it. And now he'd think she was offering. Or even worse, *asking*.

His wide grin made her even more irritated.

"Let's go or we'll be late for our reservation." She was through the door and down the steps before he could argue with her.

SHE HAD SELECTED ADELAIDE'S GARDEN, A HARBOR-FRONT restaurant only four blocks from Delaney House. She liked having the option to walk home if things didn't go well. She'd also asked for one of the tables with a view of Mallard Bay's harbor and the small lighthouse which sat on the last point of land near its southern edge. Having nothing to talk about during an uncomfortable dinner bothered her more than not being able to leave when she wanted. Reconnecting with David Farquar was proving to be more stressful than she'd anticipated.

As soon as they were seated, he ordered a bottle of a ten-year-old Sauvignon Blanc and watched the sommelier uncork it. She was relieved when he gave a brief nod after the ritual sniff and taste routine.

When they were alone, he said, "You rushed me out of your mansion so fast I left the bottle of Cristal Brut. It was for a special toast."

"Silly me. I thought it was a housewarming present." Grace felt foolish. David was all about David. An expensive gift would naturally be for him to enjoy, too.

"It is," he said, completely missing her point.

Grace sighed. It would be a long dinner if he was going to trot out every irritating aspect of his personality.

"What are we toasting?" she asked, raising her glass. "Or do I have to wait until we have the Cristal to hear your news?"

"It's big, Grace. I should make you wait for dragging me away from your very lovely bedroom."

Grace drank half the glass of wine. She got an immediate warm buzz and the satisfaction of seeing the smile slip from his face.

"That's not iced tea," he said.

"No," she agreed and smiled at the server who had appeared with menus, a lengthy greeting and recitation of the chef's specials.

Grace thanked her with a big smile. She wasn't sure she could eat and what she really wanted was to stop David from talking. She'd worked hard to put the past behind her and the gleam in his eye made her nervous.

"This is one of my favorite places," she said. "I'll order for us." Without waiting for him to agree, Grace chatted with server asking her which river the soft shell crabs came from and was the chef offering them sautéed or deep-fried. She could see David was getting frustrated, and by the time she had ordered backfin salads and the sautéed soft shells for entrees, she wanted to laugh. "Hope you don't mind," she told him as she handed her menu over to the server. "I was feeling crabby tonight, pun intended."

"I'm surprised you didn't order the cream of crab soup." His annoyed tone made her feel better. This was familiar territory.

"It's very rich, a bit too much for me. But," she called after the departing server, "do you have the Maryland crab soup?"

David's phone burst into the theme from *Law and Order.* He took his time silencing it. When he finally left the table to answer the call, surrounding diners watched him go with a mixture of amusement and irritation. Grace sipped her wine and tried to calm down by blessing counting. After health, Niki and Leo, she got stuck on freedom, silently chanting it like a mantra. *I'm free. I'm free. Imfreefreefreefree.* It helped.

So did the crab. There's no such thing as too much crab and no better crab than the Chesapeake Bay Blue, even when you eat alone. David didn't return until Grace had finished her soup and the server was presenting the salads. The delicate Bibb lettuce was the perfect bed for the pearly chunks of backfin. David pushed his plate aside to make room for his elbows as he leaned across the table into Grace's space.

"Sorry, sweetheart. It's hectic at the office right now. I've gone through two assistants since you left. It's been hell without you."

"I wasn't your assistant. I was co-counsel." She smiled at the sight of David working to control his exasperation.

"Whatever. I didn't just mean work, anyway. I can always get someone to work with."

"Wow. Way to make me feel special." Grace took a bite of crab and savored the mild taste. Heaven.

His anxious expression hardened but he carried on. "I mean it. I've been lost without you. Can't we try again? We can go slowly. Dinners, weekends. I want to show you what you're missing. You know we were good together."

"Are you going to eat that?" She pointed her fork toward his untouched salad. She thought about telling him his elbow was sitting in a puddle of salad dressing that had spilled when he shoved the salad plate aside, then decided to let it go. She wouldn't be the one trying to get olive oil out of his Brioni shirtsleeve.

"What? You want my food? Grace, haven't you heard anything I've said? I love you and I want to try again."

It took a long few minutes for her to stop coughing after she inhaled a bit of the backfin. Then the absurdity of the situation hit her and she started to laugh. She knew she was only a few degrees off hysteria, but it felt so good, she indulged herself.

"Are you through?" David said when she finally stopped and was wiping her eyes.

"Yes, and I apologize."

"I guess it is a lot to throw at you."

"You think? And in public." But she was smiling as she reached over and patted his hand. "I've told you, I will always love you, but it's the kind of love that wants to see you healthy and happy and doing well. I'm not in love with you and I've been very clear about my feelings."

The plaintive look on his face made her wince. This was the only side of David that gave her pause. He was so rarely vulnerable and it always cost her when she tried to make him feel better. She said, "I'm not the same person I was when we were together."

"Well, I miss her. You, whatever. I want it all back. What do I have to do, Grace? Just tell me what you want."

What she wanted.

Stop dithering, girl.

Avril's advice to move on with her life collided with David's plea. Grace looked at the man who'd once held her heart and tried to imagine the future with him. Was this why she couldn't seem to settle? Had she really been waiting for him to change and come after her?

"This was supposed to be beautiful." His expression hardened and he leaned back, breaking the spell. "I've lost count of the times I've apologized and tried to explain how I've changed. I know I treated you badly during your last year in DC But when you left—"

"David! You fired me, remember? That's the part you leave out of these reimaginings of our relationship. When I went through the worst time of my life, you fired me. Yes, my work was off. I wasn't producing and I was behaving irrationally at times. I was *grieving* and in shock, and I needed you to understand and support me."

Her palms were itching – not a good sign. In the old days, a fight with David meant over the top stress and brought on an itchy rash. Grace had never quite believed the man she'd loved could give her hives, but she never broke out unless she was fighting with him. She clenched her fists to keep from rubbing her hands together and concentrated on how good it felt to unload the speech she'd carried around for a year.

"Alright, alright." In a lower tone, he said, "I hear you. But, Grace, I learned from it, from you being gone. I've grown. When you called, I thought you were ready to listen to me. I know you love me. You have to."

"Have to?" She'd found her voice but still wasn't sure exactly what she wanted to say. Well, she knew but didn't think it was wise to use that kind of language in public.

"Fair enough," He tasted the wine, made a face and once more leaned toward her, elbow back in the salad dressing.

Grace smiled in spite of herself and said, "Looks like there's more?"

"Well, now it feels awkward."

"You're long past awkward here. Spit it out."

"Look, I can deal with it, your feelings, I mean. I promise not to let how I feel interfere with us day to day. We can be professional and still have a friendly business relationship, right?"

She tried to ignore the itching that had spread to her wrists. "You know I agree. I called you for Bishop. I'm assuming you'd call me if you needed help with something here."

"Yes, but I'd like more. I want, that is, the board and I want you to come back to the firm. Same arrangement, but with a concrete path to partner. And the financial package reflects the partner track. I can have the papers to you tomorrow, just say yes."

Of all the things she thought he'd say, she'd never considered a job offer. But this was David, a man with a plan and a backup plan, and an escape plan if the first two proposals didn't work. Her mind refused to consider anything other than the chant. *I'm freefreefree.*

"Do I have your attention, now?" the old smugness was in his smile.

Two things saved her.

"Look who's here!"

Grace had never been so glad to see her cousin, even if Niki was with Aidan Banks.

CHAPTER TWENTY-THREE

"I think Niki'd talk to a tree. She never shut up. Not once."

Aidan draped his stocky frame over the visitor's chair in McNamara's office, using the heel of one shoe to rock the wheels back and forth. Head tilted, eyes closed and arms hanging limply at his side, he looked like a giant toddler after a tantrum. The Chief tried and failed for the hundredth time to see what Niki found appealing about Banks' walking drama routine.

Raising his voice over the squeaking wheels, Banks said, "She kept yakking on about stupid stuff until Farquar finally left. And then, bam! As soon as he's gone, Niki demands we leave, too, and take Grace home. What the hell? She breaks up their dinner and then ruins ours. The romantic evening out she's been nagging me for cost me last week's overtime and got me absolutely nowhere. She wouldn't even let me ask for the leftovers to go."

McNamara grunted and continued reading over the report he'd be giving to the Town Council on Tuesday night. The elected officials wanted to hear about the Bishop investigation, too. There wasn't much he could do about that, though.

Banks sat up, halting the screeching wheels. "There was one good thing."

"No details." They had a rule. Banks could talk to him about anything except his physical relationship with Niki. McNamara didn't do the Dr. Phil thing.

"Not that good. But I think we may have seen the last of Farquar." He said David's name with a scowl. "He looked upset when he left and I thought Grace was gonna cry, but she didn't run after him, or anything. She also let Niki make me leave my dinner to take her home, which I have to say, isn't like her. She could have walked."

McNamara gave up and looked at Banks. David Farquar had paid him a visit an hour earlier, saying he needed information on the investigation. He'd dropped Grace's name into the conversation so many times, it made McNamara think the lawyer was interested in more than Bishop's murder. Banks' account of the ruined Saturday night date seemed to support the Chief's suspicions. "Grace seem okay?" he asked.

"She's a girl, so who knows? All I can say is she didn't take my head off the way she usually does. And she let Niki fuss all over her, which isn't normal, so could be she was upset."

Upset about Farquar and the Bishop case? McNamara thought not. Which left the romantic relationship she'd had with her former boss and McNamara wasn't going near that minefield. He couldn't see Grace with the tightly wound lawyer, but he knew they'd spent a long time together. He thought Farquar's condescending attitude alone would turn a woman like Grace off, but, as Banks had said, she was a girl, so who knew?

Banks went on with his complaints about his expensive non-event evening and McNamara's thoughts drifted to the killing. He was hoping for a call from Detective Marbury about the shell casing and scarf. Her first reaction last night had been a flat-out insistence that the MSP hadn't missed a bright yellow scarf with a distinctive bird pattern during their intensive sweep of the woods. He was inclined to agree with her. The scarf was fairly clean and in good shape. It was unlikely it had been outdoors in the elements for two weeks.

His cell buzzed and Marbury's name flashed on the screen. Maybe his luck was changing.

DESIREE MARBURY ACTUALLY SOUNDED PLEASED WHEN SHE TOLD McNamara that Quentin Bishop had done a runner.

"It explains a lot and sure makes him look like the junior version of dear old dad," she said. "He has dual citizenship, Canadian and the US, and until today moved freely in and out of the States managing his companies. He has three homes here as well and has never really been on our radar. Stellar professional reputation, if you leave off the father's antics. Garrett Bishop gave us fits, but he's homegrown. USA through and through. Quentin Bishop reads like a different animal until he doesn't get what he wants."

McNamara wasn't sure what had made Desiree Marbury so chatty, but he wasn't going to interrupt the stream of information she was giving him. He said, "And this morning Quentin Bishop wanted to leave the country?"

"Wanted to and did. Pilot didn't file a flight plan until he'd crossed the border, either. In the scheme of things, a rich dude ignoring a stay-put order on a low-level person of interest charge isn't going to send anybody into battle, you know? But when I have to use my Sunday working because an entitled bastard like Bishop Junior does what he pleases, when he pleases, it makes me really mad. But at least it's a break in the case."

McNamara had seen the red-haired, red-faced Marbury really mad. He almost felt sorry for Quentin. "What can I do to help?" he asked.

"I don't mind telling you we were two steps away from absolutely nothing. But thanks to your find in the woods, and Junior's lack of respect for a lawful order, we're back in business. He'll be returning and when he does, things will be different. He wasn't considered a suspect before he left the country this morning, but I was just notified his status changed."

"Because he left?"

"And because he wasn't listed on the passenger manifest until his plane was out of U.S. airspace. Also, seems our comrades in Baltimore finally found Garrett Bishop's cell phone and cracked it open. The last text message from his son wasn't nice."

"NOW IS NOT THE TIME TO START KEEPING THINGS FROM ME," McNamara said.

He thought Grace looked too tired for nine in the morning. Her hair was already slipping out of its braid, the shorter strands curling to a fuzzy dark halo in the humidity. Makeup apparently hadn't been an option today; the pale face looking back at him was bare and guileless. Which meant nothing since she was a lawyer.

"Not you, too," she said but motioned for him to follow her through a labyrinth of rooms until they reached a small area that had once been the business end of a kitchen. Converting a 1870s Victorian home into a commercial space had obviously had some challenges. The new office was laid out in a maze of short hallways and unexpected dead ends. McNamara hoped once the boxes were gone and some order was imposed, it would look more professional. Right now, he could be standing in the back end of a Goodwill store.

"I'm here on business," he said. On the way over he'd decided to skip their usual banter. He was still irritated that she'd ignored his warning about Quentin Bishop, and even more irritated that she'd called Farquar to ride in and help. But more than anything, he was mad because he cared enough to be irritated. "We need to talk. I'm assuming you have an office with a door that shuts? If not, let's go to the station."

She was rummaging through a box and turned back to him with two coffee mugs. "It's Sunday, Chief. Lily and I already feel put-upon because we're here. You can press charges after we've had coffee. Still three creams and two sugars?"

"Black."

She poured his coffee and took time assembling hers with heavy cream and a packet of Equal. He didn't make his usual crack about a spoonful of chemicals clearing the fat out of her arteries. Then he hated the way her face tensed as the silence stretched out.

Her office was a large room that was more organized. She sat on one of the two armchairs in front of her desk and sipped her coffee.

McNamara didn't bother trying to wait her out. "Where is Quentin Bishop?" he asked.

She looked at her watch. "Somewhere in Canada would be my guess." She picked up her iPhone and flicked through screens before handing it to him. "I got this thirty minutes ago."

Emrg in Vancvr. Gen off will hndl US auth. Very sorry. More ltr.

"Is he paying by the letter?" McNamara grumbled.

"I can translate."

"It just looks ridiculous. I understand it fine. Bishop ran off and left you to clean up after him. What's the emergency in Vancouver?"

"Let's be clear, Mac. David Farquar will be doing the cleanup, if any is necessary, but Quentin did call me last night. He said he might need to leave to handle a family problem in Canada. I reminded him of the protocol required to get permission when he was under an order to stay in the area. I'm sure he followed it."

"He's got a real big family problem right here." McNamara wanted to tell her not to even think about keeping anything from him, but decided there was no point in picking a fight. More of a fight. "If he'd followed protocol, I wouldn't be here."

This seemed to surprise her. "Detective Marbury called a little while ago asking if I knew where he was. I told her what I just told you. She didn't say there was a problem with him leaving. Do they have a warrant for him?"

McNamara hesitated. She was Bishop's attorney. One of them anyway, and he wasn't going to help her client. If Marbury hadn't filled Grace in, he wouldn't either. Instead, he said, "Maybe I should be talking to Farquar. He came to see me this morning and was pretty steamed about the case in general, but he didn't mention Quentin skipping."

"I prefer to say Quentin made a mistake and has every intention of returning as soon as possible." Her words were stiff. "What did David want?"

McNamara was disgusted with himself for introducing the subject. He did not want to talk to Grace about her boyfriend. "He wanted what all attorneys want, to exonerate their clients. I'd like to believe he didn't know Bishop was headed out of the country."

"I'm sure David's on top of it," Grace said as if that was what he'd meant. "If you want information, start there."

"Will he be in town a while? Farquar, I mean."

"I hope not."

McNamara agreed with her but kept his opinion to himself.

CHAPTER TWENTY-FOUR

More than two weeks after he was shot, Garrett Bishop's death was still the topic of conversation wherever Grace went. The overly cute Barksley Pet Spa was no exception. If Leo hadn't been so happy to see his best friend, a timid shepherd named Louise, Grace might have turned around and given the class a miss.

Once a week, a group of volunteers met in the store's training room and worked with their foster dogs. The classes helped the dogs become more socialized, while the volunteers checked in with the rescue group which sponsored them. Prospective new owners could also attend and see the available dogs' behavioral skills, or lack thereof. As the hour progressed, Grace relaxed and enjoyed the whole process. She'd missed having a dog and even though there were times she was at her wit's end with Leo, she was still glad she'd gotten involved. Working with the rescue league was the closest thing she'd had to a hobby in years and it gave her a chance to visit with her friend, Benny Pannel. The contractor and his family were on their third foster dog, a Springer Spaniel who was the best behaved of the motley group that made up the Sunday evening class.

"I think we've got her placed," Benny said when they met up

after the final activity. He pointed to a young couple who were wearing huge smiles. Grace held Leo so Louise's foster mom could coax the shepherd away from her eight-pound boyfriend. Leo was squirming and making pitiful noises as he struggled in Grace's arms.

"That was fast," Grace said as she wrangled Leo, who would not be soothed as Louise disappeared through the front door. She tucked the little dog into the crook of her arm and rubbed his chest while she watched Benny interact with a couple who were cooing over his spaniel.

"Is it a done deal?" she asked Benny as the couple left, looking over their shoulders at the spaniel as they went.

"Oh, yeah," he said, dropping a hand to rub the dog's head. "This one was easy. A real love. The only hard part will be breaking the news to the kids. They want to keep her."

"How do you do it?" Grace asked. She couldn't imagine ripping a dog away from Benny's kids, five of the sweetest children she'd ever met. They could talk her out of her last dollar.

"They're old enough to understand what we're doing," Benny said. They'll be sad for a little while, but then they'll be excited about the new dog."

Benny had been recruited into the rescue group by his friend, Henry Cutter. Benny, in turn, had recruited Grace. She thought of them as resistance fighters, working against puppy mills and trying to provide a home for hard to place dogs. At eight years old, the spaniel wasn't as adoptable as a younger dog.

"I'm glad you're here," Benny said. He looked around and then motioned for her to follow him. When they reached the momentarily quiet area of the toy section, Benny stopped and settled his dog. "Look, I need to tell you something and get it off my chest."

Grace hoisted Leo to her shoulder to give her arm a break. Benny didn't look like he was starting a quick story.

He said, "You've known me a while now and I hope you know I would never do anything to hurt you?"

She couldn't guess what was coming next. The twist of anxiety which had started that morning with Mac's visit hit her stomach with a new jab. She made herself smile at Benny and said, "I know you wouldn't. What's happened?"

"The man that was killed. That Bishop guy. He called me for an estimate on the old Morgan house. I met him out there a couple of weeks ago. I thought he owned the place."

"Is that what he said?" Grace asked, and then wished she hadn't interrupted. Whatever Benny had been about to say was lost, as he appeared to be considering every word Bishop had said.

"Nope," he finally admitted. "The subject of who owned the place never came up. I just assumed if he wanted to build on it, he owned it. I don't get time to read the papers much, and I've been working down near Vienna for the past month. But this morning I got all caught up on the news and then checked in with some of the family."

Grace knew this meant Benny had plugged into the vast Pannel family grapevine.

"Now I've got a better idea of what was really going on with Bishop, but I want you to understand how it happened, okay?"

"Just tell me, Benny, it will be okay."

"Bishop said he wanted an estimate to demolish a house and put up four stick-built buildings on the property. You know what it would mean to our business, so I was excited. I met him and got all the details to do an estimate. We spent about two hours out there the first day. I went back the next day to meet with him, but when I got there, he was with another guy and they were arguing. They were into it big time, so I waited by my truck."

Benny shoved a handful of unruly hair off his forehead and took a breath. The contractor's troubled eyes said he had come to the upsetting part of his tale. Leo was nuzzling Grace's neck and she rubbed his back as she waited for Benny to finish.

"Bishop kept looking over at me as he and the other guy yelled at each other. Then, all of a sudden, Bishop yells at *me*. Tells me to get outta there. He didn't have to tell me twice. I mean, I wanted the job, but the guy was crazy."

"I'm sorry," Grace said. "He probably wanted your estimate to help him decide how much to bid."

"See, I don't think so. Now that I know what was going on, what the papers said about the auction you were havin', I think that's what Bishop and the big guy were fighting about. Garrett was yelling he'd pay whatever it took. And he said he had the girl in his pocket and the rest of them could go home."

The last part came out in a rush. Red-faced, Benny bent down to fuss over his dog.

Grace struggled to absorb what he'd said. *The girl in his pocket?*

Without looking at her, Benny said, "I feel like I should tell Cap'n Mac, Miss Grace, but I won't if it'll get you into trouble."

He hadn't called her 'Miss Grace' in a long time. She knew he was trying to be respectful as he gave her bad news.

She made Benny promise to call McNamara, and then paid for the toy mouse Leo snatched off a low shelf. After dropping Leo at home, she drove out to the Mallard Bay Golf Course. She needed to tell Cyrus what Benny'd said and let him know she was going to kill Connie.

SHE SHOULD HAVE KNOWN THE COURSE WOULD BE CLOSING DOWN this late in the day. Mosley's cart was among the others parked for the evening in the storage barn next to the Pro Shop.

"Mr. M's over in the dining room with some friends," the attendant told her.

Grace hesitated, then went to her car. As she tried to decide what to do, her phone chirped with a text from Niki: *I have BBQ, up for company?*

She'd been expecting to hear from Niki, but she was suddenly so tired she felt weariness seep through her. They needed to talk, but maybe it could wait. Grace didn't want barbecue, or conversation, or confrontation. She wanted to be alone to process the last twenty-four hours.

She managed a hot bath, a microwave pot pie and ten minutes of sleep before the world crashed in on her again.

"You're not eighty, you can't go to bed this early," Niki said when a groggy Grace answered the phone. "Besides, don't you admire the way I've held off saying anything about last night? My goodness, girl! You said David was handsome, but really. How could you walk away from *that*?"

Grace rolled her eyes and propped herself up in bed, nudging Leo over and getting a wide doggie yawn for her trouble. "I told you, when we aren't working together, all we do is fight." She reached for the cortisone cream on the bedside table and squeezed a dollop on her hands. "We have absolutely nothing in common. I was glad you and Aidan showed up, but I hated ruining your evening. I know Aidan was mad."

"Aidan's always mad, don't give him another thought. But Grace, if you and David are good together at work, surely you could have made it work at home. He's gorgeous and rich and he looked so upset, he must be the sensitive type."

"Sensitive? David? Uh, no."

"Well, it's clear he loves you. It's written all over him."

Grace wondered if she was the only one who hadn't seen it. And how long had it been going on? In all the years they'd spent together, she'd never defined any particular expression of David's as meaning 'love'. 'Want', yes. 'Need', constantly. But never love. And now, when she was over him, he loved her. She said, "He wants to try again. He offered me a job."

Niki's squeals of surprise turned to amazement at Grace's announcement that she'd said no to both offers. Niki's arguments on David's behalf took them through the next hour and sent Grace to the kitchen for wine.

"I don't understand you," Niki said.

Grace had explained all she was going to. She didn't see how Niki could fail to understand that she and David were incompatible.

"Is it someone else?" Niki asked. "I mean, maybe you have a thing for Quentin Bishop? I've been thinking about him, myself.

He's awfully rich but he isn't nearly as handsome as David. And then there's the whole murder thing. He could be guilty, right? It's too creepy for me."

As far as Grace knew, Niki had never met Garret Bishop's son. "Is Connie talking about the clients?" she demanded.

"Are you kidding me? Yes, Mom is talking about your clients. Hellooo? You've met her remember? Loud woman, motor mouth?"

"Yeah, well," Grace hesitated. She needed sleep and if she told Niki what Benny had said, she'd be on the phone until midnight with her cousin.

"What's she done?" Niki asked.

"Just being Connie." That much was certainly true. It remained to be seen if the 'the girl' Garret Bishop said was in his pocket was her middle-aged aunt. Right now, she could honestly say she had no idea and no reason to worry Niki. She changed the subject by saying, "I slipped something into your purse when we were at the restaurant tonight."

"What?"

Grace had been walking around with a check for Niki's mortgage for the last two days, trying to figure out how to get her cousin to accept it. She'd resorted to subterfuge when she'd had the chance and had slipped the check into a small pocket on the side of Niki's purse. An apparently rarely used pocket. She heard scrambling noises then a gasp.

It wasn't easy to get Niki to agree to cash the check. Only the promise that the money was an advance on Connie's commission on the Morgan farm convinced her cousin to give in.

"You're sure she wants me to have it? I was afraid she and Dad wouldn't repay me," Niki said when she finally stopped protesting.

"If they fall behind on the payments again, you have to let me know. I'm sure they won't, but if they do, I can advance the rest of the commission to you," Grace said.

"Not if Dad has anything to say about it. It means so much that she went against him to make sure I got the money. Don't defend him; I know that's what she did. Thank you for helping her."

"Don't think about it," Grace said, trying not to think about it herself. She'd have to tell Connie before Niki thanked her or it would all blow up. "This is your money, Nik. You have to remember that. Emma gave it to *you*, not your Dad." She changed the subject away from the money and Stark's lies. Niki had no illusions about her parents, but she didn't like being reminded of their shortcomings by other people, not even Grace.

CHAPTER TWENTY-FIVE

When she was finally off the phone, Grace was wide-awake. Thinking she should make use of the time, she spent an hour on the computer trolling all the reports she could find on Quentin and Garret Bishop.

"Quentin's father married his fiancé," she told Mosley the next morning as they sat in his golf cart. She'd decided to embrace Mosley's haunting of the Mallard Bay Golf Course, at least until winter settled in. Lily was upset by the new version of her beloved boss and a distracted Lily meant trouble for the firm.

"Don't men usually marry their fiancés?" Mosley asked. "Or is that another thing I've lived to see changed?"

"No, no. Garrett Bishop didn't marry his own fiancé, he married Quentin's."

While Mosley mulled over this bit of scandal, Grace took a cinnamon muffin from the bag between them and took a bite, savoring the crunch of walnuts and the sugary glaze. Between this and last night's pot pie, she'd have to run flat out for three hours to work it all off, and that wasn't going to happen. She made a mental note to run up and down the staircase at Delaney House for a half hour and skip dinner.

When it looked like Mosley was drifting away from their new client and back to the golf game in front of them, she said, "So, you get the idea. Quentin's got plenty of motive, other than financial, to kill his father."

"Didn't you know that when you agreed to represent him?"

"That he had a motive? Yes. Just not how much."

Mosley took a look in the pastry bag and rolled it closed again.

"Not a muffin fan? I can bring whatever you'd like."

"Heart doc has me on a strict regime. He and the endocrinologist are in cahoots."

Grace frowned and tossed the crumbs from the muffin out for a circling seagull.

Mosley *tsked* at her before adding, "Diabetes. Runs in the family."

"What are you doing about it?"

"What I'm told."

She reminded herself he wasn't being deliberately evasive and phrased her next words so he wouldn't have to answer her. "I'm glad to hear you're listening to the doctors. You'll let me know if I can help you? With the doctors or grocery shopping? Anything, Cyrus."

He patted her hand. "Take care of Marjorie."

Grace bolted upright from the one-armed hug she was giving him. "You mean find her a job?"

"She has one. We need her."

"Cyrus, no," she said, even though she knew she'd give in. Marjorie had worked for Cyrus for forty years. Lack of work wouldn't be enough for him to let her go.

He shook his head and waved in answer to a call from a trio of golfers who passed them.

"Lily is brilliant. She'll know what to do," Mosley said, going straight to the heart of her concern. "She'll help you make everything work if you just trust her."

"Lily's feelings are a part of the problem. She's not going to help keep Marjorie, because Marjorie won't cooperate." How many more times did she have to say it? Grace wanted to scream. She tried out various arguments in her head while Mosley gave his attention to the golfers who were selecting clubs from their bags.

She finally settled on honesty. "I think Lily will leave us."

Mosley said, "No. Trust her. She knows Marjorie has historical knowledge. Knows where all the bodies are buried."

Grace blinked, trying to get his pronouns sorted to the right women. "Marjorie? Are you serious?"

Still watching the golfers, he nodded. "She helped bury half of them."

Grace knew Mosley was giving up a lot in his newly downsized firm. His plant-kicking tantrum had surely been born from his discomfort and yet, in one way or another, he'd come around to almost everything she asked of him. Everything but Connie and Marjorie.

"Will Marjorie be willing to work under Lily?" she asked.

The old Mosley emerged briefly in a hearty snort. "Of course not."

He would not be dissuaded. Not only hadn't Grace been able to share her own worries and get his take on the unpleasant scene Benny had witnessed, she still had the staff problems. The news about Mosley's health turned her from needy to protective. She'd have to be her own counsel and let Mosley stay in his golf course bubble.

───────

HER RESOLVE GOT HER THROUGH THE TEN-MINUTE RIDE TO THE office where she ran smack into Connie, who was face to face with Lily.

"I've been waiting for you," Connie said to Grace without taking her eyes off of Lily.

"Oh good. I was afraid I might go a day without a trauma drama." Stepping between the two women, Grace leaned toward Lily and said, "I'll handle it, thanks. Don't you have a decorator coming in this morning?"

They smiled at each other in the wake of the hiss which came from Connie. "That's supposed to be my job! I'm the office designer. You're wasting the firm's money!"

"You don't work here, Connie. But please, follow me." Grace led the way into her office, shrugging off her coat, and then unpacking her briefcase as she let her words sink in.

Connie stood in the doorway, watching. When Grace sat behind her desk, Connie came into the room but didn't sit. "I do all of Cyrus' decorating," she said.

Grace tucked the information aside to consider later. "I don't know anything about a decorating job," she said. "And I don't care. This is a new firm."

"Oh, I didn't forget the arrangement. Couldn't if I wanted to. I can't go anywhere without someone asking me what happened." Connie walked to the nearest chair and sat, moving slowly. She balanced at the edge of the seat, wincing dramatically.

"Okay, Con, what's wrong? Throw your back out again?"

"Not exactly. I fell down the basement steps. I have bruises on the backs of my thighs and sitting is painful."

Not for the first time Grace considered the possibility that Stark abused his wife. Connie could have injured herself in a fall, but bruises on the back of both thighs might also be from a blow. "You should go to the doctor."

"Everything works, nothing's broken. No need for drama. Isn't that what you said?"

"I'm sorry you're hurt, but it doesn't change anything here. Your health insurance is still in effect, though. It covers therapy." When Connie dead-eyed her, Grace added, "Therapy for your legs."

Connie would not be shifted off topic. "Are you sure there's no going back? No way we can work this out?"

Grace heard David saying the same words. How did she get here, having constant arguments with people who were so sure she would give in?

The answer came immediately. She was not going to be a doormat. Not any more. She didn't realize she'd spoken out loud until she saw Connie's face. There was nothing to do but get on with it.

"Make a new start, Connie. That's what we all have to do, but this is your chance to start over and get things right."

"Easy for you to say! I don't have an office and even my new business cards are on backorder. The card stock I picked had to be imported."

"And naturally, you had to have it. Let me guess - very unusual and expensive."

"Well, I have to make a statement, don't I? Since I'm on my own if I can't get another job. And it's hard to look like a successful person anybody would want to hire when you don't even have an office."

"You're back to that? I told you, no. You work from home."

"That's not working out for me. I need someplace to go and you know I can't afford to rent a place, not with the huge mortgage payment we're making to Niki."

"You mean the huge payment you're not making to Niki. Perhaps Stark could get a job? There's a novel idea. He spends so much time in Atlantic City, maybe he can work at one of the casinos and let them pay him for a change."

"Don't be rude, Grace. Your uncle has his challenges."

So much was wrong there, Grace didn't know where to start. Not that anything she said would make a dent in Connie's well-padded emotional armor. She was even happier she'd given Niki the money. "What do you want, Connie? Besides a place to go pretend you'll have a job in three months, what do you want from me?"

"Nothing. I have a proposition for you."

She should have seen it coming. Connie's plan to open a real estate office on the ground floor of Delaney House was doubly upsetting because it was an addendum to Niki's bed and breakfast proposal. She'd guessed she might be tag-teamed by her aunt and cousin, and was surprised to find how much it hurt. It was possible Niki didn't know what her mother was up to, but there was zero possibility she hadn't bounced her ideas off of Connie. Niki was Grace's best friend, but she was Connie's baby girl.

'No' did not go over well.

After ten minutes of wheedling and pleading and, when all else failed, tears, Connie straightened up and changed course. It always surprised Grace to see how skilled her aunt was at this. You never knew what really lay at the center of Connie's emotional productions. She'd demand gold and trade down to the silver, which had been her real goal, the whole time confusing the issue with drama and keeping everyone in earshot off balance.

"Alright, you win," Connie said. "I'll tell Niki." She rose and moved to the door, wincing pitifully with each movement.

Grace got up and followed her. It wouldn't be wise to leave Connie unattended in the office. They were almost through reception when Connie said, "Since you won't help us in any other way, will you please advance me the commission on the Morgan farm? Cyrus said I had to ask you. And before you say no, it's not for me, it's for Niki. If I don't get the money to her today for her mortgage, the bank will start foreclosure on the inn."

"No, they won't," Grace said and steeled herself.

"You don't know anything. We're in dire straits and all I'm asking for is what's due me."

Grace hung onto her temper and mentally thanked Cyrus. When she finally responded, she could manage a smile.

"Way ahead of you. I knew you'd want to do that, so I gave Niki the money for the mortgage. She's current. All you and Stark have to do is make the future payments."

"*You* loaned it to her?"

"No, you paid her back."

Connie paled. "You gave her my commission? How much of it?"

"Added to the money you still owe Cyrus for paying off Bishop's firm, it comes to a little over half your commission. You'll get the rest at settlement unless you fall behind on the next mortgage payment to Niki."

"You had no right!"

Grace said, "I know, but I did it, anyway. And you're welcome."

The nearest object to Connie's hand was a delicate Hungarian rose glass vase that had lived for thirty years on a mahogany credenza in Mosley's office. The shattering of crystal against the freshly painted wall sounded like a gunshot.

"I could *kill* you! You're a meddling, sanctimonious *bitch*!"

Grace was an inch taller and twenty pounds heavier, but she backed up as Connie moved in.

"You owe me and you *will* pay me. Don't even think about not paying my full fee or you'll be very sorry. "

"You want me to tell Niki you changed your mind?" Grace asked.

"What?"

"I told her the money was from you. That you wanted your fee on the Morgan sale to cover your loan."

Connie was trembling but she stepped back. "You don't know what you've done," she said.

Grace followed her out onto the front porch.

When Connie reached the sidewalk, she looked over her shoulder only long enough to repeat, "You'll be sorry."

CHAPTER TWENTY-SIX

An angry Anton Norse proved it was indeed possible for the day to get worse.

"I don't know what's wrong," Lily said. "He only said he was on his way over and you'd better be able to explain yourself."

The dings and chips on the wall in the entry hall looked awful, but there was no time to deal with it. She left Lily to vacuum up the glass shards and track down Benny Pannel. Maybe the contractor could get them a painter before day's end.

Closeted in her office, she hurriedly read over the Morgan farm file and the terms of Norse's offer, but her head was filled with Connie's threat: *You'll be sorry.*

"Just what I need," she said out loud to the empty room. "A curse."

An hour later, she was willing to consider the possibility that Connie was a witch.

———

"First, your man, your Chief of Police, tries intimidation. Now your local bureaucrats have their hands out. They tell me it is because of you. It is you who did not correctly gather the proper permits for this land. This is worthless." Anton Norse threw a folded packet of papers onto the desk between them. The contract to purchase the Morgan farm.

Getting information from Norse was frustrating. In his anger, his ordinarily excellent English thickened with a heavy German accent and he frequently switched to German to curse. Or threaten her. She wasn't sure which, but she didn't like it. The source of his anger was an area of the law universally hated by contractors and loved by environmentalists. Grace tried to explain that Maryland's Critical Area regulations didn't prohibit the remodeling of the farmhouse or the subdivision of the land, but there were restrictions.

"The zoning information was provided in the description of the property, Mr. Norse. The house sits less than fifty feet from the water's edge. The laws regarding construction near tidal waters aren't new. You can occupy and use the house as it is now, but if you want to do a major remodel, you'll need to raise the structure above the flood line and you can't change the existing footprint."

"If my clients want, they can change it. They have money to make it happen."

Grace tried again to explain. "A footprint of a house is the land that it covers." She grabbed a pen and drew a rectangle on a legal pad. Say this is the current house. You can't cover any more ground." She drew squiggly lines all around the edges of the rectangle. "It can only be this big, like it is now, unless you add another floor. And if you do that, you'll have to raise the building above flood level, and you'll have to connect to the county sewer system. You can't expand the septic system. Your contractor can explain it all."

"I will bulldoze it." He rose, glaring at her. "Then my clients will build what they want."

Grace considered leaving this problem for a contractor to handle, but her ethics got the better of her. "You can demolish the house. But when your clients rebuild, they will have to meet both the flood elevations and the Critical Area setbacks. That would mean whatever they build will need to be located back here, near the road. It can't sit as close to the water as the current house does."

Norse's face was turning purple.

But she'd saved the best for last. "And, they'll have to plant vegetation between the house and the shoreline." She'd done the heavy lifting; she'd let the contractor tell him the 'vegetation' meant trees. "The brochure shows the only possible subdivision of the property and the three additional houses are drawn at the roadside."

"No subdivision," Norse said. "My client's club will be waterside and it will be big. You cannot stop them when they own this place."

Grace let him spew on in German.

"*I* am not stopping you from doing anything," she said when he wound down. "*You* have contracted to buy a piece property which has specific limitations on development, and it has limitations on zoning. You need to remember it's in an agricultural-residential zone. You can't build a club and you are limited in the remodeling you can do to the current structure. All of this information was disclosed to you before you placed your binding offer of purchase. You may cancel the contract but you will forfeit your deposit."

She hoped he would do it. In his rush to outbid the Carters and get the property for his clients, Norse had put a two-hundred-thousand-dollar deposit into Mosley's real estate escrow account. Grace would prefer to take her share of the deposit and be done with the hulking Norse. Sandra Carter should be thrilled at this turn of events.

But Norse was gathering his papers and moving to the door. He looked very determined for someone about to throw in the towel. "The contract is good. I never fail a client, Miss Reagan. I *will* have my way."

When he was gone, Grace dictated notes on their conversation, detailing his words and adding background for context. As she reviewed what she'd written, all she could think of were the two threats, which had been leveled at her in the short time she'd been at work. Connie's angry face and *'you'll be sorry'* danced around Anton Norse's parting shot.

I will have my way.

She was sure he wouldn't. The laws had already been tested and litigated. But what would Norse's anger mean for Mosley's firm and its client? A protracted lawsuit over the terms of the sale wouldn't endear them to the bank, and a disgruntled corporate client was poison in a small financial community.

After updating Lily, she delved into the vast world of Critical Area legislation looking for a loophole that would allow Norse's clients to build their club in the wetlands. She didn't really expect or even want to find one, and she knew angry neighbors would rally if such a plan became public.

"One mess at a time," she decided.

But even this simple goal turned out to be impossible.

CHAPTER TWENTY-SEVEN

"Connie says you've never lost a divorce case."

It had been five hours since she'd stormed out of the office, but apparently her aunt hadn't found time to poison Sandra Carter's opinion of the law firm. Yet.

Grace searched for a diplomatic response. "'Lose' isn't a term generally applied to a divorce, Mrs. Carter. I always work to get my clients what they want, if that's what you mean."

The truth was, all of her divorce work had involved pro bono cases with clients so poor, neither party had anything but children to argue over. Grace explained her lack of experience in the world of high stakes matrimonial implosion, then leaned back in her chair and let her client run on about the need for a fast and financially rewarding divorce from her husband of twenty years. If Sandra was like her best friend, Connie, there would be no shifting her off this plan until all possibilities were explored. Or until she got bored, whichever came first.

"And that's why I need you," Sandra said when she finally wound down from detailing her husband's many flaws. "One-stop shopping, so to speak. I don't want to use any of our attorneys. They're all in Jason's pocket. Besides, you intimidate my husband."

After the morning she'd had, it felt good to hear she intimidated someone. Grace pushed the childish reaction aside and made a note to find out if Senator Carter was litigious, or if he had other reasons for keeping a string of lawyers.

Sandra went on, saying, "He checked you out, you know. Jason was impressed with the firm you used to work for. He'll just die when he hears you're my attorney in the divorce."

Grace stifled a groan. This was why she hated divorce work. But Sandra Carter's retainer would keep her from having to tell Cyrus he needed to make another deposit to the new firm's operating account. Quentin's retainer had covered the shortage for last month. With Sandra's they could meet payroll and operating expenses on Friday. And if Connie found a house Sandra liked and if the divorce went quickly, maybe this extension of her professional ties to Connie wouldn't be so bad.

Her business plan said 'real estate and family law'. You didn't get any more 'family' than divorce work. Mosley had extensive experience in the area and still handled work for his aging clients who occasionally needed to divest themselves of an unwanted spouse. A new case might perk him up.

Sandra's tale of a long-stale union finally broken apart by a young mistress was run of the mill. Grace was relieved at the lack of anger but had a hard time understanding why Sandra was approaching her divorce with the enthusiasm of a wedding planner.

"Why file now?" Grace asked. "One minute you're shopping for a vacation home together and the next, you're filing for a divorce."

"One has *nothing* to do with the other." Sandra's voice turned harsh. "The Eastern Shore house is *mine*. I'm the one who wants out of the Richmond and DC lunacy we're trapped in. I want a home in the country and a social life I don't have to share with my cheating husband's girlfriend. They aren't exactly discreet, you know. I've tried really hard to pretend it doesn't bother me, but he's behaved so badly in the past few months, I've can't take it anymore."

"Behaved badly, how?" Grace asked, still looking for a kernel of sense in Sandra's story.

"Well, you saw for yourself how he was that night at Niki's house. And he keeps saying we can't afford the homes I like. Well, I'll be able to buy anything I want when we're done, won't I?"

"I can't make you any promises," Grace warned. "He can't give you what he doesn't have. Do you know how your finances are set up?"

Sandra's shark-like smile wasn't pretty. "My brother's our accountant. Tell me what you need to know and I can have the information to you in an hour."

Grace made notes and said, "Well, that makes it easier. We'll talk about the financial aspect after I've had time to assess your situation."

"I can explain it all now," Sandra said. She leaned forward and tapped Grace's desktop with a shiny, bright pink fingernail. "I want the condo in the Outer Banks with all of its current furnishings, my Jaguar and two million dollars in cash." She paused briefly to let Grace make notes. "He can keep the house in Richmond, all of our club memberships and all of the assets he brought into the marriage." She laughed and then added, "He can also keep the Escalade we just bought. I wanted to buy it outright, but he insisted on a six-year payment plan. Let Miss Perfect drive it, he can figure out how to pay for it."

Grace repeated the list back to Sandra, who nodded her approval and said, "That should do it. Everyone gets what they want, and I keep my assets."

"How equitable is this division?" Grace asked. "Monetarily speaking."

Sandra shrugged and said, "If you mean market value and considering debt owed on the property, I'd say, seventy-thirty. I'm the seventy. And by the time he's sold everything he can't afford to keep, they'll be in an apartment somewhere deep in a suburb. But who cares. This is what's important: I want this wording in the paperwork. I want you to say that in recognition of twenty years of marriage and in return for a hassle-free divorce, I will forgive Jason's debt to me for paying off his college loan and he doesn't have to repay me for the down payment I put into the Richmond house. It wasn't much, but it will look impressive in the papers. I also want you to make sure these words are in the settlement documents." She looked at Grace expectantly.

"I write fast, Sandra. Have at it," Grace said.

"Okay," she nodded. "'*In light of my husband's long and very public affair, I am conceding to his wishes to be with the woman he loves and their children.*' There. Did you get it?"

"Children?" Grace had been having a hard enough time picturing the dour Senator in a public love affair, but kids in the mix made a whole new game.

"Didn't I mention them? My loving husband didn't want kids with me and talked me around to his way of thinking. I made peace with it years ago, and then I found out he already had a child. And now his mistress just had their second, a boy she named after his daddy, in case anyone we knew was deaf as well as clueless."

Grace was shocked, but Sandra's demand for a divorce made sense now. "How long have you known about his other family?"

"For years. I've gotten to this point several times, but he always talked me out of it. Not this time, though. He's getting meaner as he ages, and I don't like it. You saw how he acts when he's mad."

"The day Bishop died? We were all upset."

"He's been so rude and hateful lately, and it isn't getting better. This whole chain of events has pointed out to me that I'm wasting my time. Now, are you going to represent me, or are you taking his side?"

Grace decided she had more than enough to work with. Not much would trump a second family on the side. Jason Carter was in trouble. She told Sandra she'd take the case.

"Oh, and one more thing," Sandra said. "Connie is my real estate agent. I won't buy my house through anyone else. She very graciously is refusing to let me sign on as a client in her new firm, but I'm telling you, if she isn't my agent, I'm walking out of here with all my business."

"I can agree to that," Grace said, thinking Connie was a sinkhole that would never settle.

You'll be sorry.

She put Lily on research detail after Sandra left. A half hour later, they knew a lot more about their new client. Far from exaggerating, Sandra had actually been quite modest about her contribution to her marital union. Her art brought eye-popping prices, and an Internet search turned her name up far more often than her politician husband's.

In less than a week, Grace had taken on two new clients. She put them aside and returned to her review of the Critical Areas laws. Anton Norse was worrying her.

CHAPTER TWENTY-EIGHT

I t was getting dark when she pulled into the drive at Delaney House, and she almost missed seeing the man who was leaving her backyard. He was consulting a clipboard, turning back once to look at the house and briefly in her direction before hurrying away.

Grace's experience with inspectors wasn't good. She got out of the BMW and sprinted in the direction the man had gone. She reached the sidewalk at the far side of her property in time to see a van that might have been blue or black disappear around the corner at the end of the block.

Nothing looked amiss in the yard or on the porches. No tape plastered across the doors or work tents with caution signs erected on the lawn. None of the hallmarks of her last round with public officials were visible. She'd had an occupancy permit for nearly a year, but she still expected a building inspector or police officer every time the doorbell rang. Strange men walking around the house set off every nerve she had.

All the doors were locked and she thought the first floor looked just as it had when she'd left earlier, but it was hard to tell if the empty rooms had been disturbed. She was almost to the second floor when she realized she hadn't turned off the alarm. She had a clear memory of setting it that morning.

The big house was quiet in a way only a spooked person can sense. No creaks, pops or sighs from ancient floors or the modern appliances. The house was holding its breath, too.

She stood still, holding tight to the smooth banister. From here, the lights she'd switched on when she'd entered downstairs let her see all of the landing. When her right leg sent a warning tingle of an approaching cramp, she eased onto the second floor and looked down the hall. The last door on the right stood open.

Without stopping to think, she turned and ran back down the staircase, across the hall and out the front door, slowing only long enough to hit the blue 'Alarm Set' button on the small panel to the left of the doorway.

Twenty minutes later, she felt like an idiot.

Chief McNamara's face showed concern, but Grace thought it was for her state of mind, not because he thought anyone had been in the house. He and Aidan Banks had looked in every corner of Delaney House's seven thousand square feet and found nothing except a field mouse in one of the humane traps near a basement stairwell.

"Maybe you should keep the little guy as a pet," Aidan said in a rare display of humor.

Grace said if the mouse was smart enough to open doors, maybe she should. Once Aidan left, though, all attempt at jokes stopped.

"None of the utilities have techs in the area," McNamara reported. He tapped his cell a few more times and added, "None use blue or black service vans, either."

"Let me guess. None of their employees are instructed to run off when the homeowner approaches, right?"

"I think you can assume that. We've been through every room. Your alarm is working and thanks to your quick thinking, we're sure no one got out while you were calling us. The man you saw could have been someone who took a shortcut through your woods. Or was up to something back there. It doesn't look like anyone was in the house."

She was tired of arguing. She knew someone had been inside.

The rear of her property was all that remained of an ancient woodland which had once covered what was now the southern half of the village. Locals referred to the large overgrown area as 'Delaney Woods'. Last winter, a police investigation had necessitated the partial clearing of the tangled vines and scrub brush and the removal of several trees, but the undisturbed area still offered shelter to small animals and humans who wanted privacy. Grace wasn't interested in accommodating any of them.

"Do you like living here. All alone, I mean. Does it worry you?" McNamara asked.

"I'm trying as hard as I can to sell it, alright?" She was sick of everyone assuming she was dragging her feet. That she didn't know what she was doing.

"No nibbles from potential buyers?" he said as if she hadn't just acted like a two-year-old.

"No," she sighed. "Only my family wants to move in." She told him about Niki's proposal.

"Think it might be an answer to your problems?"

"Oh, yeah. That's what I need to do. Keep everything tied up here for a couple more years."

"It would make Cyrus happy."

"Three and a half months, Mac. That's all I have left at the firm."

"So, who has a key to the house besides you?"

"Niki. We share Leo, you know."

"That's right," he made a show of looking around and even checking the bottoms of his shoes. "Where is Mighty Mouth, anyway? He'd be useful if you did have a break in. Bad guy wouldn't see him but the neighborhood would be alerted."

Grace refused to give in to the smile that tugged at her mouth. "At Niki's tonight. I dropped him off there, so she wasn't here today. And before you ask if I'm sure – I am. She wouldn't come in the house without telling me. Besides, she doesn't have keys to the storage room on the second floor or to my apartment."

"And it was the storage room door which was standing open?"

"Yes. I haven't been in there for at least a month, so I didn't accidentally leave it open. I'd have noticed before now. In fact, I went down to the second-floor sleeping porch this morning to bring in the swing cushions for the winter. I'd have seen if the door was open."

"Someone was in the house and you know this because the room you find necessary to lock with a deadbolt was standing open."

She wished he hadn't said it out loud, but then he made it worse.

"Which is why you think the person had a key." He looked thoughtful, but not convinced.

She told him she'd installed locks on the storage room and her apartment when she'd moved in during the height of the renovation work. She'd continued to use them even now because the house was being shown and she didn't want her private areas opened for inspection until there was a serious buyer.

His only response, other than a skeptical look, was, "When you're ready to talk, call me."

When McNamara was gone, she reset the alarms, locked the door to her apartment and sank into a hot bath. Tomorrow she would go back to the real world, but for tonight, she was in her nest at the top of Delaney House and she told herself she was safe.

———

"I'M BACK AND I'M SORRY. GRACE?" QUENTIN BISHOP'S WORDS brought her out of a sound sleep and into a cold Tuesday morning.

She'd had a restless night and struggled to focus. "I don't know where you are, but it's 4:45 here. A.M."

"I know, and I apologize. I wouldn't be so rude if I had another choice?"

She sat up and turned on the bedside lamp. She thought his return to the every-statement-as-a-question mode was a bad sign. "Have you been arrested?"

"I think it may be imminent. I'm in the Immigration and Customs Enforcement offices in Philadelphia and I need you to pick me up."

"You aren't making sense, Quentin. Why are you calling me? Have you talked to David?"

"I called him, but he didn't know I was returning so soon and I caught him off-guard. He's trying to arrange transportation for me, but I wasn't sure how long they would let me have access to a telephone, so I took the opportunity to call you, too."

This was ridiculous. Grace wanted to say 'use Uber'. Instead, she told Quentin not to answer any questions until she arrived. If he was willing to pay a lawyer to chauffeur him, he'd called one who needed the money badly enough to do it. Mindful of the ears listening in on their conversation, she said, "You said I.C.E. has detained you? For now, just tell me what they said to you." Immigration could have any number of reasons for detaining a foreign national, but a U.S. citizen?

"Detain is a mild word. They hauled me off my jet in handcuffs. It would have been all over the news if I hadn't landed at two a.m. It's a show and nothing more, the authorities were well aware I was coming, and that my itinerary was straight to Easton and you."

"What reason did they give you?" she asked.

She heard someone speaking in the background and Quentin said, "It's complicated and the agent says I have to hang up."

"Wait! Where are they holding you?"

"The building is on Chestnut Street. You'll have to look it up." The phone beeped and he was gone.

She made a cup of coffee before the next call came in.

"I need a favor."

"Let me guess," Grace said. David sounded as tired as she was. "You want me to go to Philadelphia and get Quentin."

"Good, he called you. I wouldn't ask, it's just—"

"Things are busy and I'm closer."

"We make an excellent team, babe. Always did."

"It helps that you're so predictable," she snapped. But she *was* one of Quentin's attorneys. Now was not the time to quibble over whether or not retrieving him from the clutches of Immigration Enforcement was covered in her representation agreement. She drank her coffee and made notes while David filled her in. She was surprised to hear Quentin held dual American and Canadian citizenship.

David said, "I'm guessing I.C.E. is holding him for the FBI. It's a common enough arrangement. They would have had agents at the airport when Quentin landed. I want one of us with him when they make their intentions clear."

"FBI?" Grace asked. "Not the Maryland State Police?"

"Power chain, Gracie. The family emergency Quentin went to Canada to deal with was a showdown with his father's widow, over control of his father's business. Unfortunately, Bishop senior was playing fast and loose with his corporate books and had recently come to the attention of the authorities on both sides of the border. That attention has now shifted to Quentin and Heather Bishop."

Grace sent herself a text with the information he'd given her and scrambled to get dressed. Barring complications, she should be in Philadelphia by nine.

CHAPTER TWENTY-NINE

The first complication for her timetable was blocking the driveway. The Chief's Ford Explorer was parked behind her BMW. McNamara was sipping from a large cup of coffee and reading something on his phone.

"What are you doing?" she said when he lowered his window in response to her impatient rap on the glass.

"Me? I often spend the wee hours of the morning here. You're just never up to notice."

The teasing tone only made her madder. "Are you going to explain what's happening, or do I have to drive across my lawn to get out of here?"

"Mr. Bishop is being detained by immigration officials. The Maryland State Police are second in line for him. I wouldn't think of detaining his attorney, except you aren't that person, so I thought I'd check things out over here. Anything else happen after I left last night?"

He got out of the car and stretched, but she refused to ask how long he had been there.

"No," she said. "And just so you know, the MSP is third behind the FBI." She enjoyed his look of surprise. "David's handling all the excitement. I'm only doing courier service for my client. So, could you please move?"

"I thought you weren't going to represent Bishop in the investigation into his father's death?"

"This current situation doesn't have anything to do with Garrett's death."

"Did your boyfriend tell you that, too?"

Something snapped and the last of her patience vanished. "We, you and me, *we* are going to have a problem if you keep calling him that. Understand?" She couldn't recall ever having seen McNamara embarrassed, but there was no mistaking the look on his face. She wanted to stop, back up and start over, but the words were already coming. "And furthermore, where I go and what I do with my clients is none of your business."

The mild, slightly amused expression that was his public face slipped into place and his vulnerability was gone. Grace, on the other hand, was breathing hard and wanted to throw up. She'd been mad at David and had taken it out on Mac. Who had also been arrogant and presumptuous. Why did they both have to act like she was theirs to direct? Her anger resurfaced and she felt better.

"Understood," McNamara said. He opened the car door but turned back to her before getting in. "If you need me, I'll be here."

It was a long, miserable drive to Philadelphia.

"WERE THOSE HANDCUFFS NECESSARY?"

"We allowed him to drape his coat over them when we took him off the plane," Agent Rounder said. She didn't break her stride as she led Grace and Quentin Bishop at a fast clip down a long, drafty hallway. She was a small woman but had no trouble staying in the lead.

They were somewhere underground, moving between the Pennington Processing Center and an adjacent parking tower. Still technically in Philadelphia, Pennington was far enough away to add a half hour to her original timeline. Quentin had just been released on his own recognizance, a feat she knew was due to David's calls and not to her appearance.

Since leaving the final checkpoint of the detention tower, they had walked for ten minutes following Rounder into an elevator and down twenty floors. Another long walk brought them to the underground parking facilities. Grace thought any escapee from the I.C.E. facility would die wandering in search of an exit. They'd passed several people wearing identification badges who paid them little attention except to once-over Quentin and Grace.

"You're saying my client had to choose between being in shirtsleeves in freezing weather or wearing his coat and exposing the handcuffs? Really?"

Grace only got a shrug for her trouble.

"It's okay," Quentin said. "She's just doing her job."

"And I'm doing mine," Grace said. She put her hand on Quentin's arm and stopped walking. "This is far enough." A security station up ahead had a red 'Exit' sign. There was no way she was letting him leave the building looking like a criminal. "This is as far as you go with us, Agent Rounder. If the press is out there, I won't let you smear him because you can't make your charges stick."

Rounder had been short on details with Grace, but not deliberately rude. The agent made a pro forma protest, but Grace still won the staring contest. She and Quentin exited the building and made their way unencumbered by an official escort through the small crowd of reporters. She waited until they were on I-95 heading south before asking him what, precisely, she'd just liberated him from. Other than muttering 'thanks', Quentin had been silent, lying with his head against the headrest and eyes closed since they'd left the parking garage. Now he only managed 'sorry' as he rubbed his face with both hands. At least both words were uttered as statements.

She had plenty of time to wonder what had triggered Quentin's annoying use of the questioning speech pattern. He'd been up all night, so she gave him a break and enjoyed the silence.

After more than an hour, he said, "It's all crap."

She was startled out of a semi-serious imagining of what the

Delaney House Inn might look like if she let Niki have her way. It was a relief to turn her attention to Quentin. Niki had expensive taste.

"In what regard?" she asked.

Quentin shook his head. "I'll be amazed if there isn't at least one shot of me doing the perp walk from the plane last night. First, I had Rounder's boss, a guy named Strickland. He was a hard ass. Said I was being charged with obstruction of justice in the investigation into my father's business. All crap, you understand. Then he said the State Police in Maryland want me for the murder of my father. That one has me a bit more worried, but it's still crap."

Grace negotiated a bottleneck at an exit for a shopping center. When she was clear, she asked, "All of it is crap? With the FBI and the state? Why would they go to the trouble?"

Quentin seemed to consider his answer before saying, "Well, technically, I didn't cross every 'T' when I entered Canadian airspace. Even if I am a natural born citizen there, it was hard to convince them I wasn't running from anything here, but I guess it looked suspicious."

"That makes no sense."

"The Canadian authorities won't give me a pass, Grace. My father tormented them for years. They want our companies to stay in their country, but Dad was always pushing the envelope. I don't expect you to understand." Quentin ended the conversation by pulling out his phone and calling David who answered on the first ring. The voice they heard did not sound happy.

While the men talked, Grace was second-guessing her decision to be a part of Quentin's legal team. When they stopped in Chestertown for a late breakfast, they ate in silence. Quentin still looked exhausted and Grace decided from here on out, he could be David's problem. They were on Route 213, halfway to Centreville before he picked up the conversation again.

"It's true the Maryland police are zeroing in on me. I'm afraid I didn't realize how much trouble I was in until Rounder told me there was an open warrant for me as a witness. Even dead, Dad manages to screw up my life."

"You surely didn't think his death would go on the back burner, did you? I mean, you say what's happening in Vancouver is important but this is still an unsolved homicide."

Quentin turned his face away and watched the farm fields fly past his window.

Throwing out the decision she'd just made, Grace said, "Tell me, why did you really go back?"

"My father's wife called and said she needed me." His voice was toneless; the answer sounded rehearsed.

"So, you hopped in your private jet and violated about a dozen regulations getting to her."

Quentin continued his study of the countryside. Grace pretended she understood.

"Okay, we'll leave it for now," she said, as if she had a choice. She wanted to return to what mattered, anyway. "If the Canadian authorities let you leave, why do our immigration authorities care if you came back here?"

"You'll remember I wasn't supposed to leave in the first place. I think they were making an example of me and I was hardly in a position to complain."

"Because?"

"Because," he sighed and gave Grace an 'I give up' shrug. "I was wrong, okay? I panicked when Heather called and I didn't think of anything but getting to her. Understand now? It was stupid? I know that. She only wanted to see—" he didn't finish but his fingers drummed a static-y beat on his bent right knee.

"If you'd come?"

But Quentin had shut her out. Again. After a time, he said, "It will be fine. I have good attorneys."

"I must not be one of them since I have no idea what's going on."

"You don't need to. The one who's keeping me out of jail does."

The words and sharp tone were so out of character for the man whose usual defense was a juvenile speech pattern she was shocked.

Then furious. She felt her neck warming and knew her face was going red. "Well, he's the right one to handle your murder defense."

"It won't come to that, I assure you." His eyes never left the scenery on the right side of the car.

If Quentin Bishop wanted to pay her hourly fee for chauffeuring services, so be it. She needed the money and a high-profile client. Let David and his partners do the work. Grace took him to the Egret Inn and dropped him off. She half expected him to tip her but found she was wrong about that, too.

CHAPTER THIRTY

It took McNamara a while to convince Benny Pannel to give a statement to the State Police. It took him even longer to make Desiree Marbury understand that pushing Benny for more than he wanted to say would be a waste of energy. The only positive thing to come out of the exercise was it kept his mind off the early morning encounter with Grace.

He didn't blame her for blowing up at him. He must have looked ridiculous hunkered down in her driveway like an angry father forbidding a teenager to go out. He deserved the analogy but he didn't like it. There was a lot he didn't like about the Bishop situation and very little he could do about it.

He couldn't give Grace the information that had placed Bishop at the top of the MSP's list of suspects. Marbury had trusted him. Even if it had been legal to do so, he wouldn't betray her trust by telling Grace about the text Quentin had sent his father the night before Garret was shot.

Desiree Marbury had been a rookie trooper under McNamara's command in the MSP. They'd kept in touch and she'd leaned on their long friendship when she told him about the first big break her team had gotten in the Bishop investigation. Quentin's last text to his father had been a scathing five words: *You are dead to me.*

David Farquar would undoubtedly try to blow it off as a family squabble, but the State saw it as another threat. One the dead man's son had finally carried out.

McNamara hadn't broken Marbury's trust. Instead, he'd let Grace drive straight to a possible killer. This uncomfortable thought had bothered him all morning until Benny showed up and gave him something useful to do. After much coaxing, the contractor told him someone associated with the bidding on the Morgan farm may have planned to rig it in Bishop's favor. Even better, Benny might be able to identify Anton Norse as the person Bishop had been taunting. Desiree had been thrilled with the information and was all set to grill Benny for every last detail he could remember.

McNamara warned her and then wished her luck. Benny's side of the Pannel clan hailed from Tilghman Island. Benny would say what he thought was appropriate and after that, God Himself wouldn't get another word out of him. But McNamara knew someone who was always ready to talk. The Chief decided to pay a visit to the 'girl' most likely to have been in Garrett Bishop's pocket.

HE SPOTTED CONNIE'S CAR IN GRACE'S DRIVEWAY AND PULLED UP to Delaney House for the second time that morning. A quick look around told him Connie wasn't outside. He rang the front doorbell but didn't wait before opening the door and stepping inside.

"Well, come on in!" Connie's face fell when she saw him standing in the hall. "Oh. What are you doing here?"

McNamara smiled. "Might ask you the same thing. I was on my way to see you and found you here instead of your own house. Who are you expecting?"

"A buyer. I'm showing the place. Now tell me what you want and clear out. The last thing I need is for the police to be here and upset my client."

"Grace is letting you show the place?" The locks on the storage room and Grace's apartment suddenly made sense. If Connie had access to his house, he'd lock a few things up, too.

"Certainly! She wants it sold, or so she says. I sold the dump out on Morgan Creek, I can sell this if she gives me enough time."

"That's why we need to talk," McNamara stepped into the front parlor and admired the restoration work Grace and the Pannels had done. Over his shoulder, he said, "I heard you did a great job."

"Yeah? Tell it to Cyrus and Grace. They're pushing me out of the firm."

"Really?" He came back to face her. "Sounds upsetting. Why would they do that?"

"Grace says she can sell real estate if she has to."

He nodded and stood for a moment, hands clasped behind his back. When she started to speak, he broke in and said, "Was it over the way you handled the bidders on Morgan farm?"

"What? I don't know what you mean!"

"You made some promises, didn't you? To one of them?"

It might have worked if the doorbell hadn't gone off again. The Westminster chimes rolled through the house and gave Connie the seconds she needed to pull herself together.

She waved at someone she saw through the panel windows at the side of the front door and spoke to McNamara through a fake smile. "You listen to me. Whatever that scumbag Jason Carter told you is a lie. This is one of the reasons Sandra's leaving him. The man couldn't tell the truth with his last breath. Now she's here, and I do not want her upset. Get out." Connie left him with the air of one who assumes their command will be obeyed.

Which was why the Chief stayed for the house tour.

───────

"AND THAT'S IT!" CONNIE SAID WITH A FLOURISH. "THE MOST historic house in town. You'd own a piece of history and be the envy of everyone you know."

They were back in the entry hall, having toured the first and second floors. McNamara wasn't surprised to see Sandra glow at the picture Connie painted. She had grown increasingly excited as they walked through the rooms and Connie told stories of lavish parties and the famous people who'd attended them. She described the generations of Delaneys as if she'd just left a family reunion, omitting only the most infamous bits of family lore. Murder, assault and heavy household maintenance weren't in Connie's spiel.

"What do you think, Captain?" Sandra asked McNamara. "You're from around here. Is this house as famous as Connie says?"

"Chief," he said with a smile. "I'm the Chief of Police."

Connie glared at him, but Sandra laughed. "Of course you are," she said. "You boys and your titles. Captain, Chief, Senator. They all mean Big Man, don't they?"

His burst of laughter put color back in Connie's cheeks and drew a giggle from Sandra. "You are so right, Mrs. Senator Carter," he bowed. "I want to thank you for letting me tag along today, but I need to leave and let you and Connie get on with your tour."

Back at the office, he dictated notes on the hour he'd spent in Delaney House, taking care to describe Connie's assurance that she could get the price down by fifty thousand and Sandra's approval of the plan. At some point since Waterfowl Weekend, Mrs. Carter had added a million dollars to her house-shopping budget.

CHAPTER THIRTY-ONE

"**D**o we have a client, or don't we?" Mosley didn't take his eyes off the golfer who kept taking practice shots.

"We do. But what I'm supposed to do with Quentin, or for him, is another question. David didn't return my call this morning."

"Farquar's a good man. Your Quentin will be fine. Assuming he isn't guilty of conspiracy or murder. Even if he is, David can handle it."

"Well, I agree, but you talk like you know him. David, I mean."

Apparently tiring of the incessant triple-step, tiny-swing dance of the procrastinating golfer, Mosley turned to her and grinned. "I know *you*. I read what I could find about him. And that firm. Had to when I got involved with Miss DC"

"I told you not to call me that," Grace said, but she smiled back at him. It was good to see Cyrus happy. He had a bit of sun on his leathery cheeks and his eyes twinkled. When she'd agreed to run the practice, he'd joked that they were Beauty and the Beast and had taken to calling her 'Miss DC', laughing at her outraged protest over the contest title.

She had no idea what he had to be happy about, but whatever it was, they'd both enjoy it for a while.

"Take him at face value," Mosley said, turning back to watch the golfer, who, having finally taken his shot, stood staring forlornly in the direction of a sand trap.

"Who? David?"

"No. No. Eyes wide open there."

"Bishop?" she tried again.

"Yes," Mosley said. "Your client asked for specific things. Don't push in past that."

She knew he was right and had already decided it was the best course of action, but it rankled that he would now think she was doing what he told her to. *Oh, grow up*, she chastised herself.

She moved on to the Carters. "When was the last time you had a juicy divorce case?"

"Juicy?" The golfers lost their audience.

"A fed-up wife and a husband with a mistress *and* children."

"Husband's children?"

When Grace said yes, Mosley's laugh made the nearest golfers look at him for a change. She filled him in on Sandra and Jason Carter and he congratulated her on the firm's expanding business.

"I can help,' he said. "Divorce pays when everything else dries up. Let's see." He gave his freckled scalp a scratch. "The Carters aren't all that scandalous. Back in '66 Gerard Pinklee came home from a month-long sales trip with two teenage girls he wanted his wife to adopt. Turned out, the girls weren't teenagers, and one of them wasn't a girl. I didn't have to work too hard on that one."

He was off and running. For the next half hour, Grace listened to tales of bad marriages put asunder by Cyrus Mosley, Attorney at Law. The warm fall morning was punctuated with the calls of geese overhead, an occasional shout of 'fore!' and Grace's laughter. It was a rare return to the early days with Mosley and she realized how much she'd missed him. She also realized he could talk when he wanted to. She didn't try and figure it out, she was just grateful.

When she left him safely situated near the tenth hole with a boisterous foursome of friendly golfers, she was happy. The feeling lasted right up until she crossed the threshold of the new office and entered the real world again.

HER TRIP TO PHILADELPHIA HAD BEEN BRIEF BUT SHARP. A WHIPLASH taste of her former life. She'd worn a suit and heels and if her brief-case had only contained blank legal pads and a laptop, it was still her armor. Quentin Bishop might consider her a second-tier employee, but for a little while she'd been back in the game and had held her own. She was glad she still looked the part of managing attorney as she tried to decide how to deal with Marjorie Battsley's return.

No offer Grace made was good enough for the Bat. Lily wouldn't bend from her demands, either. Grace had to referee some kind of settlement if Marjorie was to make it to year forty-one as Mosley's employee. She was entertaining the idea of buying the Old Bat a golf cart and sending her off with Cyrus, when she opened the front door to the office and heard only the hum of the copier. It was tempting to circle to the through the small sitting room, sneak into her office and lock the door, but she resolutely turned left and into Lily's domain.

There was a panicky moment when she found Lily's space empty, but then she heard Marjorie say, "I think that does it."

She found them in the small room between the two partners' offices. It had been used as a temporary storage area, but all the boxes were gone. Lily's desk from the old office was sitting in front of a large window overlooking the rear garden. Both women smiled at her, but Lily's grin looked triumphant.

"I'm taking this office," Lily said, adding, "if it's okay."

"I'll handle the front desk and the phones," Marjorie said. "Since Connie won't be here, I should be able to do all of the filing and other support work, too."

"Who are you people?" Grace said.

At some point while she had been confronting Connie, alienating McNamara and getting Quentin out of custody, Lily and Marjorie had reached a detente on their own. As Lily explained it later, faced with the inevitable, she'd decided to set her own terms for surrender. For her part, Marjorie turned out to be a pragmatist who knew a final offer when she heard it. Lily's proposal of a 'front of the house/back of the house' arrangement had been worked out and was being implemented. Grace doubted the truce would last, but she was too grateful to poke holes in it.

"Works for me," she said and checked her watch. "Staff meeting in thirty minutes. I'll fill you both in on our new clients and their far-flung problems and you can tell me how we're going to get the work done."

The staff meeting lasted three hours and was an eye-opening event. Far from not having any work for Marjorie, Grace and Lily soon realized they would be in trouble without her. The Carter divorce and Norse's declared intent to challenge the zoning on the Morgan farm were both labor-intensive projects. They had two other sales going to settlement next week, and while they required little work at this point, anything could happen before the parties signed the final papers. And then there were the clients who were coming in to transition from Kastner to Grace and Mosley. These meet and greets weren't billable but took up time and energy.

It was a daunting schedule but an exhilarating one. Mosley's new firm was off to a good start. Cyrus had been right about the firm needing Marjorie. Grace knew he would use up a week's worth of words to make sure she knew he'd bested her. She pushed the thought aside and smiled at the pleasure it would give the old guy. If Lily and Marjorie could maintain their forced goodwill and Grace could keep her sanity, they might just be successful.

Grace took her 'ifs' and went home. She needed rest before seeing what tomorrow would bring.

FOR TWO DAYS LILY AND MARJORIE WORKED OUT THE TERMS OF their new work life and set up the office operations. Grace worked on

Sandra Carter's divorce and cleaning up odds and ends of work for Cyrus. The weather held in a streak of increasingly warm days and Cyrus' office visit on Wednesday was short and cheerful. When Jason Carter appeared on a Friday morning and threatened a malpractice suit, the jolt was almost a relief after the unreal calm in the office.

"I'm not a confrontational person, Ms. Reagan. I'm an insurance agent by trade, as well as a politician. Suing folks would be bad for my image, if you get my drift. So understand I'm not making this threat lightly. You were working for my wife and me and now you're helping her divorce me. I'm hoping by talking this out with you now, we can clear things up and avoid any further unpleasantness. But understand, I'll sue you if you help her leave me."

Grace took a moment to study the man who sat across from her. For once she was glad she'd agreed to take Paul Kastner's 1950s era executive desk. She disliked the heavy double pedestal style, but today she appreciated its bulk. Jason Carter was angry and the bigger the desk between them, the better.

She said, "I'm afraid I can't talk to you, Mr. Carter. I'm Mrs. Carter's attorney and she's suing you for divorce. If you want to talk, we need to have your attorney present."

"That's just it! Sandra and I worked everything out years ago. We don't need you; we can file the paperwork through our lawyer and go through the process. But I'm saying this all wrong. I won't give in to a divorce; Sandra has to get past this. We've done it before."

Grace frowned. Sandra had alluded to long-standing problems, but she hadn't mentioned a prearranged settlement. Jason Carter seemed sincere. Sincere and very agitated. He was barely recognizable as the pompous man she'd met at Niki's on the night the auction plan blew up. Today he looked vulnerable, sitting on the edge of his chair, hands gripping his knees as he waited for her response. She ignored a fledgling tingle of sympathy. He wasn't her client.

"I don't know anything about a previous settlement between you and Mrs. Carter," she said. "But you'll be receiving her terms for the divorce by the end of next week. I urge you to contact your attorney."

He closed his eyes and mumbled something which sounded like, "I don't want to." A tear rolled down his cheek.

Grace looked around and made a mental note to add tissues to the office supply list.

Carter cleared his throat and said, "Sandra knows how this has to work. I have a public image to protect. I've never hidden anything from her. She has much more money than I do, so there's never been any reason for me to be secretive about where my money goes. And she's never cared, except when she gets like this. Please help me slow things down and I can turn her around, I know I can."

Grace opened her mouth and closed it again. A mistress with two children, one a new infant, would set any wife off. Either Jason Carter was monumentally insensitive, or there was something she was missing. She had no business talking with her client's husband, but she had warned him about needing counsel. She pushed the desk phone's intercom button for Lily.

"Coffee?" Lily asked.

"No, just come in and bring a notepad, please."

"I wouldn't mind coffee," Carter said.

Grace got up and opened the door to her office, pretending not to hear him. If Carter still wanted caffeine when she was finished, he could go down the street to the coffee shop. But she thought a bar would be a more likely next stop.

CHAPTER THIRTY-TWO

When Lily arrived, Grace said, "Mr. Carter, I've asked Ms. Travers to join us so she can make notes of our conversation."

Out of the corner of her eye, she saw Lily's eyes widen. Grace knew not a word said between now and Carter's exit would be missed. "You came here today to talk to me and have done so even though you understand I'm your wife's divorce attorney. I have twice recommended that you have legal counsel present when you talk to me. Are these statements accurate?"

Carter hesitated, then looked at Lily and said, "Yes,"

"Do you have an attorney to represent you in the divorce?"

"No." He leaned forward again.

Lily tensed, then stood and moved her chair closer to Carter's. She sent a worried glance to Grace, then kept her eyes on Carter.

"Senator Carter," Grace said gently. She waited a moment while Carter raised his head and composed himself. "I don't want to be unkind. I don't want to say things that hurt you."

Carter said, "I understand you're my wife's attorney in our, our, uhm…"

"Divorce," Grace said.

"Divorce," Carter echoed. "I know I need my own attorney. But the ones I use are for my business or are involved with my political campaign. As far as I know, none of them handle divorces. Our family attorney also represents Sandra's father. He doesn't like me."

Grace didn't know if Carter was referring to the attorney or Sandra's father and she decided it didn't matter. Carter looked as if he was about to cry again. Grace tried to catch Lily's eye, but Lily was still watching Carter's every move.

"I'm sure one of the lawyers you use can handle your interests in the divorce. Until then you shouldn't be talking to me."

"I want to," Carter said. "Nothing I say to you will make matters worse and you might be able to help."

Grace made notes of her own. After a minute, she said, "You started your visit today by indicating you would sue me for malpractice because my firm represents the sellers of a property you and your wife bid on unsuccessfully. You veered off of the topic, but I'd like to address it now and make it clear that you have never been my client. I've had no business dealings with you other than to communicate with you regarding the offer you placed on my client's property. After that transaction, I was retained by your wife as a buyer's agent. She also retained me to represent her interests in a suit for divorce against you. Do you have any other questions regarding my business relationship with Sandra?" She hoped Lily had total recall because her secretary hadn't written a word and her focus on Carter was bordering on bizarre.

Grace's words had a galvanizing effect on Carter. A hint of the man she'd first met emerged as he said, "There's no need for the deposition tone. I understand what you're saying and you don't have to keep repeating it. I'm talking to you at my own risk. I've got it."

"Good," Grace said. "I can't make you leave, but I'm not encouraging you to talk to me, either."

"Alright, already! I get it. Now listen to me. Sandra knows if she really wants a divorce she can have it, but under certain terms. It's sort of an undocumented prenup. That's what I've been trying to make you understand! This isn't some new decision on her part, she sometimes gets this way — upset, I mean — and she demands a divorce."

Grace waited and then gave in. "How often?"

"Over the years, I'd say four or five times. It's been several years since the last one, though. I thought we were past it. She has her bad days, but not like this. She's an artist, an eccentric person. And then there are complications. She has issues, but they mostly stay under control."

"Issues?"

"She didn't tell you?"

Grace didn't answer. She'd warned him, but she saw no reason to rub his wife's attorney-client privilege in his face. She didn't want him to stop talking.

As she'd hoped, Carter grew more nervous in the silence and answered his own question. "Sure, Sandra told you. When she gets mad, she tells everyone I'm unfaithful. What'd she say? I have a mistress? Two kids, right? One's a new baby?"

Now Lily's pen was racing across the legal pad. Grace waited for her catch up before saying, "Is that an accurate description of the situation?"

"No! When Sandra gets in one of her moods, she's a jealous, crazy woman. She's always been that way. We got married when I was in college and I was very naive. I had no experience with women at all when I met her. She's older than me, and I was out of my mind for her. She was a dream. I fell hard and I still love her." His voice cracked as he wound down. "It sounds silly, but there was a time I thought her jealousy meant she loved me so much, she couldn't stand for any other woman to, well…"

"Have your children?" Grace said.

Carter groaned. Grace was surprised to see Lily scoot to the edge of her chair. She was staring at Carter again. Grace decided they would have to have a talk about professional etiquette.

"There aren't any children," Carter said. "I'm sterile. There. Are you satisfied? Do you want the details? I can prove my sperm count if it will make you believe me. No children, just one neurotic wife that *I* must be crazy to want to hang on to."

Grace thought he looked sincere, but so had Sandra. "One of the kids is named after you."

"Do you know how common 'Jason' is? Half the boys born in the 90s were named Jason. I admit I had an affair with a married woman about ten years ago. I'm not proud of it, but I did it. She had a two-year-old at the time and I never convinced Sandra the affair was brief, or that the child isn't mine. Sandra insists on believing I've cheated on her all through our marriage. I haven't seen the other woman or talked to her in a decade, but a few months ago, she had another baby. It's ridiculous, but Sandra insists the boy is mine."

"Is he?" Grace asked.

Carter had calmed down as he told his story, but now he came bolt upright again. "No! And confessing my sins to my wife is the dumbest thing I've ever done."

When he was finished with his tale of woe, Grace remembered yet another reason why she didn't do divorce law. No winners, only losers and the attorney stuck in the middle. And she was well and truly stuck. There were a million questions she wanted to ask, but most of them would violate her client's confidentiality. According to her husband, Sandra Carter periodically went off the deep end, convinced he was cheating again and embarrassing both of them with public confrontations.

"It's a miracle I got elected and then re-elected with all the gossip out there, but I don't think I'd survive another round of Sandra's lunacy. For both our sakes, you've got to get her to either drop this craziness or go along with the divorce arrangement we agreed to."

Grace was astounded to learn the agreement gave Sandra more than she'd told Grace she wanted. Carter would have to repay his student loans and the down payment on their house. The one thing it didn't have was the language Sandra wanted recording her husband's infidelity. "I'll talk to my client," she said.

When Carter was gone, Lily said, "What is wrong with people?"

"Which people are we referring to?" Grace asked. "Our client, who may be unstable, or her husband who, if he isn't a liar, is certainly a masochist?"

"Both," Lily said. "I remember when we had normal clients, but that was before you got here."

"But your life is so much more interesting now."

"Ever so much. Let me know when you're ready to discuss my hazard pay."

Grace abruptly changed the subject. Lily had mentioned that another raise would be welcome. "Carter has to know he'll have to produce medical records if he's going to prove he hasn't fathered any children. I'm inclined to believe him."

Lily gave her a look that said the issue of salary would not be forgotten. "Poor guy slips once and pays for it forever. Why didn't he let Witch Wife go?"

"Poor guy slips once? Whose side are you on? And it's Paying Client Witch Wife to you."

"I'm giving you my opinion as a woman who doesn't take cheating partners lightly. And if I don't give you the truth about our clients, who will? The woman's not right in the head and you know it."

"He cheated, he admits it."

Lily threw up her hands in exasperation. "Yes, he confessed and look what happened. He's a walking advertisement for keeping your cheating mouth shut."

Grace stared at her secretary. Here was a side to Lily deserving of a girl's night out and martinis.

"Don't get all nosy," Lily said. "I just watch a lot of TV."

"Uh huh."

"Will you tell the Missus about this visit from her soon-to-be ex?"

"Yes. In fact, give Sandra a call and see if she can come in this afternoon."

Lily shook her head. "It's a mistake. At least don't tell her every-thing. I think she could be trouble."

"Could we go back to me, Boss, you, Not Boss?"

"Sure," Lily said agreeably. "But that will take us back to the salary discussion. However there is one more thing you should know before you decide to keep the Carter divorce. I meant what I said about our client being trouble, but besides that, her husband is carrying a concealed handgun."

"What?"

"I saw the outline of the holster under his jacket when he leaned forward the first time you upset him."

"No! It could have been —"

Uncharacteristically, Lily cut her off. "It's small, a Glock of some kind."

"You saw the gun well enough to know the size and model?"

"I know what I saw."

"How?" Grace was looking at a different Lily now, one who seemed resigned to crossing some boundary she'd set for herself.

After a moment, Lily set her pad and pen down, unbuttoned her left sleeve and rolled up her shirt cuff. First the petals of a rose tattoo emerged a few inches above her wrist, then an intricate script. Lily held her forearm closer so Grace could read it.

"'*Semper Fidelis*'? You're dating a Marine?"

"I *am* a Marine. Military Police. Reserves now."

Grace knew her mouth was open. She didn't shut it.

Lily gave her a tight smile. "Yeah, well. Two tours in Afghanistan." She rolled her sleeve back down and buttoned it. "The Senator was packing and really agitated. It's not a good combination."

Grace fought the urge to say 'Yes, Ma'am'.

Lily paused at the door. "Be careful with both of them, Grace. He doesn't feel right to me, and she's more trouble than she's worth. A woman who looks for ways to stay miserable isn't going to suddenly get rational just because she has good legal counsel."

Lily was right. Grace knew it and couldn't do anything about it. She'd do what she could to keep Jason out of the office, but they needed Sandra's business. At this point, there was no such thing as a client who was too much trouble.

CHAPTER THIRTY-THREE

McNamara closed his office door before returning to the telephone he'd answered five minutes before. Detective Desiree Marbury wasn't known for her patience, but the Chief had more leeway with the by-the-book detective than most people. He resumed their conversation, and Marbury reported the latest findings in the Bishop murder and the MSP's next steps. Now that he was officially in the active investigation, he wished he wasn't.

Marbury knew how he felt and had curbed her enthusiasm for the new break in the case. "I'll send some reinforcements, sir. I know this will be awkward, and you'll need the help."

McNamara wanted to refuse the offer, but he knew it wasn't in his department's best interest. He also wanted to tell her not to call him 'sir', but it would be a waste of breath. It was an official conversation and her response would be that he outranked her and even retired, he did.

Instead he said, "Let me ask you something. Those issues with the lab in Baltimore a few years back. That's all cleaned up, right? Is there any chance the evidence was compromised?"

"The shell casing? No chance at all after you handed it over to us. The fingerprint is a partial, the ID won't hold up in court but it was enough for the search warrants. That and Banks' identification of the scarf."

"Have you've let go of Quentin Bishop as a suspect? What about the text he sent his father? *'You are dead to me'* is incriminating, don't you think?"

"It is," Marbury agreed. "Until you read the reports from Vancouver and the interviews with Garrett Bishop's wife and their friends. It looks like the son was finally making a clean break from a life-long battle with his father. I believed Quentin Bishop when he said the text was meant literally. He was cutting all ties, but Garrett Bishop kept badgering him to forgive and forget. Dear old Dad wanted one big happy family with his ex-fiancé in the role of step-mom."

"Thanks, Desi. This is good work."

"Thank you, sir," Marbury said. "We're satisfied with Quentin Bishop's alibis and explanations. We've turned the Bishops inside out and all that's there is a rich, dysfunctional family intent on tearing each other up. No murderers, at least not for our case."

They discussed logistics for the day and McNamara accepted a short-term loan of two MSP Troopers. Banks wouldn't appreciate being restricted to traffic and tourist duty, but there was no other option. Three hours later, the Chief and the MSP detectives executed three search warrants. Two hours after that, Connie Delaney was arrested.

"I'M NOT HAVING THIS CONVERSATION," McNAMARA SAID.

The morning had been stressful, but Saturday afternoon was lousy. Banks blamed him for Niki breaking up their so-called relationship, and now Grace was staring him down in an argument he had no hope of winning. He didn't even want to.

"You know I can't discuss this with you," he tried.

Grace didn't budge and since they were in her house, it was hard to make her leave. He'd have to arrest her and he couldn't make himself do it.

"This is bull and you know it, Mac! You can't let them search my home! I'm Connie's attorney. This is harassment, pure and simple."

"Read the warrant, Grace. There's ample cause."

The truth was, he thought 'ample' was a stretch. The causation argument was solid for the searches of Connie and Stark Delaney's home and the Victory Manor Inn, but this afternoon's tossing of Delaney House felt excessive. Not that McNamara had anything to say about it. He'd been relegated to keeping Grace out of Marbury's way, and was grateful he didn't have to add to the awkward situation by combing through the third-floor apartment.

Grace saw no redeeming aspect to their roles. "Just because Connie is over here occasionally, the police found a judge to say my house could be searched for the gun that killed Garret Bishop. It's insane! Connie's at the Acme Market and Starbucks occasionally, too. Are they searching there? And if they have a warrant for my house, why don't they have one for the office? Let me guess, no compelling evidence, right? What the hell aren't you telling me?"

"Read the warrant, Grace."

"I've read it."

"Read it again."

It was a long afternoon.

"I GET IT. YOU COULDN'T STOP THEM. AT LEAST THEY DIDN'T FIND anything at our houses. Yours and mine, anyway." Niki tucked Leo under her left arm like a white, over-inflated football, and picked up speed. At this pace they would finish the entire five-mile walking trail in record time. Leo's daily walk had become a legal strategy session neither Leo nor Grace could keep up with.

"Well the police aren't chasing us now, so slow down, will you?" Grace left the path and collapsed on a nearby bench. She had longer legs than her petite cousin, but nobody matched Niki for stamina.

"You need to keep moving." Niki set Leo down at Grace's feet and began to jog in place. "Keeping your heart rate up is key during aerobic exercise. We're not getting younger and if you don't make more of an effort, you'll have real problems in a few years."

"Real problems - as opposed to what? Do I have imaginary ones now?"

Niki ignored the question but stopped jogging. "Well, your cop boyfriend didn't let your mother get arrested."

"Nik, quit making me defend Aidan. It feels unnatural. He couldn't do anything to help her. And now the Chief has him on restricted duty to keep him in the clear where the investigation is concerned. We've got Connie out on bond, and I'll do everything I can to exonerate her, but she isn't easy to handle."

"Now there's a news flash. It's a miracle she and Dad aren't both in jail after the way they behaved when the search warrant was served. She's always been a drama queen and Dad's an ass, but Mom didn't kill Garrett Bishop. Why would she? What possible reason would she have for killing a potential buyer? This is stupid!"

Grace shook her head. Niki's defense of her mother said all anyone needed to know about Connie's character - even her daughter didn't say 'she wouldn't do it'. Niki's only argument was that Connie didn't have a good enough reason to commit a murder. They both knew from experience she was capable of it. Last winter, Grace had witnessed first-hand her aunt's willingness to fire a gun in anger.

To make Connie's defense even more difficult, she was an excellent shot with a rifle and had the competition medals to prove it. The medals she'd won in college, an assortment of firearms, the Delaneys' computers and DNA samples had been taken during the search of their home.

Niki finally sat down on the bench. "How long can you represent her?" she asked.

Grace was grateful for the wording of the question. Her cousin understood the importance of Quentin Bishop's business to the struggling law firm. "For now, it's fine. Quentin isn't being charged with anything." She didn't add that if he were, his power lawyer would take over. She hadn't heard a word from Quentin or David. Quentin's retainer was spent and she hoped she wouldn't have to come up with a way to refund it.

"Do you think Mom did it?"

"No, I don't." Grace made her words firm and was rewarded with a tremulous smile from Niki. A suddenly revived Leo kept her from having to produce more reassurance. Instead, she said, "Okay, let's get moving and see if you and Mighty Mouse here can keep me from those real problems in my future."

They ran the last two miles of the trail, passing the dog between them like a canine relay baton. Leo was the only one still grinning when they reached the small parking lot where they'd left Niki's SUV.

McNamara was waiting for them.

"Oh, for heaven's sake, what now?" Grace shoved Leo at the Chief and bent at the waist, hands on hips, to catch her breath.

"I'm sorry," he said. "It's Cyrus. You need to come with me."

HARD AS IT WAS FOR GRACE TO THINK OF THE BAT AS BEING A relative of the Chief's, it was even harder to see her as a compassionate woman holding Cyrus' hand, and wiping his face with a washcloth. Grace stood in the doorway of the emergency room cubicle and worried she would never get the sight out of her mind's eye. It was just wrong.

A voice cut through the background chatter from the central nursing station. "Are you Mr. Mosley's next of kin?"

Grace said 'no' at the same time that Mosley said 'yes'. They looked at each other, and Grace felt ashamed. She wasn't sure why, but her answer had hurt him.

"I'm his friend," she told the doctor who moved past her to join Marjorie at Mosley's side.

"And my medical power of attorney, as well as my attorney in fact. I consider her to have next of kin status." Mosley's tone was weak but clear. The doctor looked back over his shoulder at Grace, who nodded.

She was relieved that Mosley sounded as if he had retained all of his faculties. The heart attack had been serious, but he'd pulled through. Again.

Turning to Marjorie, the doctor said, "And you are?"

He was no match for the Bat. The cubicle was crowded with the four of them, but they got on with the business of sorting out Mosley's care.

Grace and Mosley only had a few moments alone before he was whisked away to the cardiac wing. She walked alongside his gurney to the elevator.

"Sorry about this," he said. "I'll be fine in a day or so."

"You'd better be," Grace said. "I need you."

His look of surprise was comical, but it made her cry.

"I'll bring work to you," she managed. "It's only the golfers who'll have to do without you for a few days."

But he was asleep, gone even before the elevator doors closed him off from her.

"They'll do the surgery and he'll be fine," Marjorie said.

Grace turned to find she'd followed them at a respectful distance. She closed it now and took Grace's hand.

"He's a force of nature, that one. This procedure won't be anything to him. Isn't even surgery."

The doctor's description of inserting stents into two of Mosley's heart valves sounded like surgery to Grace. Anything involving hospitals, anesthesia and poking something foreign into a person's body was surgery.

Marjorie kept talking. "He loves you, Grace. I've never seen him sadder than when your mom took you away when you were little, or happier than when you came back here and joined the practice. He's not leaving us now, life just got good again."

Grace was still in her sweaty running clothes but Marjorie gathered her into a hug. And in this day of surprises, Grace let her.

CHAPTER THIRTY-FOUR

I n the usual manner of such things, the surgery wasn't as simple as Marjorie had promised or as dangerous as the doctors warned.

Two stents did the trick, but Grace spent a difficult night at the bedside of a fractious Mosley. He didn't want her there, and he wouldn't let her leave. She moved between his room and the hallway, where she waited each time a nurse came to fine tune one of his drips or bandages. Mosley turned out to need more privacy than a teenage girl.

Dawn brought Niki and Avril and a chance for escape. Grace managed four hours of sleep before presenting herself in court on Connie's behalf.

The arraignment was difficult, but Connie was released pending trial. Grace traded heavily on the 'lead counsel in the hospital' plea and it bought them time.

It took the remaining equity in both Stark and Connie's house and the Victory Manor Inn to secure bail. The only upside of the tense afternoon was that Connie was so intimidated by the process, she stayed silent, moving and talking only when Grace told her to. Even the presence of an enraged Stark didn't distract his wife. She ignored him and as soon as he'd signed the guarantee documents for the bail, Stark disappeared without a word. Connie either didn't notice or didn't care.

She was still docile after they left court. None of them had eaten lunch and Grace agreed with Niki's suggestion they eat something before convening at Grace's office to go over the next steps. It was a mistake to let Connie order an Old Fashioned before the food arrived, but the real damage was done when she ordered a second one while Grace was checking in with Cyrus. Six ounces of bourbon and sugar cubes sent Connie from terrified to angry to fiercely bitter. None of these behaviors worked well in the restaurant.

Niki kept patting her mother and crying, so Grace sent her home and took Connie to the office, where she proved even more difficult to handle.

"It's time to use those military skills of yours," Grace hissed at Lily as they watched Connie pace around the conference room, wobbling slightly and muttering to herself.

"If I only could," Lily said in a silky tone and then cracked her knuckles. "I'd —"

"Okay, okay, never mind. Bad idea."

"You sure?" Lily asked. "For real, one shot to the back of the knees and —" she stopped and smiled at Grace, apparently satisfied with the look on her boss' face. "I can handle her. Properly I mean. I do have skills."

"I'm sorry. Really sorry." Grace shut out Connie and gave Lily the apology she'd been thinking about since the meeting with Jason Carter. Until then, she'd never taken the time to get past her surface opinion of the young woman who'd become a significant part of her life. She'd only considered Lily as an element of Cyrus and work and hadn't looked further.

"I'm sorry I doubted you, underestimated, and probably dissed you when I didn't even know what was happening under my nose. I made assumptions and they were wrong. I should have gone through your file sooner and read your resume. I should have asked Cyrus. I should have known how skilled you are, and I'm sorry."

"Is this where you thank me for my service?"

"I mean it, Lily, I feel awful. You're important to the firm, and you're important to *me*. I won't be here much longer, but while I am, I'll see to it that you're taken care of, professionally speaking. I've always known you can take care of yourself and the rest of us, too. I didn't need to see the tattoo to know how capable you are."

Lily smiled. "It's been three years since I decided I wasn't going to make a career in the Corps. I'm still coming to terms with a few things, myself." She glanced over at Connie and said, "I've got this."

Grace couldn't hear the words Lily said when she stopped Connie mid-pace and whispered in her ear, but Connie took a seat at the conference table and glared at Grace.

"She's all yours," Lily said. "I'll be at my desk if you need me."

Grace opened a take-out box of food and gave Connie her untouched chicken and avocado salad from the restaurant. "Eat it," she said. "Eat the roll first, then the chicken. Eat it and then we talk."

"Lily was rude to me! I want her fired! Do you know what she said?"

Grace smiled and said, "No, I don't, and I also don't care. Eat."

"I can't! I'm too upset!"

"You're drunk, too. Eat it now."

"I'll throw up!"

"Good. Go ahead and do that and then eat. If I'm going to keep you out of jail, you have to stop whining and help me."

Connie trotted out the tears again. "I can't," she wailed.

"You'll wear orange jumpsuits in jail, Auntie. *Orange.* No root touch-ups, no highlights. Rubber flip-flops."

Connie rubbed her eyes.

Grace didn't let up. "Common showers."

"Stop it! Please, stop it!"

"Bunkmates."

Connie grabbed the roll and stuffed it in her mouth.

There really wasn't much new information but Grace kept going over the days before and after the shooting, and every detail Connie could remember of the day Bishop was shot. Not surprisingly, the alcohol loosened her mouth and Grace filled pages of her legal pad with notes. She didn't think much of it was helpful, but she wrote for as long as Connie talked, and there was one surprising tidbit.

"You were at the Morgan farm the morning of the murder?"

"Well, I was supposed to be. I was going to look at the property again with Sandy and Jason. I followed them out there, but he pulled off the road before we reached the farm and said he was going to walk through the woods and get a feel for the area." Connie stopped and frowned into her coffee cup. "I don't like him."

"Who? Jason Carter?"

"Yeah. Sandy always brags about being a senator's wife, but he's not all that. He yells. A lot."

Grace was amazed that this would bother Connie, whose entire marriage had been an emotional war zone.

"Anyway, I pulled in behind them and got out to see why he'd stopped and I could hear him yelling. Then he got out and stomped off into the woods. Sandy rolled the window down and told me they'd meet up with me later. She said Jason wanted to be alone, and she just wanted to get to St. Michaels."

"So, you left her there?"

"Yes. What else was I going to do?"

Grace decided Connie had sobered up enough to tackle the critical questions. "Are you sure the scarf they found is yours?" she asked.

"No! The police and that nasty prosecutor only let me see it for two seconds, and it's not like I owned it for very long. I lost it the day after I got it."

"Are you sure about the timing?"

"Only because Sandra harped on it. I swear she wore hers just to rub it in that I'd lost mine. Sometimes she isn't very nice."

Grace left the understatement alone. "We can get the store owner to testify both you and Sandra bought matching scarves. That's something they should remember. I'll find out how many others they sold and try to get a list of buyers."

"No! You can't do that." Connie was agitated again. "I won't let you embarrass Sandy. I can't lose her as a client."

Grace double-checked her watch. It was two hours since Connie's last drink. The effects of the alcohol were still there, but she should be sober enough to know how ridiculous she sounded. This was confirmed by the redness of the face that was avoiding her.

She tried again. "I'm not going to accuse her of anything. I'll ask her for her receipt and get yours and ask the store how many other scarves like those were sold, and to whom. No accusations at any one person, just a clear point that you aren't the only one who could have dropped the scarf and the shell casing in the woods."

"But they said the scarf's label had a fingerprint!"

"A partial print and only some of the points matched yours. You probably touched it when you were in the store, looking through the scarves. That doesn't mean it's the one you bought. The store clerk's testimony will be helpful, I'm sure of it."

"No! The police will go right to Sandra, won't they? After all, she really wanted the Morgan farm. Well, Jason did, anyway."

"The police won't necessarily think they killed Bishop for it. That wouldn't make any sense unless they killed Anton Norse, too."

"See, even you go right there!"

Grace fell back in her chair and stared at her aunt. Was it possible three of her clients could be suspects in the same investigation? She desperately wanted to go to the hospital, shake Cyrus out of his drug-induced sleep and talk this out. She'd been crazy to take on Connie's defense and now Sandra may need representation, too. And then there was Quentin. She couldn't even call David.

"You can't ask Sandra about the scarf." Connie was crying again.

"Why not?"

"I can't take anymore, Gracie. I just can't."

"You'll have to. We have to look at every possibility."

"Then look!" Connie exploded. "Look and leave the damned scarf business alone, okay? I don't need more humiliation. Look at all the other people who could have killed Bishop."

The words lay between them for a long moment.

"You think I did it," Connie whispered.

Grace decided no good would come from responding to that. Instead, she said, "Right now, I'm your attorney. If you did it, you don't have to tell me, but don't lie to me. You have to hear me on this. Whatever you tell me, do *not* lie to me. Not about anything."

For the first time since she'd met her aunt, Grace thought Connie looked her age. Older. The beautiful woman was gone. Her scared and shaking client broke down, and Grace let her cry.

CHAPTER THIRTY-FIVE

"**O**f course they stole the scarves," Niki said. "Those two on a martini high would do any stupid thing you can think of."

They'd put Connie in the only room on the second floor of Delaney House that had a bed. She'd refused to go home to the still manic Stark, and Grace didn't want her comparing notes with Sandra, who was once again in residence at Niki's inn. It had taken Niki and Grace and the promise of more bourbon to get Connie's cooperation, but eventually, the day was over, and she wound down. Niki took her mother's car keys and purse to make sure any midnight escape wouldn't involve impaired driving.

"I can see the shop clerk on the witness stand now," Grace said as they sipped tea in the downstairs kitchen. "I'll just ask her, 'Other than my clients who shoplifted these matching silk scarves, who else might have stolen or purchased one?' Should clear things up. Connie and Sandra can share a cell."

"They deserve it, but promise that you won't let it happen," Niki pleaded. "Just because they had a silly bet, and got away with it doesn't mean either one of them killed Garrett Bishop."

Bet or not, it didn't help Connie's defense, but Grace didn't point

204 | CHERIL THOMAS

it out. She sometimes thought Niki lurched through life, bouncing off one family disaster and into another. When her cousin started laughing, Grace felt equal parts relief and pity.

"Maybe Mom can share a cell with Winston," Niki gasped. "It would be proper punishment for him. Her too."

They never discussed Niki's brother, and Grace couldn't think of anything to say. Winston Stratford Delaney the Fifth had seven more months to serve of his sentence for distribution of heroin and assault. It wouldn't be helpful to point out that Connie wouldn't be in a minimum-security facility if she were convicted of murder.

Instead, she said, "Connie and Sandra are still going to have to confess and get it on the record that they both had scarves. I'll check with the store and see how many they have left. Connie said there were six or eight the day they were there. They selected the bird pattern because there were enough that two going missing wouldn't be immediately obvious."

"Clever even when drunk. My mom's claim to fame."

"She said it was Sandra's idea."

"I'm sure she did."

Grace knew her honesty lecture hadn't fazed Connie, other than to make her feel hopeless. Telling Connie not to lie was like telling rain not to fall.

Niki got up and gathered her purse and jacket and Connie's things. "Are you sure you don't want me to stay, too? Mom's an argumentative drunk, but she's mean with a hangover."

"Believe me, I know. Nope. Go home and get some rest. And keep an eye on Sandra for me." Grace would have to tell Sandra tomorrow that she couldn't represent her in the divorce or the purchase of property. While she wasn't positive her representation of the two women in three unrelated legal matters actually constituted a conflict of interest, she didn't want the Attorney Grievance Commission to have to make the call. Plus, the whole mess had an incestuous feel. Unless—

"Nik, there's something you and Connie need to talk about as soon as possible. I haven't handled a criminal case in several years, and when I did do them, I was always assisting David. You need someone better, with more experience."

"No!"

"Listen to me. I'm not abandoning Connie. I will never do that to *you*, understand? But I want the best defense for her, and I don't think I'm it. I'll do for now, but we need to think about the long run."

They hugged, Niki hanging on longer than usual. Grace picked up the little tremor that shook her cousin's slender frame. "It will be okay, Nik. I know it will," she whispered. A tingle of fear grabbed her as the words left her mouth. Because it wouldn't. And the next day proved it.

SANDRA CARTER WORE WHITE SILK PAJAMAS AND HER FACE WAS dewy with night cream, but she looked as alert as if she'd been up for hours. "No, I haven't seen Connie," she said. "And I don't appreciate being dragged out of bed at this hour."

It was nearly eight a.m., but they'd had a hard time rousing Sandra. The small sitting room of her suite was crowded with the three of them and there was no place to sit. Both chairs and every other surface were covered with Sandra's clothing, shoes and shopping bags.

"When was the last time you talked to her?" Niki demanded. Her hair, a short blonde version of Grace's wiry curls, stuck out at odd angles and dark smudges under her eyes testified to a sleepless night. "She's gone and we have to find her. She could be in trouble."

Grace knew Niki meant Connie *was* trouble. *Their* trouble if she'd left the county and violated the terms of her bail.

Sandra yawned and stretched into an exaggerated yoga bend. When she was upright again, she said, "I can't think before morning tea, but I'd say she's with Stark. Where is he, anyway?"

"He went straight to Atlantic City after he left court yesterday," Grace said. "That's the problem. She's alone and upset, and we need to find her." She left out the part about babysitting a very drunk

Connie, waking to find her gone, and finding the contents of Grace's own tote bag dumped out on the kitchen table. The small amount of cash she'd had was missing, but at least her car keys were still tucked safely in the pocket of the jacket she'd worn the day before. Niki had taken Connie's purse and keys, so wherever she was, Connie was on foot with only five dollars to her name. They hoped.

Sandra moved over to a mirror, studied her reflection, then picked up a brush and went to work on her hair.

"You have to help us," Niki said. "She wasn't listening well yesterday, and you know how impulsive she is. I need to find her."

"I'm sure she'll turn up." Sandra put the brush down and went toward the bathroom. "And when she does, remind her we're going shopping. She promised we'd do Easton before I go back to Virginia. I'm getting bored waiting around here for her."

Fortunately, Sandra didn't look back at them and missed Niki's one finger salute.

"I FOUND HER." NIKI SOUNDED TIRED AND IRRITABLE WHEN SHE called Grace at work an hour later. "She drove out to the Morgan farm."

"How? Why?" Grace was dumbfounded. Connie wouldn't spend five minutes at the old house when she was being paid to do it. She was rarely out of bed before ten, let alone out visiting murder scenes. And she had to have a monster hangover.

Niki said, "Mom called Sandra, said she needed a car and didn't want to deal with us to get her keys back until she'd taken care of some business. While you and I were driving ourselves crazy looking for her, Sandra slipped out and took Mom her car. And here's the best part. Mom just called and asked me to come get her."

Grace checked her calendar and saw she had two hours until her first client. "Oh, no," she said. "Let me."

"I thought you'd want to talk to her. Just don't kill her, Grace. She's my mother and I call dibs."

CHAPTER THIRTY-SIX

W hen Grace turned off the state highway and onto the bumpy country lane, she felt even more sure something was very wrong. Connie always looked for the easy way out. Driving miles into the countryside and poking around in an abandoned house would be the last thing her prissy aunt would do.

Then she remembered the marksmanship medals and Connie throwing the antique vase. *You'll be sorry.* Connie had been right. Grace was indeed sorry she was out here in the middle of nowhere on a bitterly cold December morning looking for a relative she'd rather not find.

Sandra's Jaguar was parked next to the house. Grace was barely out of her car when she heard a woman scream, "Help me!"

Moving as fast as she could, she picked her way around the soft spots in the porch floor and saw the lockbox hanging open on the front door handle. She called Connie's name as she stepped inside and was answered with another scream.

At first she thought the roof had collapsed in the upstairs bedroom. Papers and bits of drywall littered the floor like the aftermath of a tornado. But it was the legs dangling from the ceiling that got her attention. Grace recognized the material of the wool slacks Connie had worn to court the day before.

A tremulous voice said, "Niki?"

"No."

"Oh, Gracie! Are you alone?"

Grace sighed. "Yes. But I'll get help. Don't move."

"Wait! Are you still my attorney?"

Grace had her phone out but paused over the 'emergency call' symbol. "For now," she said. There'd be time enough to sort it all out once they were back in Mallard Bay.

"Do I still have client confidentiality?"

Grace looked at the legs. Scratched and dirty bare feet said Connie's undoubtedly expensive shoes had been lost when she crashed through the ceiling. Toes with cherry red nail polish wiggled impatiently.

"Grace? Gracie!"

"Yeah, Connie, you have confidentiality."

"Then get yourself up here and help me!"

The attic access was a narrow staircase at the back of the room. After a brief internal debate, Grace climbed the creaky steps and emerged in a partially floored, turn of the century attic, complete with an old trunk and a lot of cobwebs. Connie sat a dozen feet away, straddling one beam while clinging to the adjacent ones with visibly shaking arms.

"Don't just stand there," she pleaded. "Get me down! But don't call anybody. I don't want to be seen like this."

"I'll look around for a ladder." Grace started back down the steps, only to be pulled up short when Connie let out another yell.

"Don't leave me! I can't hold on!"

There was nothing of use in the attic that Grace could see. A box sat next to the steps, but it looked to be full of papers. No help there. She didn't want to do it, but after another squeal from Connie, she climbed the remaining steps and carefully stepped out to the edge of the floorboards. Connie was too far away to reach.

"Stop it!" Grace said as Connie opened her mouth. "Not another scream. I need to think."

"I can't hold on!"

"Then don't."

"What?" Momentarily startled, Connie stopped shaking and focused on Grace.

"You won't fall if you stay calm. Now let go of the beam in your right hand and grab the one you're sitting on. Then do the same thing with your left hand and stretch out."

Grace lay down and inched as far out onto the ceiling joist as she could while still keeping most of her body on the floor. "Like this, see?" When she stretched out her hand, she was only a foot short from meeting Connie's. "You can reach me. I'll help you get over here."

"I can't!"

"Easy peasy, Con. Come on."

Either Grace's fakey-calm coaxing or the lack of options made Connie move. With a good deal more damage to the ceiling plaster, she made it to the floor and collapsed across Grace. "Are you hurt?" Grace asked when they were untangled.

"Yes, I'm hurt!"

"I mean, do you need medical attention?" Grace said, recognizing the onset of a fresh round of hysteria. "Are you injured? Bleeding?"

"No. I don't think so." Taking stock of herself distracted Connie long enough for Grace to get to the steps and start down. "Wait!" Connie yelled. "I need help!"

Grace pulled the box of papers onto the top step above her. "No, you don't. Come over here and get down the same way you got up. And if you start screaming again, you're on your own, you hear me?"

CHAPTER THIRTY-SEVEN

"What's in this box?" Grace demanded as Connie gingerly picked through ceiling rubble for her shoes.

"It'll take too long to explain. You said we have to get back to Mallard Bay."

Grace looked at the top layer of papers. Income tax forms. She put the box on the floor and knelt next to it.

"Those are my personal papers!"

Grace ignored Connie and dug into the box. Copies of IRS forms filled the top half and then she found the receipts and ledgers. An ugly idea took shape. She looked up at Connie and asked, "What are you doing with these??"

Connie had one shoe on and the other in her hand. The Mephisto flats would need professional help. "Don't jump to conclusions. Just give them over and I'll explain."

"Not a chance," Grace said. She took a closer look at the receipts and felt the blood began to pound in her head.

On a green ledger sheet, someone with neat handwriting had recorded credits and debits under columns titled with names of Atlantic City casinos. Stark Delaney had lost much more money than he'd made, but the spreadsheet covered a five-year run and several columns showed big wins. These were in columns with only initials as identifiers.

"Yes, it's what you think it is." Connie's hands went to her hips, elbows and neck out, eyes narrowed. "We had to have money, something *you* wouldn't understand. Cyrus wouldn't be reasonable with Stark's trust fund, but he certainly kept the money flowing to you and your mother, didn't he? Stark didn't have any choice."

It was an argument that wouldn't die; one Grace would never win. Every despicable thing Stark and Connie had done over the years was blamed on their belief that Grace and her mother had gotten more than their share of the family estate. The subject was also Connie's favorite diversion when she wanted to deflect attention from her own actions.

Grace ignored the taunt. "Are you determined to go to jail, Connie? Why would you keep these?"

"They don't show *me* doing anything wrong."

Connie's smile made Grace want to give up and leave. Whatever Connie was planning would be a disaster. "How much?" Grace asked.

"Doesn't matter." Connie bent at the waist and raked her fingers through her hair. "I feel nasty, like there are bugs on me."

Grace resisted the rude retort that sprang to her lips. Instead she said, "Did Cyrus know?"

"We told him about the wins, yes. It's not illegal to be a professional gambler, you know, so don't even think about threatening me. You're still my attorney, anyway." Connie moved on from her hair to swiping dirt and cobwebs off her clothes.

"A *professional* gambler? What do you call an amateur? He lost a lot of money, Con."

Connie snatched the sheet out of Grace's hands. "You're looking at the bottom line. When he won big, we were rich. It was fabulous."

"And when he lost, there was Emma. His mother paid the bills, didn't she? And when she couldn't, Cyrus stepped in." She scrambled through the pieces of paper and held one up. "And there were always the antiques to sell. That's what happened to all the furnishings that were supposed to be divided between us."

The proof was in the box that sat in front of her. But why? Why pack a box with records of gambling losses, sales of stolen furniture and income tax returns? "What else is in here?" she asked.

"None of your business," Connie snapped. "It doesn't affect anything the police are accusing me of, but why give them any more evidence? They're going to bring out every speeding ticket and missed credit card payment to prove we have money problems."

"Probably. But Connie, it will only show you had a reason to want Garret Bishop healthy. He had the most money and would have paid a lot to win the bidding."

Connie's face looked hot as she reached down and picked up the box. "There's another one way back under the eaves. You're young and limber enough to get it out. We need it, too."

Grace grabbed Connie's wrist and hung on. "Tell me the truth. What are you keeping from me?"

"You said to be careful, remember? You made it sound like you didn't want to know."

"Did you kill Bishop?"

"No! But everyone thinks I did. You think so, don't you?"

"Tell me what you did."

Connie jerked away from Grace but didn't lose her grip on the box. "Anton Norse paid me to guarantee he would have the highest bid. Fifty thousand, in advance. He didn't like the auction you came up with, but I could have handled it. I'd have found a way to sneak a peek at Bishop's bid and let Anton know the amount he needed to beat. I thought Bishop would just write Anton a check for his trouble and get the property from him, but in any case, I'd have been in the clear with money from both of them. I didn't need to kill Bishop, but who will believe me?"

"Certainly no one with any sense," Grace said. As usual, Connie's plan was full of holes and wishful thinking, but it didn't make her a cold-blooded killer. Only a prime suspect for the police. "You're saying your defense against a murder charge is that you committed extortion and agreed to make sure the dead man lost the bidding? *After* you took money from him for unspecified future services."

Connie slapped at her ankles, then shook her hair out again. "It wasn't like that at all. I can explain everything, but later, okay? I've got to get a shower. I feel like my skin is on fire."

They heard car tires crunch over the oyster shell driveway.

"Expecting someone?" Grace asked.

"My ride. The Jag got stuck in the mud." She pulled her phone out of her pocket. "One bit of luck - I had this with me. Nothing else worked out right. I couldn't even trust my own daughter to help me."

Grace didn't point out that Niki had sent help. Connie was already busily reconstructing the truth and casting herself in the role of victim.

"Right," Grace said. "And you have nothing at all to do with it." She stood up and wiped her hands on her slacks. "You packed up two boxes and brought them out here. Why?"

"After the police searched the office, I decided to pack up everything at home that might be misunderstood. They'd already searched here, so it's the perfect hiding spot. I was right, too. That snotty detective would be all over this stuff. But don't worry, I'll get the boxes back from you as soon as I can, so you can honestly say you don't know anything."

A car horn sounded.

Ignoring it, Grace said, "Thank you so much for your concern for my reputation."

Connie narrowed her eyes. "You're my lawyer. I wouldn't have told you anything if you weren't. Now do your job. Get the boxes back to town, and if you want to cut me loose after that, fine. But if you aren't going to stick with me, I suggest you don't look through the rest of the papers or your rigid little soul will be conflicted into a tizzy, and there won't be a damned thing you can do about it."

They heard footsteps on the porch. "Connie!" Sandra sounded like she'd arrived for a cocktail party.

Grace blocked Connie as she tried to pass. "You listen to me. I don't know how this will end, but I'll make you this promise. You jeopardize Niki's inn and you'll see what my rigid soul can do. You do *not* leave this county or do anything else to risk your bail. Got it?"

Connie left without answering. A moment later Grace heard the creaking staircase, and then Connie and Sandra talking over each other as they left the house. A look out the window told her Sandra had managed to get Niki's SUV.

With a sigh, she pulled out her phone and called Lily. They needed to regroup.

CHAPTER THIRTY-EIGHT

"**Y**ou might have called and told me your aunt cleared our client." David sounded happy, and Grace knew she was supposed to respond in kind and be thrilled to be of use. But she was five minutes from the office and had no time to spare for David or, if the conversation went bad, a case of hives.

She said, "My client was arrested and charged with murder in the second degree, but she's out on bail. The charges will be dropped, so don't get too cocky." She glanced in the rearview mirror at the two boxes in the back seat. She needed to go through them as soon as possible and find out what Connie was up to.

"It's only Murder Two because they can't prove premeditation, yet," David said. "But with her sharpshooter medals and flimflam scheme to get money from Bishop, she's way out in the lead. And if, for some reason, she's cleared, I've got Anton Norse charging around the woods with a rifle and leading the local cop right to the evidence against Connie Delaney. Norse looks good for the shooting, too, you know. Once the police move away from Quentin, I'll be happy to take Ms. Delaney's case for you."

"I don't think so," Grace said as she pulled up in front of the office.

"You're going to keep a criminal case?"

"David, you're more than welcome to Connie. If I could, I'd turn her over to you now. Only one little problem. She doesn't have any money. None at all. She's in debt over her head, and I'm working pro bono. You remember your law school Latin, right? I'm working for free. Still want her?"

"Now that you mention it, my plate's pretty full."

"I thought so." Grace had always found money to be the way to drive David off any topic, and he stayed true to form.

"No, wait." He hesitated and then said, "She's your aunt. I'll do it."

"What?"

"I'll do it. The firm will represent her." There was another short silence. "Pro bono." It sounded like the words hurt him. "Quentin cut me lose this morning. He thinks he's in the clear and didn't like my last bill. I won't handle her personally, so there won't be any question of conflict, but you know we have the manpower to see she's taken care of. You'd like the two new attorneys that came on after you left. If you would just come back, we'd be a powerhouse again, babe. Think about it. But whatever, we'll take her. You hang in with her while I move a few people around and I'll send somebody over in a week or so to interview her."

She heard voices in the background and David said he had to run. He rang off, leaving her to digest this new turn of events and wonder where the catch was in his offer. She didn't reach any conclusion before finding that Quentin Bishop was waiting for her in the office.

Lily caught her in the reception and motioned her into the empty client sitting room. "I put him in Cyrus' office," she said. "He's got coffee and a magazine, but he doesn't look happy."

"Did he say what he wanted?"

"To talk to you. He just got here, though. I didn't even have time to call you. He can't complain about the wait."

The wait was the only thing Quentin Bishop didn't complain about.

Gone was the hesitant, nervous man who'd talked her into representing him. The irritability she'd seen a week earlier when she'd picked him up in Philadelphia was still firmly in place. He managed a civil greeting before saying, "You might have told me one of your other clients has been charged with my father's murder? I could have left three days ago."

She poured a cup of coffee from the service tray Lily had left on the small conference table. "That would have been unethical, Quentin. Your attorney is well aware of the recent developments. You should talk to David." She waited to see if he'd mention firing his attorney.

He ignored her statement. "You said you couldn't represent me regarding my father because you'd found his body. You didn't say anything about representing the real killer!"

"I'm not." She set her cup down gently, suddenly realizing how it must look to him. She hadn't spared a moment of thought over the last three days to anyone other than the Delaneys and Cyrus. "Quentin, I'm defending my aunt. Connie Delaney is my family." She was amazed the words came out without a hitch.

He gave her a calculating look. "That complicates things, doesn't it?"

"Possibly," she agreed. "It depends on the work you have for me. I have no problem with reviewing some contracts unrelated to the situation here. That's what you hired me for."

"Look, when I initially came to you, I did need representation, and I'm grateful you referred me to David. All of that was sincere. But it wasn't the only reason I wanted to talk with you."

"No college friend referred me?" she guessed. It had always sounded contrived.

"To be completely honest, I didn't think I needed a lawyer. I had alibis, and I'd never set foot on the Eastern Shore. It wasn't until I got here and was talking with you, and then David, that I realized I might be in trouble."

"So, why did you hire me?"

He looked so uncomfortable, it made her uneasy.

"I'll tell you everything, but first I need to know how well you knew my father." He leaned back in his chair and watched her.

"I thought we covered this when we met." Grace couldn't think where he was going, but added, "I had several face-to-face interactions with him, none of which were private. We talked on the phone maybe a half dozen times. During most of those conversations, he either argued with me or threatened me. I was not a fan. I went out to meet him on the morning he died because he said he had a contract for me to purchase the Morgan farm. Now that I haven't told you anything you didn't already know, why don't *you* tell *me* what's going on."

Bishop's expression didn't change as she talked. He was still frowning when he said, "Did he give you anything?"

"Other than a hard time?" Now she was getting angry. "No."

"Did you sleep with him?" Grace was half out of her chair when he held up his hands. "Okay, I'm out of line, but I have to know. It's critical."

"You're not only out of line, you're out of your mind. No, I did not!"

Quentin didn't look like a man who believed what he was hearing. He leaned forward in a 'we're all friends here' pose.

"Let me ask it another way. Please, please hear me out. I'm not judging you. I don't even care, except — here's the thing. Apparently, my father was having an affair with someone and if it is proven to be a fact, it changes how his assets are distributed. Some couples have prenups, my father also had to offer a death contract to get his current wife to marry him. One rather odd clause says if she's unfaithful before his death, even if they don't divorce, she gets nothing when he dies. If he's unfaithful before his death, her payment from his estate doubles."

Grace was momentarily distracted from her outrage. It was the second odd pre-planned divorce arrangement she'd heard in the past week. "Is there a 'Get out of Jail Free' card, too?" she asked. "Sounds like a game of Monopoly."

Quentin shook his head. "Just high stakes matrimony. To make it more entertaining, my foundation turns out to be the only beneficiary of the will, other than the mandatory bequest to Heather, his widow. If there is proof of adultery, we lose a lot of money. Money which could make something good out of my father's miserable life."

"How do you know he was having an affair?" Grace asked.

"Being the sensitive person he was, he bragged about it."

That rang true. Garrett Bishop was always bragging about something, Grace thought.

"I'm sorry. Really. I used you, but in my own defense, it was for a decent reason. The foundation needs that money. I went back to Canada to talk to my father's business manager. He's been a friend to both of us for a long time, and I'm relying on him to guide me through all of this. That's why I left when I did. I had business there with him, and I needed to try to talk some sense into Dad's wife. She was making some demands."

"Did it work?"

"The talk or her demands? Never mind, the answer to both is 'no'. We'll probably settle on an amount that makes both of us unhappy. Unless she can prove he was unfaithful."

"What evidence does she have?"

"Right now, she's fishing. But she's hired a private detective firm to find out how Dad spent his last few weeks. I know it sounds crazy, but Dad told his business manager to ready a seven-figure cash transaction because he was buying a property in Maryland from a beautiful woman, and the deal was in his pocket. Heather heard the rumors and she's determined to get the penalty payment."

When she trusted her voice, Grace said, "Your father must've had big pockets. Seems like he put a lot of things in them."

"What? Oh, you've heard him say that. The man was a walking cliché."

"These private detectives your stepmother hired—"

"Please. Heather is only my father's wife."

"The private detectives. By any chance does the firm use dark blue vans?"

Quentin looked confused and Grace told him to skip it. She was too angry to be relieved at having a benign answer to the mystery man who'd broken into Delaney House. A new alarm system was being installed in a few days, anyway.

"Well, Mr. Bishop, if you've gotten what you came for, I'm busy and I know you have other things to do." She stood. "Let me be clear, I did not have any kind of personal relationship with your father. And in case we don't speak the same language about such things, I'll be blunt. I didn't have sex with him. Further, I don't know if anyone else did."

Quentin rose. "It's 'Mr. Bishop', is it? You're angry and I don't blame you, but I had to know, you understand? And I need to warn you Heather can be relentless. You may hear from her, or someone connected to her. She's sure you and my father, well. Let's say Heather thinks you're the key to a windfall for her."

Grace went to the door and opened it. She wanted him gone. "Good to know. As a matter of fact, I believe your stepmother's employees may have been responsible for a break-in at my house a few days ago. The cost of my new alarm system will be added to your bill. I trust there will be no objections?"

"None. I really am sorry." He sounded sincere and looked miserable.

Grace didn't care. "I think this concludes our professional arrangement. I'll total the hours I've worked against the retainer, add the expenses and either send you a refund or a bill."

It was a refund, but not as large as she'd feared. It turned out she'd spent quite a bit of time on Quentin's behalf and all of it because he wanted to know if she'd cost him a chunk of his father's estate. After dispatching notices to his corporate office and to David, she tried to put both men out of her mind. Her pro bono client needed all of her attention.

CHAPTER THIRTY-NINE

McNamara finished his notes and got up to refresh his coffee. It felt odd to be at home on a Tuesday morning, but he'd needed quiet to work and the police station was the last place he was going to find it.

Aidan Banks was so agitated he could barely function. He could hold the office together by himself as long as the Chief or one of the MSP detectives wasn't around. Give him someone to 'what if' or 'how come' and Banks would drive himself and everyone around him crazy trying to put his life back to rights. Connie was looking good for the murder, and since Banks had identified her scarf, his romance with Niki was growing cold, fast. Until Connie was exonerated or he was proven blameless in her conviction, Niki wasn't going to take him back.

McNamara took his coffee out onto the deck and considered walking down to the water's edge and the narrow beach that framed his land. He could stand with the row of pines behind him and the water lapping at his feet, and let the Wye River bring him around and settle his thoughts. He didn't want to leave the phone in case Aidan called, and he had a hard and fast rule about no phones on the beach.

What was the point of owning such a peaceful place if you were going to defile it with noise and conflict?

His time had been well spent this morning. He'd made lists of the main suspects in Garrett Bishop's death, then categorized the scraps of information he'd picked up. When all of it was laid end to end, he'd found one angle that hadn't gotten any attention – at least not from him. He didn't have enough to act on and he wasn't going to Desiree Marbury with a half-baked idea.

Needing something constructive to do, he got a bag of birdseed from the pantry and went out to top off the feeders. The first snow of the season was forecast for the next morning, but all the preparations were done. The roses had been put to bed for the winter. New mulch on the flowerbeds around the house and Merri's perennial garden lent a spicy wood smell to the damp air. He loved this place. In one way or another it had always been home to him. He'd brought life and happiness into it when he was a young man, reviving it from his aging parents' care and filling it with his hopes and Merri's plans. Now in his fifties, he felt peaceful and grateful to still be here. He tried not to think about what would happen to the old place when he was gone.

At the last feeder, he shooed a squirrel away and reset the allegedly rodent-proof cap in place. He collected advice and gadgets dedicated to foiling the cagey animals, but they always seemed to win in the end. They never stopped trying to get what they wanted. Stop them one way and they fell back, regrouped and came at their goal from another perspective. They won by persistence. He stood for a time looking out through the pines to the water flowing past his dock and thinking.

"Need some help?"

McNamara was relieved to see Avril's cone-shaped sun hat pop up from behind the headstone. She'd ignored his arrival and he was beginning to wonder if she'd died while weeding a grave. It had to happen sometime and he felt sure she wouldn't go quietly in her bed.

"Typical," she said as she grabbed onto her grandmother's stone marker and started to pull herself up. "A man arrives just as I've finished the hard part."

He helped her get upright and admired the clean, well-tended rows of graves.

"I have help," Avril admitted. "Just not today. Rory's got the flu that's going around and I told him to stay home. I'd prefer to work alone out here than then get a bug and be knocked out for a week."

"Rory Bailey helps you out with this place?"

"Isn't that how you found me?"

"Yes. I suppose he called you?"

Avril ignored the question. McNamara thought it was a step up from telling him to mind his own business. It hadn't been easy to coax information out of the irritable farmer, either. McNamara had no doubt it was only his connection to Marjorie Battsley that made Bailey cooperate at all.

"He was pretty sick, Avril."

"Oh, he'll be fine. I'm sure you and Rory had a lot to talk about even without a murder." In case he missed her reference, she added, "How's his great romance going? Will we be having any little Baileys running around soon?"

The mental image of his sixtyish sister-in-law producing babies with Rory Bailey made McNamara laugh out loud. "Wouldn't that be something?" he said. "They'd both stay busy and out of trouble. But, actually, we talked about Garrett Bishop."

Avril said, "I told you to do it a month ago." She pulled a cloth out of a deep pocket in her canvas coat and went to work wiping down an obelisk-style tombstone. Zachariah P. Oxley may have died in 1898, but his great-granddaughter still took care of him.

McNamara said, "I passed everything you told me to the State Police. They interviewed Rory in the early days of the investigation. I even went out and talked to him myself."

"Let me guess, he didn't have anything to say."

"Oh, he talked a lot. Told me all about how he was happy Bishop was dead and out of his hair. Threatened to pump buckshot into the folks walking across his land to get a better look at the spot where Bishop died. He says one reporter trespassed to get a photo of the back of the old Morgan house with the Bailey family cemetery in the foreground." He expected a reaction to this last bit and he got it.

"That would set Rory's hair on fire, alright. Mine, too, if it happened out here. No respect for the dead at all. Did he tell you there were locals out there, too? Not only reporters but people who should know better."

"He mentioned a few names."

Avril had moved around to the far side of the obelisk. McNamara couldn't see her face, but he was pretty sure she was smiling. This was the kind of game she loved, an information standoff. He cast about for a throwaway tidbit.

"He said the two of you had theories, but not one you both agreed on."

"Rory's got it in his mind that there was a love triangle. After he found out how young Garrett Bishop's wife is, he decided someone killed Bishop to free her up. Or she hired somebody to do the deed."

"You don't agree?"

"I have a brain. No one is going to track Bishop down to the Chesapeake Bay and kill him where both they and he would stand out. They'd run him down in New York, or someplace else where it's easier to get away."

McNamara was impressed but only nodded. He bent down and squinted to read a small stone. *Angel 1929* was the only inscription.

Avril said, "My brother. Or he would have been. Died at birth. They didn't name them back then. The little ones who didn't survive, I mean. My father said it was bad luck. I can't imagine why." She reached down into a box and took out a small pot of winter pansies. "Make yourself useful. There's a cup there just at the base. Pop these in."

McNamara bent down and found a metal cup had been inserted in the ground near the headstone. Without the flowers, the greenish copper cup blended into the grass. The three-inch pot of pansies fit perfectly.

"Good. You may continue," Avril said in a queenly tone. She sat on a canvas stool and watched the Chief of Police place flowers down the row of tombstones.

"Avril, this is a lot of work for you. Who's going to see these flowers?" He was baiting her and they both knew it.

She rose to the challenge. While McNamara doled out pots of flowers and used his Swiss Army knife to gouge out a few invading weeds, Avril talked about the importance of keeping her family together and honoring them, even centuries after they'd gone.

"They wanted to be here. These people didn't leave their home, they stayed right here. The house is gone," she waved toward the faint outline of an overgrown brick foundation pillars a hundred yards or so away, "but they're still here."

"And you look after them."

"And when I'm gone, Rory will do it. And when he's gone, there's a trust. I've set it all up."

"Why Rory?" McNamara adjusted a copper cup before popping the pansies in and standing back to assess the results.

"He's a cousin, didn't you know that?"

"Of yours?" He was surprised. Avril was vocal about being the last of her line.

"Well, on paper, anyway. His mother married my uncle when Rory was about ten. He's not an Oxley by blood, but there's a connection. He helps me here, and I help him at his place. Rory's younger than me, but he's alone. I go out to the farm from time to time and cook for him. I tell him when it's time to paint and get new furniture – he's oblivious. And I help him with his genealogy. He decided a while back he wanted to know about his mother's people. About damn time. If he doesn't get the records down before he goes, there'll be no more first-hand information, so to speak."

"His farm was in his mother's family?"

"Keep up, Lee. You're the one who wants to know about Rory

and his theories. Are you telling me you haven't done a little snooping around before coming to talk to me?"

"I know his wife ran off about twenty years ago and took their daughter."

Avril took off her hat and ruffled her close-cropped hair. "There're a lot of ways to kill someone. Most of them are legal, that's what gets me. Humans can do the most awful things to each other, maim and kill without lifting a hand in anger. Poor Rory never was right afterward. They'd been living in Baltimore but he came back here and hunkered down. Fancies himself a gentleman farmer. Mostly he takes every opportunity to be angry and let out some of the pain. Naturally, he thinks Bishop's wife killed him."

"And you think?"

"Could be a family affair. Could be an accident. Could have been one of those people in my photos shot Bishop, got rid of the gun, then joined the crowd to watch the police."

He looked back to find her watching him. He almost told her he'd gone over every one of those shots, studying each face, identifying each person and evaluating their reasons for being at the scene of a murder. Instead, he patted the last pot of pansies into its cup and stood up. If he gave Avril any encouragement, she'd never let him out of her sight.

After warning her about the impending snow and receiving her usual rebuke, McNamara drove back to Mallard Bay thinking about grudges, greed and single-minded determination. He decided Rory and Avril and the squirrels were onto something. He just had to figure out what it was.

CHAPTER FORTY

I t took three hours, but Grace and Lily copied and cataloged every piece of paper in the two boxes Connie had hidden in the attic of the Morgan farmhouse. Grace copied and Lily created a spreadsheet. Each document went back into its original box in order. Lily didn't ask why they were going through the obsessive exercise, and Grace was grateful.

"It might be easier if you'd let me do the copying," Lily said as she cleared the machine of a clog. "This thing freezes when it sees you coming."

"I want a fresh perspective when I look at everything," Grace answered. "If I did the spreadsheet, my mind would be made up by now." Looking at Lily's face, she knew she was right. Lily had an opinion she was itching to share.

It was mid-afternoon before Grace set her pencil down next to her notepad and rubbed her eyes. Her last cup of coffee had grown cold, but she drank it anyway. She needed the caffeine. Four pages of notes listed every financial sin Stark Delaney had committed in the last six years. At least she hoped it was every sin. It was hard to imagine her uncle had been busier than these records indicated. Innocent looking tax returns were covered in neon blue sticky notes. In her girlish writing Connie pointed out one lie after another, including bogus charitable deductions. Unreported sales of various antiques could be explained away as gifts from his mother. *Didn't report cash sale of piano* was clipped to the same tax return as a photograph with *Giuseppe Palinti etching $1,000 cash* printed on the back. Her anger grew as Grace recognized snapshots of family portraits and antiques she thought had been sold by her grandmother in the later years of her life. According to Connie's notes, Stark sold all of them and kept the money.

He had a particularly flush year in 2009. His tax return said he earned eighty-three thousand, and had ten thousand in charitable deductions. Connie's records claimed he'd sold an eighteenth-century inlaid sideboard and a mahogany Federal period secretary, and kept the cash in a safe deposit box. Theft of the items would be hard to prove since there was no one alive to testify against him.

What was the point of Connie's meticulous records and damning revelations?

The thought nagged at her as she locked the office, picked up Leo from Niki, and drove home. The little dog ate better than Grace did that night. Wine and a pack of peanut butter crackers passed as dinner and did nothing to help her sleep. Morning didn't bring any bright ideas, but as she read over her notes again, she could only think of one reason for what Connie had done. Why does anyone write down anything? To make a record. For themselves or someone else.

THE NEXT MORNING HEAVY CLOUDS MAINTAINED A PREDAWN bleakness and a weather warning flashed on the iPhone's screen. Grace ignored it as she drove to the office, her mind sorting through the various options open to Connie. She was relieved to arrive at work and have someone to talk to.

"Insurance?" Lily asked. She joined Grace at the small conference table where they'd left Connie's boxes. "Against what?"

"Leverage with Stark," Grace said. She pulled 2012's tax return out and handed it to Lily. "By this time there wasn't much of value left in Delaney House that Stark could easily take from his mother. But look at this." Attached to the returns were two photographs of a pair of emerald earrings. Connie's notes said they were valued at forty-eight thousand and Stark had sold them for twenty thousand cash. "This bugged me all night and I finally realized why. I remembered Cyrus said Stark's mother sold these in the late eighties. I know because Cyrus had the records and showed them to me. There was so much to take in back then, it took me a while to piece all the memories together."

"Then Connie's lying?" Lily waved a hand at the boxes. "About all of this?"

"Connie lying. Imagine that," Grace said. "I think most of what's here, her accusations, are true. Enough to tie Stark up in knots, anyway. But maybe she didn't think it was enough so she embellished things a bit."

"I don't know," Lily said. "This required planning and thought. Does that sound like Connie to you?"

"A motivated Connie? Possibly. She starts out strong with the truth - Stark's probably lied on his tax returns his whole life, but at least he was smart about it, never underreporting what could be proven. But then Connie got greedy and added claims like these earrings. Now *that* sounds like her."

"This is one seriously messed up family," Lily said, then added, "But again, why? What's she going to do with all this?"

"I can only think of one thing she would want from Stark so badly that she'd go to this much trouble to hold something over his head. I'm going to go find her and see if I'm right."

GRACE DIDN'T BLAME CONNIE FOR WANTING A DIVORCE IF, INDEED, that was her motivation. She'd hatched a blackmail scheme that might work on her despicable husband. Stark would never let Connie

230 | CHERIL THOMAS

leave unless he had to and if he had to, he'd want her to go empty-handed. Unfortunately, the IRS would look at both signatures on the returns. Grace doubted Connie realized she had implicated herself in tax fraud along with Stark.

The drive out to Stark and Connie's house was scenic, but today Grace negotiated the winding country roads without giving a glance to the frost covered fields dotted with cows and horses. Even the little stone bridge that marked the entrance to Queen's Brooke Estates failed to get her attention as she crossed it. Usually the pretentious bridge, which straddled a drainage ditch, ramped up her blood pressure since it led to the equally pretentious houses that sat in a semi-circle in the middle of a former soybean field. The enormous McMansions were phase one of a multi-phase development that had been over-leveraged and under-financed. Connie and Stark had gotten the house at rock bottom prices, but Queen's Brooke Estates would remain a collection of half-finished community infrastructure with a dozen angry property owners until the economy improved.

Sandra Carter's name flashed across her phone for the third time as Grace pulled into the driveway of her aunt's faux-French country chateau and parked next to the three-bay garage. She said 'hello' in a tone she hoped would shorten the conversation.

"Thank goodness!" Sandra sounded frantic. "I didn't think you were going to answer and I don't know what else to do. I don't want to make things worse for Connie."

"I'm at her house now. What are you talking about?"

"Is she there?" Sandra sounded surprised.

"Doesn't look like it," Grace said. "No cars here. Why?"

"She called me very upset. She said you were turning against her and she'd end up in jail and it would kill her. She said she didn't have any choice but to leave the country and she asked me for money."

"*What?*"

"Yes! She's leaving. She said Stark wouldn't help her, you wouldn't help her, and she was on her own, so she was leaving. She wanted fifty thousand and said to tell you it was her fee for selling your house to me, so you should take it off the purchase price."

Grace gaped at the steering wheel and the little green 'active call' light.

"Did you hear me?" Sandra said. "Hello?"

"You're buying my house?"

"Well, I guess you *are* surprised. You've been horrible to Connie, but I've fallen in love with Delaney House and I want it. I'll even pay the ridiculous price you're asking. But right now we need to focus on your aunt. If she'll be in trouble for leaving the county, I'll bet leaving the country would be a lot worse, right?"

"Hang on," Grace said. She got out of the car, ran up to the house and jabbed at the doorbell, then pounded with the ornate brass knocker for good measure. No sounds came from inside. After a quick look through the front windows, she returned to the car and told Sandra to start over.

"I'm trying to tell you where she is, if you'll listen," Sandra snapped. "I just talked to her. She asked me to meet her at the Morgan farm. She left something in the house, but she wouldn't tell me what. I did what she said, I'm here and her car is here, but I can't find her. I don't like being here alone, this place is creepy and it's starting to snow. How long will it take you to get here?"

THREE MORE CALLS HOUNDED HER ON HER WAY OUT OF MALLARD Bay. She didn't take Niki's or David's. She didn't want to deal with either of them and she needed to concentrate on driving. It wouldn't be long before the back roads would be a mess.

The third call was from Mosley's doctor, but at least it was good news. The patient was discharged and on his way home in Marjorie's care. He'd be delivered into the hands of the home care nurses Grace had hired. The doctor sounded sympathetic when he wished her luck in managing Mosley's recovery. Grace thought she'd take the cranky old man any day over her fool of an aunt.

Connie was all over the place, gathering evidence against Stark, demanding money from Sandra and talking about running away. She was acting like a person on the edge of a breakdown. Until David's firm could take over Connie's defense, Grace was on deck, and her client seemed to be doing everything she could to guarantee a conviction of murder with a side helping of extortion.

SANDRA'S JAGUAR AND CONNIE'S AGING MERCEDES WERE THE ONLY signs of life at the old house. Grace sat in her car for a moment. She wanted to gather her thoughts before joining whatever circus was going on inside. Just as she got out of the car, the front door opened.

"What are you waiting for?" Sandra called. "She's in here!"

It was snowing in earnest now, and a sharp wind pushed the car door against Grace. The wool coat that had been warm enough when she'd left home now felt like a sweater. She hurried into the house, head down and holding the hood of her coat to keep it over her head.

"You took your sweet time!" Sandra said as she shut the door behind Grace. It was nearly as cold in the house as it was outside, but Sandra, in only a sweater and slacks, was perspiring. "Connie came charging in a few minutes ago, acting crazy. I think she's drunk again. She says she's hiding, but she's crying and isn't making any sense. She's in the kitchen looking for something."

Grace heard noises coming from somewhere in the rear of the house.

"See?" Sandra demanded. "I don't know what to do with her. You have to help me get her out of here and back home."

"Maybe I should call Niki," Grace said. Now that she was actually faced with having to handle Connie, dragging her back to town and getting her calm before involving Niki seemed unrealistic. In fact, the whole situation felt surreal. Sandra in her expensive clothes and cloud of perfume looked like an apparition in the dim light. The house creaked and moaned around them and snow drifted in through the broken windows.

"Please," Sandra tugged at Grace again. "You have to do something with her. Help her!"

A loud moan from the kitchen ended Grace's indecision. She found Connie slumped on the floor, clinging to a sagging cabinet door.

"Oh, my God!" Sandra cried. "I'll call 911. See if she has a pulse!"

Grace bent down to reach for Connie, but pain exploded up her arm. The next second she was on the floor, and a scream was still echoing around the old walls.

"Shut up!" Sandra stood over her with a black object in her hand. "I'll kill you if you make another sound."

A *Taser*. Grace tried to wipe the sudden tears from her face with her uninjured hand, but nothing seemed to work right. All she could see was Sandra looming over her and the butt of the Taser pistol as it came down.

CHAPTER FORTY-ONE

"I won't do it! You're crazy. My God, I never realized how crazy you are!"

"Then you'd better go while you can."

"Listen to me, it's not too late."

Grace strained to hear what Jason was saying to his enraged wife. Their voices faded in and out, and she hoped it was only because they weren't nearby. Connie was gone and she didn't know how long she'd been unconscious. Blood trickled down her face from a cut on her scalp. The argument taking place somewhere near the front of the house meant Jason wasn't joining forces with Sandra. She felt a surge of hope.

"You never take my side on *anything*. Why can't you just for once do what I ask you to?"

Grace knew she had to move. Glass and plaster crunched under her as she painfully got to her feet, but the Carters argued on. If they'd heard her, they didn't care.

"I'm not going to carry them out to the woods. I'm going to get them to a hospital. We can fix this, honey." Jason again. "I love you, you know I do. Twenty-five years! You have to know we're a team, right? Oh, Sandy. No."

It was the odd note in his voice that made Grace stop as she reached the staircase near the front door. She looked around the doorway into the living room and jerked her head back. They were at the far end of the room. Either one of them could have seen her if they hadn't been absorbed in each other. She took another quick look.

Jason was pleading. One more look told her Sandra held a gun.

Sandra was talking again. "Oh, honey, *yes*. I'm an artist, not a child. You don't get to *fix* what I do. You don't get to make decisions for me, and you don't leave my shoes at home."

"Your shoes?"

Grace stopped. Where was Connie? She hadn't been in the kitchen and Grace couldn't remember her leaving. A glance out the nearest window told her it was snowing harder now.

Sandra was laughing. "Yeah. I put up with all the cheating and lying and disrespect, but you know what did me in? The day we came out here so you could check out the hunting. The day Bishop died. The day you killed him. You left my shoes at home."

"Now, wait a minute. I didn't kill —"

"I decided to get my boots out of the trunk. My feet were cold, and I wanted my boots. You were out stomping through the woods making sure it was a good killing ground. Remember? 'I'll have my own hunting preserve,' you said."

"So what?"

"You left me in a cold car and I wanted my boots! But when I opened the trunk, my shoe bag wasn't there. You know what was there? Your rifle cases. *Three* of them."

"Sandra, My God! What did you do?"

"I shot you, darling husband. Damn good shot, too. Would have been perfect if I'd targeted the right man. Just like killing a farmer's cow, you know? Same mistake, only a bit more serious."

Grace had to go. However the Carters' argument ended, it wouldn't be good for her. Her hand was on the doorknob when the doorframe next to her face exploded. Momentarily blinded, she dropped to the floor. Another shot rang out and hit the door panel above her head. Someone started screaming, but this time it wasn't her. Jason and Sandra were yelling. She yanked open what was left of the door and ran.

She was halfway to her car when she realized her keys weren't in her coat pocket. Neither was her cell phone.

Fours cars in the driveway and no keys in any of them, but at least hers was unlocked. She grabbed the tire iron from the trunk and ran to the back of the house, praying that she could find Connie before Sandra started looking for both of them.

She had just reached the back steps when she heard another gunshot. Later she couldn't remember how long it took her to break out of her shock and move onto the porch. Her head throbbed and her thoughts were fuzzy, but one thing was clear in her mind: Connie was still inside the house and Sandra had a gun.

"Don't make me shoot you."

The words came from behind her.

"ISN'T THIS BETTER? MUCH WARMER IN HERE OUT OF THE SNOW."

The gun jabbed into Grace's back and she bit her tongue to keep from crying out. Sandra had threatened to shoot her if she said anything. Jason's body on the floor was ample evidence that she would do what she said.

"Get upstairs now where we can talk without this little distraction."

Another poke from the gun barrel. Grace moved as directed.

Sandra had used the Taser a third time to stop her from swinging the tire iron. It was only a short zap, but Grace felt damaged. Not injured exactly, but not right. Her feet were clumsy but still worked. She tried not to let Sandra see her hands spasm.

The climb up the stairs was painful and the closer they got to the second floor, the more afraid Grace became. When she stepped onto the landing, Sandra moved quickly up behind her, yanked her around and pushed her against a bedroom door. The rotted wood gave way and Grace fell backward. Sandra was at her side in an instant.

"Get up!" The hand holding the pistol swung at her face and caught Grace's mouth. "Get. Up!"

Grace stood but bent at the waist, letting the blood streaming from her split lip splatter the dusty floorboards.

"Well, this is convenient." Sandra sounded happy again.

Grace couldn't think. The sight of her own blood pooling on the floor mesmerized her.

"Come on, now. Only a few more steps and I'll let you go."

This did penetrate the fog. Grace looked up and around. They were in the room where Connie had broken through the ceiling only the day before. Sandra was standing near the doorway to the attic staircase. The gun was pointed at Grace, but Sandra was smiling.

"I know you want to get away from big bad me, but come on over here. Promise it won't hurt. One more flight of steps and you're done. I'll leave you alone."

The gun was steady and was pointed at Grace's chest. She went, plaster and debris crunching beneath her feet. As she passed Sandra, she noticed the yellow scarf she wore. It seemed important, but she couldn't remember why.

"A little faster, okay? I have things to do." Sandra jabbed her again with the barrel of the gun and Grace tried to make her feet run. Sandra's laughter was still in her ears when she reached the top of the attic staircase and heard the door slam shut below. "Safe and sound like I promised," Sandra called. "But if you try to open this door before I'm gone, I'll kill you, understand? Grace? Say you understand or I'll —"

In a croaky voice, Grace yelled that she understood and heard Sandra laugh again.

"Just rest up there. Give me an hour and you can come down. It won't matter anymore then."

Grace lay down on the attic floor and prayed to hear the sound of the Jaguar's engine.

———

SHE WAS AT HOME, IN THE LITTLE ROW HOUSE IN ARLINGTON. HER mother was in the kitchen making tomato soup and grilled cheese sandwiches for dinner. She was sick, that's why she was getting her favorites tonight. She was hurt. She'd been cold but Mom had made a fire. It smelled so good.

She looked around the room she loved. Her little desk against the wall, next to Mom's big one. The picture window overlooking the snow covered walkway. A Christmas tree ready for Santa, and her red felt stocking hanging from the mantle. The row house was almost perfect, but something was wrong. She felt worse as the sweet dream faded. The Arlington house didn't have a mantle for stockings. It didn't have a fireplace.

She never knew what woke her. Her head was pounding, but her hands and feet worked again. The smell of fire followed her into consciousness. Beneath her, the attic floor was warm. The pain in her head made moving difficult, but she knew she should get up. And do what? She couldn't think.

Another lapse and she was awake again. The pain was there, but panic pushed it aside. The floor was hot. She moved to the far side of the attic where she had saved Connie the day before. She couldn't read her watch. The attic light was too dim, and her eyes were unfocused. She had to get out now. Smoke was wafting up through the holes Connie had made in the ceiling. A loud popping sound told her the fire was growing.

She moved clumsily along the narrow floored section to the front of the house, took off her left shoe and used it to break out the few shards of glass that remained from the original window over the front porch. When she leaned out, the first thing she saw was the police car pulling in the driveway. After a brief burst of joy, her heart sank. The steep pitch of the tin roof below the window would send her sliding straight down to drop over the walk. If she didn't break every bone in her body in the fall, it would be a miracle.

She turned back, looking for safer access to the backyard, but she couldn't see past the staircase. The attic was filling with smoke and she was starting to choke. Out of options, she sat on the edge of the windowsill and swung first one leg, then the other out into the air.

The narrow, decorative trim under the attic window proved to be sturdier than it looked. She braced her feet on the five-inch border and inched upward, pulling herself along the window's edge as she came upright and managed to grasp the hooks of an old storm shutter frame. She stood, clutching the upper corners of the window opening, gasping for air and crying with relief at the growing wail of sirens.

When her hands began to cramp, she eased a foot to the left, staying flattened against the rough wood siding. She had no idea if the narrow strip of wood would hold her weight for long and she didn't dare look down, even when the sirens grew to a fever pitch. Help was in the yard below, people were screaming at her, and over it all she heard something else.

Sandra was calling her name. She was close by.

Grace turned her head and looked away from the window. Ten or so feet to her left, a copper downspout met an ancient rain gutter. If she could make it that far, she could hold onto the gutter and steady herself. But after only three side shuffling steps, she could go no further. She couldn't let go of the shutter hook.

"Look at me, Grace," Sandra called in a singsong voice. "Be a good girl and look over at me. I can almost reach you."

Grace took another step, angling as much of her body as she could away from the window. She didn't look back. If Sandra was reaching for her, she didn't want to know.

"Help's here," Sandra called. "Just in time to watch me try to save you. Take my hand, Grace. Look at me and take my hand."

Grace squeezed her eyes shut and concentrated on the snow patting her face. She let the shutter hook slip out of her fingers and slid another inch away. She'd jump if she had to, but she wouldn't look back. She made it to the downspout and trusted the fireman who told her to let go and slide down the roof. He caught her and eased her into the bucket lift, telling her over and over again that she was safe.

It would be a long time before she believed him.

———————

SANDRA HAD SET A FIRE IN EACH ROOM OF THE HOUSE. GRACE couldn't have gone back into the attic if she'd tried. And Sandra couldn't have called out to her as she clung to the window frame. By that time Sandra was already dead in the kitchen next to her husband who was still wearing his empty shoulder holster.

He was finally hers and hers alone.

CHAPTER FORTY-TWO

"I guess you could say Mom saved you."

It was getting harder to fake amnesia, shock, or any other condition which would allow Grace to ignore her surroundings. Besides, she couldn't leave Niki's comment unchallenged.

"You have got to be kidding me," she said, pleased to find her voice, while raspy, still worked.

"I knew that would do it!"

Her cousin's laughter hurt Grace's head more than the sunlight streaming through the hospital window. The room was crowded with two beds, assorted medical equipment, and three anxious people hovering over the patients. Connie broke through the noise to demand a latte and a bedside manicure. Niki scolded her mother, and Avril began punching the intercom button, asking for more juice. Grace decided to try and bribe the staff to roll her bed out to her car. If she could only make it to the driver's seat...

"The doctor said you'll be fine, sweetheart. You can go home tomorrow." David was holding her hand, as he had been every other time she'd drifted near consciousness.

"Now," she said.

She got her wish. Easton Memorial was slammed with a flu outbreak and every bed was needed. By late afternoon the day after Sandra tried to kill her, Grace was on the third floor of Delaney House with an anxious David in attendance. He said Avril was in the kitchen coordinating the food that was coming in from friends and neighbors, and Cyrus was supervising her from the rocking chair.

"I can't get either of them to leave," David said as he stretched out next to her and brushed a stray curl off her face.

"Welcome to my world." She felt better, or could pretend she did if she didn't move her head or any other body part. Nothing was broken, but plenty was dented, scraped and bruised. The concussion was the worst of it and David had vowed to stay until she was well. Grace thought he might make it until tomorrow morning, but only because he could, technically, sleep with her.

She tried to maintain a healthy skepticism, but David was gentle and funny and seemed to be settling in. An old happiness was tugging at her and she wasn't fighting it, much. After a ten second stare down, Leo accepted him and moved to the foot of the bed to make room for the interloper. When David scooted closer, Grace decided she didn't mind. Nothing itched and she hadn't needed to count her blessings since she'd left the hospital. It felt like most of them were in Delaney House with her.

RORY BAILEY WAS THE KEY AFTER ALL.

Jason Carter had annoyed him by trespassing on the morning Garrett Bishop died. Rory heard the killing shot a few minutes later but put it down to overly enthusiastic hunters. He didn't connect the events until Chief McNamara's visit set him to thinking about the day of the murder and Rory got mad all over again, remembering the trespassers. He was trying to decide what to do with this newly remembered information when a bleeding and incoherent Connie banged on his front door. Rory didn't bother with 911 but instead called the one person he knew would get something done. Avril came through with police, fire trucks, two ambulances and enough excitement to entertain him for a year.

Connie was able to fill in most of the remaining blanks. For once, she mostly told the truth, and with her statements, the last loose ends were tied up. Quentin Bishop's foundation was going to lose part of its inheritance and his stepmother would be a happy widow. Connie had broken out of her miserable marriage to an abusive man for a fling with an egomaniac. No one had trouble believing her story.

After interviewing Rory, Grace, Connie and Niki, the MSP moved their investigation on to the Carter home in Virginia. They didn't really need confirmation of the couple's contentious relationship but Detective Marbury and her team were thorough. Between the day Sandra Carter mistakenly shot Garrett Bishop and the day she finally killed her husband, she was busy incriminating her best friend. From planting Connie's scarf and a rifle shell in the woods to encouraging Connie to leave town, Sandra had constantly been on the lookout for ways to deflect attention from her own actions. On the last morning in the old Morgan house, when both Connie and Jason refused to follow her instructions, Sandra started eliminating her problems, one by one.

Quentin Bishop left for Canada without waiting for anyone's approval. Other than a couple of indignant protests from Detective Marbury, nobody cared. That was one annoying outsider gone, but Marbury and McNamara — especially McNamara — were disappointed that there was nothing to arrest Anton Norse for. The arrogant German would get the Morgan farm for his clients and go on to do battle with the zoning officials, which meant he would stay in the Mallard Bay spotlight for a while. McNamara wasn't looking forward to the upcoming town meetings.

The Chief went through the motions of tying up loose ends and generally shepherding life in the village back to normal. Some of the changes that came out of the chaotic weeks following the murder were easily reversed. Others left marks that would take getting used to. Christmas found Niki and Aidan reunited, Connie and Stark separated, and David still in residence at Delaney House.

McNamara decided he could put up with all three for the pleasure of seeing Grace smile.

Before You Go...

Thank you for reading *A Commission on Murder*! I hope you enjoyed it, and that'll you try all of the Mallard Bay books. Book 3 of the series, *Bad Intent*, is available now. You can read a free sample chapter in the next section.

Your time is valuable, and I am humbled that you chose to spend it with me. If you have another few minutes to spare and would like to leave a review on Amazon, Goodreads, or anywhere else, I'd be very grateful.

I hope you'll stay in touch with me for the latest updates on the Eastern Shore Mysteries. My website has all the book news, plus a little taste of Maryland's beautiful Eastern Shore. I'm also on Facebook and Twitter. Drop me an email — I'd love to hear from you!

Come back to the Eastern Shore soon!

Website: www.CherilThomas.com
Email: Cheril@CherilThomas.com
Amazon Author Page: www.amazon.com/author/cherilthomas

COMING NEXT IN MALLARD BAY

Grace's contract with Cyrus Mosley only has one month to run and she's dreaming about the south of France. This time when she leaves the Eastern Shore, she'll put an ocean between herself and her disaster loving family. She only has one or two things to clear up before she goes. Unless, of course, there's a murder.

BAD INTENT

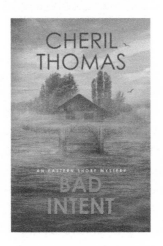

WANT TO READ A SAMPLE OF *BAD INTENT*? JUST TURN THE PAGE!

BAD INTENT

Melanie and Whitney Overton weren't the strangest clients Grace Reagan had handled in her brief tenure with Cyrus Mosley and Associates, Attorneys at Law. Top honors in the strange category went to a murdered billionaire, with honorable mention to a pair of neighbors in a death feud over a six-foot python and three dead chickens. Grace liked to think she'd learned from both cases, and yet here she was listening to another set of clients who needed a magician, not a lawyer.

"You should work with the police," Grace said, keeping her voice even and her words short. The women didn't look like they could handle complicated. The Overton sisters were trouble, plain and simple, and she didn't want to represent them in their search for their missing husband. A runaway polygamist would definitely rate a slot on the Strange Client list.

"We can't," Melanie wailed, tears leaking from her brimming eyes. "They already think Heath's a car thief."

Whitney backed her up with a glum nod.

They favored each other in the way of before and after photographs. Both were on the short side with dark hair and large blue eyes. High cheekbones and oval faces made them pretty, but only Melanie made an effort beyond that. Despite her I'm-on-the-edge persona, she'd taken time with makeup and wore a sundress with wedge sandals. Whitney's messy bun, loose tank top and yoga pants said she'd gotten dressed, and that was all anybody was getting from her.

"We want you to do that for us," Whitney said.

While Whitney had explained the reason for their appointment, Melanie had listened anxiously, wrapping her stick-thin arms around her bent torso and crossing her legs. Now she gave herself an extra twist by tucking one foot behind the chair leg, locking herself into a pretzel shape. "The police think we're crazy, but they'll believe you, Ms. Reagan," she said in a breathy voice.

"Our firm doesn't do this type of work," Grace tried again. "If you don't want the police, I can recommend a private detective."

"No. You're the one we need," Whitney said. "We need to find out everything the police know about our husband. You're a friend of the Police Chief's, so you're perfect for the job." She reddened slightly and added, "I'm sorry, that came out wrong. I should have said our neighbor recommended you."

Grace didn't have to ask which neighbor. The keeper of all gossip in Mallard Bay, Maryland, lived next door to the house the Overtons were renting. Avril Oxley had been talking about the large family for weeks.

"I appreciate that," Grace said, trying not to sound sarcastic. "But I'm not sure I can help you."

The silence grew as Grace waited to see if her words were sinking in. Billable minutes ticked by. The screensaver on her computer monitor changed from a vineyard in Bordeaux to a lavender field in Provence, and she wondered if it would be in bloom when she arrived in France in six weeks.

Whitney Overton broke the impasse. "We haven't been in town long, and we don't have any connections here, except our neighbor. You have to help us. When the police came to our house yesterday morning, they said Heath stole a rental car. I was only trying to protect the family, and now I see that was a mistake."

"She lied," Melanie said.

Flicking her sister an irritated glance, Whitney said, "I made a mistake."

Grace rechecked her notes. Between tree pollen and Benadryl her head felt like a hot, soggy sponge. She was still adjusting to the sisters' tale and assumed her slowed reflexes had caused her to miss a vital piece of information. Such as the part of the Overtons' story that would make sense. "What kind of mistake?" she asked.

"As I said, unfortunately, we had to lie — "

"*You* lied," Melanie corrected in a whispery voice.

Whitney briefly squeezed her eyes shut, then started again. "I lied about knowing where my husband — "

"Our husband," Melanie said.

Grace wanted to slap duct tape over the woman's mouth just so her sister could finish a sentence. "What did you lie to the police about?" she asked, looking at both sisters to cover her bases.

Whitney looked exasperated. "I told them we knew where Heath was when we really have no idea because he's *missing*."

"Since last Monday, May 7th. Got it." Grace circled the date on her legal pad.

Whitney's top knot had been sliding loose as she talked. Now she yanked on the elastic holding it together and resumed her story while finger combing the mass of hair that fell past her shoulders.

"Heath flew into Baltimore a week ago Sunday, rented a car, and drove over to see us. He went back to Atlanta on Monday. On Wednesday, the rental car company called me because they had my number as an emergency contact. He hadn't returned the car before he flew back home. The daily charges were still being paid by the credit card, so they'd let it slide for forty-eight hours, but he wasn't answering their calls, and they wanted their car back. I smoothed things over and authorized an extension to the lease."

"That was the first lie she told," Melanie said and dabbed at her eyes. "We have to protect the family, but if they'd called me, I might have handled it differently."

"By crying and handing me the phone?" Whitney snapped, then

colored. "Sorry, we're both very upset. Anyway, except for us being worried to death, and not being able to reach Heath, nothing else happened until the police showed up yesterday. Without saying anything to me, the rental company reported the car stolen despite the extended lease."

Both women looked expectantly at Grace.

"Why did you lie about knowing where your husband was?" Grace asked.

The sisters looked at each other in surprise, and Grace hoped they were reconsidering their choice of law firms.

Whitney scraped her hair back up and began twisting it while Melanie nervously fiddled with a perfectly coiled curl of her own. Neither of them answered Grace, who was thinking the Overtons' bathroom drains must be perpetually clogged with all that hair flying around.

Topknot secured once more, Whitney said, "I had to lie because of who we are. The Overton family? *The Plurals Next Door?* I'm sure you've seen the promo ads on the Different Lives channel? We can't risk the press getting wind of Heath's disappearance. It's totally counter to our family's mission statement."

Grace was trying to remember the last time she heard anyone refer to a family mission statement with sincerity when Melanie untwisted herself and stood up.

"We need you to find our husband. Can you do it?"

Grace meant to say no. She even opened her mouth to say no. If the billionaire's murder and the snake case had taught her anything, it was that some clients aren't worth the money. Cyrus Mosley had barely recovered from the newspaper headlines generated by those clients. Two sister wives searching for their husband would probably kill the old coot.

She'd be leaving Mallard Bay in less than six weeks. When — if — she returned, it would only be as a visitor. There was plenty of work to occupy her until she left. Good, steady, boring work.

Whitney said, "We'll pay double your regular hourly rate."

France was expensive.

Grace said, "Where would you like me to start?"

Want more?

Check your local bookstore or library for
BAD INTENT
or
use this link for Amazon:

https://www.amazon.com/author/cherilthomas

THANK YOU FOR READING!

AUTHOR'S NOTE

A Commission on Murder could not have been written without the assistance of many talented people. I take full responsibility for all errors within these pages; goodness knows the individuals named below did their best with me.

Helen Chappell – Editor, mentor and one of the funniest people I know. Thank you for working your magic once again.

Olivia Martin, www.oliviajunemartin.com – Editor, amazing resource and my go-to for all things *au courant.*

Thank you to Charlene Marcum for proofreading services and generous support. A special thanks to Douglas Devenyns for the Wild Bill Hickok obituary and history. The talented Kate Thomas provided the sketch of Gracie Mae, the Wonder Doodle.

Ron Thomas, Clara Ellingson, Cindy Haddaway, Tarah Kleinert, Olivia Martin and Roxanne Tury are Beta Readers Extraordinaire! Without them, Grace's shoes would morph from sneakers to loafers and Mosley wouldn't know what a Mulligan was. Grace would have 'called' Uber. You have her thanks and mine for saving us from that particular embarrassment. The hours you all spent on our behalf are sincerely appreciated.

The people who make the best part of my life are always on every gratitude list. My wonderful family is a blessing every day. I can never say thank you enough.

This book is dedicated to my heart and his furry sidekick. I love you both.

Easton, Maryland
March 2018

ABOUT THE AUTHOR

Cheril Thomas is the author of the Eastern Shore Mysteries series: *Squatter's Rights, A Commission on Murder, and Bad Intent.* She is also the co-author of a mystery novel, *Whispers,* and is a published short fiction author. She lives on the Eastern Shore of Maryland with her husband and a shaggy black dog named Gracie Mae.

Thomas, Cheril, A Commission on Murder, (An Eastern Shore Mystery). 2020. Second edition.

ISBN: 9781733412117

TRED AVON PRESS
Easton, Maryland, USA
www.TredAvonPress.com

Book cover by Mibl Art Studio

Made in United States
Orlando, FL
21 November 2022

24823598R00161